M000027539

Mail-Order Refuge

Dayna
Enjoy!
Cindy Regnier

by
Cindy Regnier

SMITTEN
HISTORICAL ROMANCE
LIGHTHOUSE PUBLISHING of the CAROLINAS

MAIL-ORDER REFUGE BY CINDY REGNIER
Published by Smitten Historical Romance
an imprint of Lighthouse Publishing of the Carolinas
2333 Barton Oaks Dr., Raleigh, NC 27614

ISBN: 978-1-946016-89-8
Copyright © 2019 by Cindy Regnier
Cover design by Elaina Lee
Interior design by Karthick Srinivasan

Available in print from your local bookstore, online, or from the publisher at:
ShopLPC.com

For more information on this book and the author visit:

All rights reserved. Noncommercial interests may reproduce portions of this book without the express written permission of Lighthouse Publishing of the Carolinas, provided the text does not exceed 500 words. When reproducing text from this book, include the following credit line: "*Mail-Order Refuge* by Cindy Regnier published by Lighthouse Publishing of the Carolinas. Used by permission."

Commercial interests: No part of this publication may be reproduced in any form, stored in a retrieval system, or transmitted in any form by any means—electronic, photocopy, recording, or otherwise—without prior written permission of the publisher, except as provided by the United States of America copyright law.

This is a work of fiction. Names, characters, and incidents are all products of the author's imagination or are used for fictional purposes. Any mentioned brand names, places, and trademarks remain the property of their respective owners, bear no association with the author or the publisher, and are used for fictional purposes only.

All scripture quotations, unless otherwise indicated, are taken from the Holy Bible, New International Version®, NIV®. Copyright ©1973, 1978, 1984, 2011 by Biblica, Inc.™. Used by permission of Zondervan. All rights reserved worldwide. www.zondervan.com. "NIV" and "New International Version" are trademarks registered in the United States Patent and Trademark Office by Biblica, Inc.™.

Brought to you by the creative team at Lighthouse Publishing of the Carolinas (LPCBooks.com):
Eddie Jones, Robin Patchen, Shonda Savage, Pegg Thomas, Stephen Mathisen, Sue Fairchild, and Ann Knowles

Library of Congress Cataloging-in-Publication Data
Regnier, Cindy.
Mail-Order Refuge/Cindy Regnier 1st ed.

Printed in the United States of America

Praise for *Mail-Order Refuge*

If you love stories of mail-order brides you will want to read Cindy Regnier's *Mail-Order Refuge*. Cindy has penned a debut novel full of charm and mystery. The setting in the Kansas Flint Hills, the dynamics of a young woman inheriting a ready-made family, the angst of fear of being discovered and the need to confront the *other* woman all work to create a delightful story. I'm anxious to read more of Cindy's writing.

~ Julane Hiebert
Author of the popular *Brides of a Feather* Series

With engaging characters, a touch of intrigue, and a love story that will tug at your heart, Cindy Regnier's *Mail-Order Refuge* brings a fresh, new voice to historical romance with cowboys. I highly recommend this debut novel by a talented author.

~Myra Johnson
Award-winning author of the *Flowers of Eden* series

Mail-Order Refuge is not your typical tale about a mail-order bride. While this sweet and suspenseful debut from Cindy Regnier is filled with the love and laughter readers expect from a ranch romance, there are plenty of twists and turns to keep you guessing to the end. *Mail-Order Refuge* delivers more than historical romance fans ordered.

~ Candee Fick
Author of *Sing a New Song*

Acknowledgments

With heartfelt thanks and love to my husband who has supported me with every writing venture I've undertaken and is my cheerleader, confidant and friend. I couldn't do this without you. I treasure your "pink notes" and keep them close to my heart.

To Ty, Rachel, Nolan, Kasey and Randon, thanks for putting up with me when I always seemed to be "working on my story." Your love and encouragement have pushed me farther than I ever dreamed I would go.

To my mom who loves every word I've ever written just because her "baby" wrote it. To my dad who gets so excited when he's reading he might even miss supper.

To my sister, my awesome beta reader and friend.

To my brother who has offered me fantastic story suggestions, most of which I will never use, but that character of Timothy is one brave and courageous dude.

My grandparents who instilled in me a love for the Kansas Flint Hills and what life was like "back in the day."

Many thanks to Pegg Thomas, Robin Patchen, and all those at Smitten who made this dream of mine a reality.

My undying gratitude to my mentor Tina Radcliffe and all of my writing sisters. Your encouragement is priceless—and comes with that all-important icing.

Dedication

For my dad, who gave me a love for all things cowboy,
including how to speak the language.
May you whoop and holler to your heart's content.

Chapter 1

"Tommy, wait!" Carly Blair screeched as she bounded off the depot platform after her brother. Her shout was swallowed up by the shriek of the train whistle. She missed the last step and plunged face first into the dust of the small-town train station. A horse and cart rumbled past as a hand jerked her upright.

"Tommy." She struggled to free herself from the grip on her wrist, searching the crowd frantically for her brother.

"Are you hurt?" The voice was deep, slightly raspy and, quite possibly, on the verge of laughter. When she still struggled, the man added, "The boy is safe, miss."

Safe? Carly whirled around to see her little brother standing beside a stranger. Thank God. The man gripped Tommy in one hand and her in the other while her gaze traveled up, up, up. Blinking twice, she stared into a pair of pale blue eyes nearly hidden by shocks of chestnut hair beneath a wide-brimmed straw hat.

"I ... I'm fine," she managed, sucking in her breath. The handles of her satchel dug into her free hand. "Thank you."

The man had saved Tommy from being trampled in the streets of this Kansas town, but why was he still gripping her wrist? Twisting from his hold, Carly searched the area for their trunks. Fear crawled up her throat. Oh, what had she done?

What you had to do.

She'd been telling herself that she'd done what she had to do since she and Tommy boarded the train back in Baltimore. Lester McGraw would never find them in this place.

Carly held out her hand for Tommy. He ignored it, still staring at the stranger. What had gotten into him? "Come, Tommy. We must collect our baggage and be on our way."

The stranger fixed his gaze on Carly. "Perhaps I could be of assistance?"

"Oh, no, thank you, but I'm sure we can manage." She paused. On second thought, what could it hurt to ask? "Actually, would you be acquainted with Mr. Rand Stratford?"

The man grinned as if her question amused him. "Why, yes I know Rand well. If you would tell me your name, I could introduce you."

"That won't be necessary." She wasn't going to give her name to any stranger who asked. Maybe she should turn her back on this man with the maddening grin, but how was she to find Mr. Stratford? Her chin inched up. "Perhaps you could point him out to me?"

The man's smile relented into a low chuckle. He thrust his right hand toward her. "I'm Rand Stratford, ma'am, and I presume you're Carlotta Blair?"

"You're supposed to call her Carly," Tommy said.

This was the man she'd come to marry? Thank goodness Tommy had answered for her. Carly couldn't get a word past the lump in her throat. The heat crept into her cheeks, and she silently cursed the unbecoming blush that plagued her in awkward situations. Fingers trembling, she touched his for the briefest moment. Not trusting herself to speak, she stared down at the tips of her shoes peeking from beneath her skirts. For goodness sake, she was covered in dust. She resisted the urge to brush it off.

"And who might this be?" Rand's accusing question jerked her eyes back to his. It had definitely been a mistake to not tell him about Tommy in their correspondence. But would he have agreed to their arrangement if she'd announced she'd be bringing her younger brother?

Tommy looked up at Rand. "I'm Tommy Blair, and I'm seven. I'm gonna live in a place called Kansas and maybe ride a horse. Is this Kansas?"

Rand knelt beside him but sent her a glare.

Carly expelled a sigh of relief when the man's probing gaze shifted to her brother. What would Tommy say next? She'd told him that part about riding a horse in hopes that he'd be excited about the move.

Perhaps that had been wrong too. She bit the edge of her lip. Could she do nothing right anymore?

"You're in Kansas, all right, and you certainly will ride horses. Every cowpoke needs to know how to ride a horse. Did your mama tell you that?" He gestured at Carly without looking at her.

"Oh, no," Carly said, "he's not—"

"Nah, my mama lives in heaven with Jesus. Carly done told me about horses."

"Tommy is my brother," she managed. Goodness sakes, her voice echoed all the fear overwhelming her heart. "He's right. Do call me Carly, please."

Rand stood once more, his height as intimidating as his frown. "I don't believe you mentioned a brother, Miss Blair."

"Tommy will be no trouble, I assure you." Her heart stuttered. Mr. Stratford had to let Tommy stay. What would she do if he didn't?

The man's face shifted into a tight smile. "Well then, let's collect your things and head to the parsonage. Pastor Philbrick is waiting to perform the ceremony."

"*Now?*" The word came out as little more than a squeak. Carly made a mental effort to unravel her tongue and make it speak the words she needed to say. "I … I thought perhaps we'd have a few days to get to know one another, see if we can make this work out."

Yanking his hat down, Rand didn't even look at her. "You came here to marry me. I expect we better get it done." He grasped Tommy's small hand in his larger one before striding away.

Carly had no choice but to follow.

Clumsy, a tad dishonest, and bringing another child to worry over. Rand set his jaw with a tight clamp of his mouth. Whatever else his new bride was or wasn't, at least she was pretty. Downright stunning with that auburn hair and those emerald green eyes. He'd have to be careful. Just don't look at her, that's all. He couldn't afford to get his heart tied up in this deal. This was about Jenna and Mary Jo, and he'd best not forget that.

Anyway, having the boy along might not be such a bad idea. He could work on the ranch when he got older, and if there was one thing Rand had plenty of, it was beef to fill the boy's belly. He sure hoped cattle prices would edge up soon, though. Pretty sorry state of affairs when a cattleman had to eat his own beef to make it pay.

"That's my trunk." Carly pointed at a battered piece of luggage sitting on the baggage platform. "The small one beside it is Tommy's."

"May I take your satchel for you?" Rand extended a hand.

"No." Her grasp tightened on the tattered bag.

Rand shrugged and shouldered the larger piece, then carried it to his wagon. At least she hadn't brought more than one trunk. Had it been his ex-fiancée, Myra, she'd have had at least three, if not more. There'd be no need of fancy dresses and feminine frou-frou on the ranch.

He threw a glance Carly's way. Why did the woman look like she'd burst into tears any moment? He didn't take kindly to female tears. Myra could turn them on and off at will, whenever it suited her purpose. Must be something women learned from their mamas to beguile men. Whatever the case, it wouldn't hurt him to be polite. The girl looked scared spitless.

"I've spoken with Pastor Philbrick, and he's aware of our— circumstances. He won't ask you to promise to obey me."

Even so, he expected her to do just that, didn't he? Everyone on the ranch obeyed him. He gave an order and considered it done. Only Myra had dared defy him and look what happened there.

"I—all right. Thank you." Carly stared at her shoes. Those black tips off the edge of her skirt hem must be all-fired interesting. Maybe he should try to curb a little of that anxiety she was trying so hard to hide. It was making him nervous too.

He offered his hand to help her into the wagon, but she pretended not to see it. At least, Rand was pretty sure she was pretending. And then she nearly fell. He caught her before she went down and lifted her into the seat. Tiny little thing. His big hands could nearly span her waistline.

Rand stowed the trunk in the wagon box, returned for the smaller one, then lifted the boy in behind them. Rand climbed in beside her and took the reins, bouncing them lightly over the horses' backs. They plodded down the dusty street. It wasn't far to the parsonage, but trying to think up something to talk about during the short drive made it seem a rather long journey.

"Sure is a hot one today. Late August gives us some scorchers like this."

"Yes," she whispered, gaze riveted to those dadburn shoes.

She was no help a'tall. "Probably cool off a little once we hit mid-September."

Apparently that remark didn't warrant any reply.

"The girls fixed up a room for you back at the ranch. I reckon they can find a room for the boy, too, unless he wants to stay with you."

The creases in Carly's forehead smoothed at his words. Hadn't he made it clear in their brief correspondence that she could have her own room? Surely, she hadn't thought …

"I think he'd like to stay with me for a while, at least until he gets used to the new surroundings." The girl looked plain relieved. Good. He'd managed to do something right, then.

"I'll get one of my men to stuff another straw tick and bring it in for him." Uh-oh. The creases were back. Now what had he gone and done?

"That's kind of you," she murmured. "How many men live on your ranch?"

"Four of them year-round. I usually hire on extras in the spring for calving and branding. Bunkhouse sleeps eight, ten if a few don't mind a pallet on the floor." Rand had no idea why she wanted this information. Did his answer make her feel better or worse? Her lack of response gave him no clues.

"Your letter said you were twenty-one." Rand's words sounded more like an accusation than a question. Well, maybe it was. She didn't look much older than Mary Jo.

"My birthday was last month."

"I'm twenty-eight."

"So you said."

The parsonage finally appeared. About time.

"This is it." He pulled on the reins and stopped in front of the cottage. He glanced at his bride. What in the Sam Hill? Carly was positively green. Was she going to be sick? Not in his wagon, not if he could help it. Dropping the reins, he barreled over the side, ran around the team, and lifted her from the wagon seat. Mercy, the girl needed a few more potatoes in her. She was light as a newborn foal.

"You all right?" He steadied her on her feet, unwilling to let go lest she crumple to the ground.

"I'm fine." The answer was as terse as it was unbelievable.

He scratched the back of his neck. What was that kid's name again? "Um, you there in the wagon, jump down and come help your sister. I think she'd do well to use you as a leaning post while I see to the team."

Obedient as if he were one of the ranch hands, the boy did as he was asked.

"Thank you, Tommy."

Carly's voice was firm, her face filling with color once more. *Tommy.* Rand had to remember that. Common enough name. It would have been nice if he'd had some idea ahead of time that the boy was coming. There had to be more to this story than she'd told Rand in the one letter and the few telegrams they'd exchanged, but that would be a discussion for another time.

He pasted on his brightest, however fake, smile. "Shall we go get married?"

Chapter 2

Nausea crawled up her throat, and Carly forced it back. Not that it felt better in her stomach. She just didn't want to make a spectacle of herself. She'd known she was coming to Kansas to get married. Why did it all of a sudden seem so real? So frightening?

Leaning on Tommy a bit more than she wanted Rand Stratford to know, Carly followed the man along the worn path to the front door of the clapboard house that was a small replica of the church off to the left. At least this little town had a church. She'd wondered about that. Did Rand make the drive in from the ranch on Sunday mornings, or was it too far to come for weekly services?

The door opened as they reached it, and Mr. Stratford spoke. "Pastor Philbrick, I'd like you to meet Miss Carly Blair, and this young fellow is her brother Tommy."

Carly heard Rand speak the words, and somehow her hand ended up in the pastor's firm handshake.

"Pleased to meet you, Miss Blair." He ushered them inside and produced a small Bible from his inner jacket pocket. He opened it and motioned for them to join him on a braided rag rug spread across the waxed wooden floor. "Shall we begin?"

Rand hadn't been joshing about the pastor being ready for them. Before Carly even had time to chide herself for agreeing to such a ludicrous plan, she was standing before Pastor Philbrick at his fireless hearth, waiting to promise her life away.

"Just say I do," the pastor whispered when her pause grew uncomfortably long.

Rand frowned. "She does."

Carly narrowed her eyes and stood straight. "I do."

Her tone lacked any hint of the firmness and confidence she'd hoped for in her answer.

"I now pronounce you man and wife for as long as you both shall live."

Carly swallowed hard. Did the man have to make it sound so final? Like a prison sentence? Maybe it was. Rand's letter said she could leave if ever she felt he hadn't lived up to his end of the bargain. But she couldn't leave. She had nowhere to go except back into the clutches of Lester McGraw. She'd do whatever she had to in order to save herself and Tommy from that evil man.

"Don't you want to kiss the bride?" The pastor had the most ridiculous grin on his face. Carly's cheeks went hot as she stared at the floor. She wouldn't make it easy for him.

"Nah, we need to do some getting acquainted first," Rand said, a hint of humor in his voice. Was he enjoying her discomfort?

She dared a quick glance at Tommy, who was watching the whole thing with great interest. Well, that was probably good. At first, he'd been so upset about leaving Baltimore and his dog Riley. That's why Carly had told him wonderful things about Rand's Kansas ranch, most of which she'd only guessed. Now, Tommy was all ready to ride into the picture Carly had painted, and she had no idea how much of it, if any, was true. Horses and cows. What ranch didn't have horses and cows? And Rand's dog, which she'd promised Tommy would love as much as he'd loved Riley.

Did Rand have a dog? She hadn't dared to ask. Carly squared her shoulders. If he didn't, he better be prepared to get one real soon. No matter what she had to endure, even if it involved pleading with her new husband for a dog, Tommy would be happy in Kansas. It was the only thing that mattered.

A short, plump woman—Mrs. Philbrick, Carly assumed—entered the room, an apron wrapped around her ample waist. "Would you folks stay for some tea? I just pulled a black walnut cake out of the oven, and it smells really good." Black walnut cake? Carly wanted to stay to find out what such a confection might taste like. The aroma wafting from the kitchen made her mouth water.

Rand pulled a watch on a gold chain out of his pocket and glanced at it. "Thank you kindly, ma'am, but we'd best be getting on home."

Tommy's face fell at his words. How long had it been since he'd eaten? Carly made sure he got a few biscuits for breakfast, but … What time was it now?

"Wait just a moment," Mrs. Philbrook said, "and I'll wrap up that cake for you to take home. I'm sure the girls would enjoy a piece too." She bustled out of the room.

Carly smiled encouragement to Tommy, or tried to anyway.

A few minutes later, the wedding certificate was signed with Mrs. Philbrick and Pastor Philbrick's mother, who lived with them, as witnesses. The pastor pocketed the bill Rand discreetly handed him, Carly picked up her satchel, and the three of them were in the wagon once more. This time the horses headed north out of town and onto the open prairie.

It was beautiful country with the rolling hills and rough rock outcroppings, but Carly couldn't enjoy it. Ready or not, mostly not, she was about to embark on a new stage of life. She would now be mistress of a large Kansas ranch, caretaker to two young girls she'd never met, and … she was now *Mrs. Rand Stratford*. Carly winced.

The woman clutched the basket so hard she likely squeezed the black walnuts right out of Mrs. Philbrick's cake. Not the woman. His wife. He blinked as he tried to comprehend the word. He was married. It'd take some getting used to, for sure. At least she'd finally agreed to letting him stow that blamed satchel thing in the back. She'd held onto it since she'd stepped off the train.

She'd told him in her letter she could cook passably. What did that mean? Well, whatever the case, the meals she turned out had to be better than what Mary Jo had been ladling up these past few weeks. His oldest niece was even worse in the kitchen than his bunkhouse cook, Tubby Jackson, but Rand couldn't very well eat with the men in the bunkhouse anymore. He had a family now, and he had to belly up to that supper table in the ranch house, no matter what was on it.

Maybe Miss Blair—er—Carly, could teach Mary Jo a few things in the kitchen. Jenna, too, while she was at it. At any rate, they'd have a decent dessert tonight even if the rest of the meal wasn't that tasty. That was, if Carly would let loose her clench on the basket. What was wrong with her anyway? Her knuckles had gone plumb white.

He cleared his throat. "We'll be there soon. Just a few more miles is all." Was that good or bad? Rand's words brought no reprieve for the squashed basket. "Anything you want to ask about before we get there?"

She glanced at him long enough for him to see the questions swarming around in those big green eyes of hers. Maybe she just couldn't get them to her lips. A slight tingle ran down Rand's spine when he focused on those lips. So he shouldn't think about her lips. It wasn't as if he was gonna be taking the pastor up on his suggestion any time soon.

"You raise cows?" Her words trembled.

Was she really that naive about what folks did on a ranch?

"We raise cattle. Cows are necessary when it comes to producing the steers we take into market."

That adorable pinkness dusted her cheeks again. *Look somewhere else, Stratford.*

"I guess what I meant was, do you have any dairy cows? You know, milkers?"

Rand suppressed his chuckle. "Yeah, we got a few to provide the milk we need, cream, butter and the like. Have you ever milked a cow Miss Bl—er, Carly?" He had to get used to thinking of her as Carly. She wasn't Miss Blair anymore, and he sounded like an idiot when he called her that. But it had been less than an hour ago he'd spoken those two little words he'd sworn he'd never say to a woman after Myra left. *I do.* They echoed inside his throbbing head, because sure as shootin', he did.

"No, I'm afraid not, but I'm sure I could learn."

She sounded awfully uncertain.

"I have," Tommy piped up from behind. "Sometimes Leo'd let me help him milk Betsy. I can make the milk spurt out real good."

"I'll bet you can." Good to know the boy was prepared to do some chores. He was just a little kid, but there was still plenty of work for a tyke his age. Who was Leo? He'd figure that out later. "How about we let you try it with Tubby come morning?"

"Tubby?" She actually lifted her gaze from her shoes, though the apprehension was back in her voice.

"One of my men," he explained. "He does the cooking in the bunkhouse."

Now, why did she look so relieved? She even let go of the basket with one hand to brush away a tendril of auburn hair that had fallen from the knot at her nape. Finally. His fingers had been itching to do that very thing. Her hair looked so soft, and it was such a pretty color. Myra's hair had been nearly black. Beautiful in its own way, but more likely a mirror into her heart. Why hadn't he noticed?

"Your nieces, um, Mary and Jenna. Do they cook?"

"Mary Jo. She's particular about that. And yes, they've been in charge of the kitchen since coming to live at the ranch." No point in telling her he'd eaten burnt oatmeal for breakfast more times than he wanted to think about in the last few months.

"How old did you say they are?"

"Mary Jo is twelve and Jenna is almost seven. They're good kids but still grieving their parents. I reckon having you around will help make the ranch seem more like home to them." They were the whole reason he'd gone and done this mail-order-bride thing. He'd do anything for Mary Jo and Jenna, including hitching himself to someone he didn't even know, but by thunder, it sure wrenched in his gut to think of himself as a married man.

"I hope so."

Not much of a reply, but what did he expect? She hadn't even met the girls yet.

"Are they adjusting well?"

If only he could say yes, but she'd find out soon enough it wasn't true. "Mary Jo is handling it pretty well."

"And the younger one?"

Curious little thing. Rand shook his head. He'd better just up and tell her.

"Jenna hasn't spoken since her parents died. She saw the accident. Doc says she'll come around. We just need to give her some time."

Instead of the horror he expected to see in Carly's expression, all he found was sympathy and concern.

"How long ago was it they lost their parents?"

"Almost two months." Rand dropped his voice to a whisper, the words tight in his throat. "Their barn caught fire in a lightning storm. Dan and Maggie were trying to get the animals out when the loft collapsed on them."

Carly's quick intake of breath told him she was not unmoved by the plight of his two orphan nieces.

Rand missed his sister every day, but it was the worst when silent little Jenna, who looked so much like Maggie, crawled up in his lap and sobbed her heart out. All he knew to do was hold her and let her cry.

Every day, Rand had asked God why it had to happen. As far as he could tell, God never answered him. Finally, Rand quit asking. He hadn't talked to God much lately.

"Do you have a dog?" Carly wanted to know.

That question brought him out of his reverie. Where had that come from, and why did it matter?

"Two actually. Bo is my cow dog. Had him for a coon's age, but he's a good one, all right. The girls brought their dog, Vinnie, when they came to live at the ranch. She's just a mutt, but they love her." And they did. No way he could be talked into separating Jenna from Vinnie, even if his new wife didn't care for dogs.

"Oh, that's good. Tommy was hoping you'd have a dog."

Now that was a surprise. He'd figured Carly would be the type to be afraid of a strange dog. "We could get another one, a puppy maybe? That way Tommy could have something that belonged to him."

Was that going too far? Truth was, Hiram Shagnatts from the farm across the creek had a litter of new pups that looked a lot like Bo, the old rascal. Wouldn't hurt to have another cattle dog on the ranch.

Carly actually smiled. Must have been a good idea. Rand would talk to Hiram first chance he got.

The peaked roof of the main barn came into view, and Rand pointed to it with a burst of pride in his chest.

"We're home."

Carly's smile disappeared.

Chapter 3

No going back now. Carly was a married woman, and this was her home. She dared a look around. Beautiful country, big ranch, an ominously large two-story house, and a dog running to greet them. What more could she want?

She'd be safe here. Tommy would be safe. But would Rand's nieces like her or resent her? According to what he'd said about someone named Tubby, she wouldn't be responsible for cooking for the ranch hands as she'd feared, but would she be able to manage this house, three children, and a husband?

A girl with brown braids and a blue calico dress stepped onto the porch and stared at them, not a hint of expression on her thin face. Carly forced herself to smile at the girl. This must be Mary. *Mary Jo.* She had to remember to get the girl's name right. A smaller child peered from behind the older one. She had the same brown braids and thin face, but her skin had a pallor the other girl's didn't. Jenna, the child with no voice. Could Carly help her find her words again? As Rand helped her down from the wagon seat, Carly ignored the tingles that seemed to run out of his fingertips and down her spine. Jitters.

Rand called, "Mary Jo, Jenna, come on out here. I want you to meet someone."

Carly turned just in time to see Mary Jo send a glare toward Rand as she made her way to the wagon Rand had parked in the barnyard. Her little sister followed.

"Who's that?" Mary Jo's greeting was somewhat less than welcoming.

Carly nibbled on the edge of her lip. Gracious sakes, had Rand not told his nieces about her? Surely they'd been expecting her. Rand said they'd made up a room for her.

"This is Tommy," Rand answered matter-of-factly. "He is Miss Blair's … I mean …" Rand shrugged, a sheepish expression on his face. "Tommy, meet Mary Jo and Jenna."

Carly released a sigh as Tommy nodded to the girls. Seemed Rand was as nervous as she was. She took comfort in the fact that Mary Jo's rude comment hadn't been directed at her. Of course, they hadn't been expecting Tommy.

She reached out a hand. "I'm Carly. Pleased to meet you, Mary Jo."

Mary Jo took her hand for a brief moment but didn't smile or speak. This was going to take some getting used to. Carly turned to Jenna.

"So nice to meet you, Jenna." Again, she extended her hand. To her surprise, the little girl grasped it, clinging for several moments before letting go. The trembling smile on her thin face betrayed both her broken heart and her joy at once again having a woman around. Carly could never replace their mother, she wasn't fooling herself about that, but if she could help, she did so want to do that.

"Mary Jo." Rand hefted her trunk from the wagon and dropped it into the dust of the barnyard. "You and Jenna take Carly and Tommy on in the house and show them around. I'm going to go take care of the team." He turned to Carly. "I'll have a couple of the boys haul these up to your room."

"And you won't forget about the straw tick for Tommy?" Carly regretted the question the moment it left her mouth. It almost sounded like an accusation. Of course, he wouldn't forget. Rand's only answer was a nod.

Jenna was already pulling on her hand. Carly handed the basket with the cake to Mary Jo and grabbed her satchel. Tommy was staring at the barn and two saddled horses tied to the hitching rail. He started toward them. "Come with me, Tommy."

He gave her a disgruntled look but said nothing as he walked to her side. The three of them followed Mary Jo as she plodded silently toward the porch, head down and shoulders slumped. Carly's heart ached for the girls. It was clear they were hurting. Mary Jo, at least, seemed to have formed the opinion that their uncle's new wife would be more of a nuisance than a help. Carly would just have to prove her wrong. Unless of course, she was right.

Mary Jo took them on a brief tour of the downstairs. Sitting room, kitchen, parlor, and a large area off the sitting room that Rand seemed to use as an office. Tommy gasped at the sight of the rifle hanging over the door. "Maybe I could learn to shoot that."

"We'll see," was the only answer she'd give him now. They'd have a talk about that later, in private. All the rooms were spacious, the walls papered. A rock fireplace rose to the ceiling on the outer wall of the sitting room.

The house just needed a little cleaning. A few swipes with a dust rag would shine up the handmade furniture, and a little elbow grease on the smudged windows would let the light in. Maybe pulling back those heavy draperies would help too. Yes, a feminine touch here and there was needed, but all in all, Carly was pleased with her new surroundings.

With a word to her sister to take "the lady" upstairs and show her the room, Mary Jo excused herself to the kitchen. The back door slammed. Could it be that Mary Jo was less than pleased with the new arrangements?

Carly was eager to unpack, arrange her things in the large bedroom Jenna showed her, and make it feel more like home. Even the kitchen had an allure, beckoning Carly to create meals for this new family of hers. She could picture the five of them sitting around that big round table, a home-cooked supper spread before them.

What were Rand's favorite foods? What did the girls like to eat? So much to learn. Maybe she could ask that Tubby person Rand mentioned. He should know what her new husband expected and appreciated in a meal. But would she be treading on Mary Jo's territory? Rand said she'd been doing the cooking. Would she resent it if Carly took over? Carly would have to make an effort to include both girls in the household tasks.

Tommy was engrossed in the view from the second story window. Carly quickly slid the satchel she'd held all the way from Baltimore under the big four-poster bed. She'd find a place to hide it once she became more familiar with the place. No one must ever see what was in that bag.

A loud thud and the click of boot heels on the stairway preceded a male voice calling, "We've got your trunks, ma'am."

"Open the door for them, Tommy." He rushed to do as she asked, then continued watching with big eyes as two men entered with their heavy loads. "Put them there, please." Carly pointed to the space beneath the east window. With Jenna still holding onto her hand, Carly grabbed Tommy's wrist with her other. Her face went hot as the strange men invaded her bedroom, but weren't they just carrying out Rand's orders? Should she introduce herself?

The tall, lanky man with a shock of carrot-red hair doffed his hat as soon as he'd placed the trunk on the floor. "Be right back with the straw tick, Mrs. Stratford."

She blinked at the use of the unfamiliar name but forced out a "Thank you, sir."

"I'm Nate Walker, ma'am. That there's Clarence Crawford." He pointed to the short, red-faced man with a graying beard and kind eyes. Nate jammed the hat on his head, shuffling his feet and casting a furtive glance at his companion. Without another word, they edged out of the room. A moment later quick footsteps descended the stairs. They had probably been as uncomfortable in her bedroom as she'd been to have them there.

"What's a stick tick?" Tommy wrestled his wrist away from her. "Will I like it?"

"Straw tick, and of course you'll like it. It's a mattress stuffed with straw. I'm sure it'll be a comfortable place to sleep."

"I'm hungry. Can we have cake now?"

Carly expelled a shaky breath. Better go downstairs and see what Mary Jo was planning for supper. She needed to help put the meal on the table. Her stomach was growling too. Not that she had any appetite.

Stooping to hug Jenna, who clung to her like a cockleburr, Carly spoke with a brightness she didn't feel. "Let's go find your sister."

And whatever else awaited.

They'd known he was bringing home a wife. Why were his ranch hands walking around with goofy grins and sending him sly winks? Rand scowled at Nate and Clarence as they stuffed handfuls of clean straw into the ticking.

"You can quit your smirking. I ain't blind, you know."

"Yes sir, boss." Nate bent over his work with a stifled chortle and a sideways glance at Clarence.

Rand almost gave them a frustrated foot stomp or two before he stormed out of the barn, but curiosity got the better of him. "You wanna tell me what's so all-fired funny?"

The two looked at each other and back to the mattress. A chuckle behind him made him whirl around just in time to see Tubby wipe the grin off his face. Hands on his hips, Rand stared him down until Tubby spoke.

"We was takin' bets on what your new missus was gonna look like. Clarence had her pegged as a fat woman with squinty eyes and Nate there figured she'd be old and bossy."

The two straw-stuffers scowled. "Tubby thought she'd be frumpy as an old maid schoolmarm," Clarence added. "Parker figured she'd have a mustache."

Rand choked back a laugh, keeping his face grim. "Just who do you figure won this here bet?"

Tubby was the only one who'd give him a straight answer. "Appears you won, boss. That lady you brought home is a real looker. You're a lucky man."

Why, then, did these hooligans think they were stuffing a straw tick? Yeah, Carly was pretty, all right, but it wasn't like she was gonna be curled up next to him at night. She was here to look after the girls. Period.

"Get all that snickering outta your system and get the straw tick inside. We got work to do around here, and it ain't gonna get done unless you get at it. Nate, you've got guard duty on the south range. Clarence and Parker, get the stalls mucked, and Tubby, you better get to baking these boys some biscuits and rustle up some beans to pour over 'em. They're gonna be hungry before I'm done with 'em tonight."

Rand turned on his heel and left the three staring after him. No point in letting them see how their innocent teasing hit right on that sore spot in his gut. They didn't know all the details about his arrangement with Carly. Yeah, she was a lot prettier than he'd expected. A fellow had to take his chances when he did something as dumb as advertise for a wife. She was a nice person to boot. Jenna had taken to her right away. Mary Jo would come around, and it would all work out. For everybody but him.

It would be a sight easier to crawl into his bed alone every night if his in-name-only wife was frumpy or cantankerous or disagreeable, but he wasn't doing this thing for himself. Mary Jo and Jenna were all that mattered. He should probably head on inside to see how they were all getting along. If they weren't … getting along, that is … what was he going to do about it?

Parker came out of the dairy barn with the milk bucket. At least one of his ranch hands was working.

"Want me to take that?" Rand asked. "I'm heading up to the house." Why did Parker look disappointed? Oh, yeah. He probably wanted a chance to gawk at Rand's new wife too.

"Sure, boss. Thanks." Parker handed over the brim-full bucket. "I reckon Tubby might need some of that once it's strained."

Rand sighed. No getting around it. "Come on by the house a little later and Mary Jo will have it ready for you." *And take a gander at Mrs. Stratford while you're there, see what all the fuss is about.* He didn't say that part out loud, but maybe his expression communicated his thoughts.

Parker grinned and headed off to the big barn. Guess the expression thing hadn't worked. Served the cowboy right to have to muck stalls before supper.

Rand couldn't avoid the inevitable any longer. He had a bucket full of milk to get to the house. Would his new bride be in the kitchen? Not likely. She'd be settling into her room, unpacking and such. With any luck, he wouldn't have to see her again just now.

The screen door swung open as he approached the back door. Rand nearly tripped over Vinnie as the little mutt raced out. He managed to remain upright, though he doused the dog with a milk shower. He stifled the curse that threatened to rise from his throat.

"Sorry, Uncle Rand." Mary Jo reached for the bucket. Most of the milk had stayed inside. Confounded dog. And he'd just promised to get a puppy for the boy. One more thing underfoot.

Relieved of the milk, Rand shuffled on into the kitchen and stuck his hands under the water pump. Maybe he should help Mary Jo with the meal since they had guests. Well, not really guests. This was their home now. It was Carly and Tommy's first night here, and he wanted to make a good impression. Why it was so important to him, he couldn't have said.

Mary Jo stood by the stove stirring something in a pot. The table was set, and something smelled real good. Where was Carly? He scrubbed his hands up to his elbows with the lump of soap on the windowsill. Maggie had made that soap, and the supply was almost gone. Did Mary Jo know how her mother had made soap? Did Carly? Maybe he should have included that in his ad for a new bride. *Soap-making skills required.*

Rand turned to reach for the towel hanging on the bar by the door and ran smack into Carly. His mother would have been ashamed at his lack of manners, but all he could manage was a grunt.

"Sorry," she murmured, handing him the towel. "Supper is almost ready."

Rand tore his eyes from the pretty face and looked again at the kitchen table. It was set with Maggie's china dishes, and the aroma from steaming serving bowls beckoned him nearer. He hadn't seen the china since they'd hauled it over here. Why had Mary Jo gotten it out now? Why was he glad she had?

Carly avoided his gaze. "I hope you don't mind. I found the china in a cupboard when I was looking around the kitchen. There were only four of the tin plates, so I thought it might be all right if we used your good dishes, at least for tonight." Her words sounded half apologetic. No need to be sorry for using dishes on the supper table.

"I can pick up a few more tins when I'm in town next." Dumb as a post. *Think of something stupid to say and then don't say it, Stratford.* He cleared his throat. "Using the china is fine with me as long as Mary Jo doesn't mind. It was her mama's."

"That's what she told me." Carly deposited a plate of biscuits on the table. Rand stared at her, then fixed his gaze on his oldest niece. Mary Jo looked at the floor, a slight smile playing at her mouth.

"Smells good." Rand sniffed again. *Yeah, and then some.*

"Mary Jo made biscuits and gravy," Carly announced. "We found some garden beans, so Jenna and Tommy picked them and snapped them for us. Mrs. Philbrick's cake will make a fine dessert."

If Mary Jo had made the biscuits and gravy, forcing them down would be like eating soggy lumps on hardtack. Hopefully, Carly and Tommy wouldn't say anything to embarrass her. Rand forced a grin. "Call the children and let's eat." He pulled out his chair and sat just as Jenna and Tommy ran into the kitchen. Good thing he had a table with six chairs. That had come from Maggie's house too.

"Wash your hands, please," Carly reminded as she and Mary Jo took their places.

Rand reached for the plate of biscuits, but Carly's purposeful clearing of the throat had him looking up. She gave him a disapproving frown. Oh, yeah. He swallowed hard and put the plate back. He wasn't used to minding his manners. She'd want to say a prayer over the meal. He'd started out doing that with Jenna and Mary Jo when they first came to live here, but the habit had fallen away. Lately, none of them seemed to have the heart for it. He folded his hands back into his lap and waited for the younger ones to seat themselves.

Mary Jo was actually grinning. What was wrong with her, anyway? She never smiled at meal time. Or at any other time for that matter. Not since Maggie ...

"Rand, would you ask the blessing, please?" Carly's voice was soft yet firm.

The children bowed their heads, so Rand forced himself to speak. "Father God, we thank you for this bounty before us." Maybe that had been a tad dishonest? Bounty? Mary Jo's biscuits and gravy could hardly be considered bounty. He grabbed the plate and searched for the smallest ones to save Carly and Tommy from breaking a tooth their first day there. These were different than Mary Jo's usual biscuits though. They sure smelled good, and he couldn't find the small ones. In fact, they all looked pretty much the same size. He took two and passed the plate to Jenna. He'd eat them even if he was up all night with indigestion.

The plate was passed. Uh-oh. The boy took three. He might have taken more if Carly hadn't frowned at him. Heaven help them all.

Chapter 4

Carly stole a glance at Mary Jo. The girl hadn't wanted to take her suggestions with the biscuit dough, or the gravy for that matter, but she'd done it. Probably because her uncle had made her promise to be respectful to his new wife or some such thing. Now, she watched her uncle with a smug smile. Smug or not, it was worth it if Mary Jo was actually smiling. Such a sullen, unhappy girl. Carly was going to have to find a way to get through to her. Maybe a few cooking lessons would be a good beginning. Anyway, Mary Jo wasn't the only one enjoying the surprised expression on Rand's face.

The gravy was being passed around the table behind the biscuits. Rand's mouth almost fell open when it ran over his fluffy biscuits in a smooth flow from the ladle. If Mary Jo hadn't mixed her flour with water before she added it to the gravy, it would have made for some lumps. Carly had stopped her just in time. Everyone at the table was watching Rand, though Carly tried not to be as obvious about it as the children. He forked a bite to his mouth. Hopefully she hadn't advised Mary Jo to use too much salt if he wasn't used to it, but the girl hadn't added any until Carly told her to. Lumpy gravy with no flavor? Is that what they'd survived on the past few months?

"Mary Jo, honey? You baked these biscuits?" Rand sounded like he didn't quite believe her.

"Yes."

"Hmm." Rand looked thoughtful but pleased. "You do something different this time?"

What would she say? Mary Jo glanced at Carly, and Carly gave her a quick wink of encouragement. "Not really. I just put a little more milk in 'em than usual, and some of that stuff in the can. I didn't ever know what it was for until, well, until I figured it out tonight."

"In the can?" Rand was puzzled. No doubt he didn't know what baking powder was either. "I see." Obviously he didn't see. "How did you get 'em all the same size like that?"

Mary Jo flashed Carly another furtive glance. "Instead of cutting them out with a knife, I decided to use a drinking glass upside down. Worked pretty well."

"I'll say." Rand's appreciative nod caused his niece's face to beam. "Mighty fine gravy there, girl." He nodded at Carly. "Good beans too."

Carly held her expression solemn with an effort. At least he gave her credit for knowing how to boil beans. A little bacon fat in the water did wonders for the taste, but Rand didn't need to know that either.

Tommy shoveled food in his mouth as though he'd never eaten a meal, but Rand didn't seem to notice. She tried to send her brother a warning glare, but he hardly looked up from his plate. He seemed happy enough and would be more so now that he'd eaten. Maybe this place would be good for Tommy.

Jenna, too, seemed to be enjoying her meal, though she glanced up often. Sometimes at Tommy, more often at Carly. Whenever she caught the girl's eyes, she'd offer a smile.

They ate in silence. The food was good. Delicious, in fact, after the meals on the train. Any help Carly might have given Mary Jo was rewarded many times over when Carly watched the girl's face as her uncle helped himself to more biscuits and gravy for the third time. When they'd finished the meal, the black walnut cake Mrs. Philbrick had baked was sliced and served on delicate china saucers. The children and Rand seemed delighted by the sweet, nutty taste of the treat, but Carly couldn't finish hers.

"You feeling all right?" Rand asked as she slid her cake onto Tommy's saucer. "You didn't eat much."

"I'm fine, thank you." She pushed her chair back and stacked plates, then carried them to the sideboard. "I believe I'll start on the dishes since Mary Jo has the water heated." She tossed a smile toward the older girl, who returned it with a rather reluctant upward tilt of her lips. Truth was, the darkness that had fallen while they ate sent anxiety through her that seemed to culminate in her stomach. Soon it would be bedtime, her first night in the new surroundings. What would it be like for her and Tommy to begin a new life in a new place? Would they be happy here? Would they be safe?

Rand kicked off the sheet and thumped his pillow. Sure was hot. Sultry even. Usually the heat didn't bother him, but tonight he couldn't get comfortable. Was it the August night or the woman in the bedroom down the hall that wouldn't let him sleep? Just knowing she was there sent a quiver through his gut that was a far cry from sleep-inducing. Rand turned over yet again and stared at the other wall. The moonlight shining through the open window was pretty bright. Maybe that had something to do with his wakefulness.

A scream rent the silence. *Jenna.*

Rand flew from his bed, pulled on the pair of trousers he'd shucked earlier, and grabbed a shirt, not taking time to button it. How long would the girl have to endure these horrible nightmares? He flung open his bedroom door and raced to the room where his youngest niece slept.

"Jenna, baby, it's all …" His words clogged his throat when Carly turned in surprise. She'd perched on the edge of the mattress, and Jenna was clinging to her the way she usually clung to him. Only tighter. Closer. His niece was already grasping the comfort Carly offered. It had taken Jenna much longer to find that comfort with him.

Carly's green eyes widened, betraying her shock and fear, but her voice was calm, barely more than a whisper. "This has happened before?"

Rand nodded. "Many times. I think she relives the accident in her dreams." Try as he might, he could not pull his eyes away from the sight of his wife with her long auburn hair loose, falling over her shoulders in slight curls. She was bathed in the moonlight from the nearby window.

"I think she's starting to calm down," Carly said. "I'll stay with her until she's asleep. You can go back to bed." Carly smoothed Jenna's hair with one hand and stroked her back with the other. She was right. Jenna's sobs had lessened. How had Carly done that?

Rand stood rooted to the spot.

What was she was doing? Humming? Singing? The words were almost without form, but the sweet lullaby Carly whispered into

Jenna's ear was making a difference. Jenna relaxed in her arms. As the song faded into the sultry night air, which suddenly seemed far less oppressive, Jenna closed her eyes and let a slight smile play about her lips. With a muffled hiccup, she lay back on the pillow and snuggled peacefully under the thin sheet Carly pulled over her. Rand stared as Carly dropped a kiss on the girl's cheek and rose in a soft movement.

She stood and turned, catching sight of him still standing in the doorway. She folded her arms, apparently realizing she wasn't adequately dressed. Rand forced himself to divert his eyes, choosing to look at the floor and the tips of his bare toes. He fought the inner notion that begged him to take this beautiful woman in his arms and hold her close.

She flicked her hand toward the hallway, snapping him out of his daze. He backed out of the doorway, and she slid past him, careful not to touch him. Like a flitting apparition in white, she made her way down the dark hallway. The door clicked into place behind her, and Rand shook his head to shut down the mesmerizing idea of following her.

Not knowing what else to do, he retreated to his own room, undressed, and crawled back into the big four-poster bed where he'd slept most of his life, suddenly finding it quite large and lonely for one person. He hadn't expected the turmoil now burrowing through him, and he didn't know how to deal with it.

Carly had done exactly what he'd brought her here to do, so why did he feel so ... so envious? She'd quieted Jenna's nightmare in just a few moments with a simple song and a soft touch. Obviously, he had neither of those things. Sometimes it took him half the night to get her calmed down enough to sleep again. Carly'd done it as if she'd been comforting traumatized children all her life. And how beautiful she'd looked doing it.

But his marriage wasn't about him or even about Carly. He'd married for the sake of Mary Jo and Jenna, and they were what was important here. Tommy too, now that he was here. And apparently, despite all his blunders and misgivings through the process, he'd found just the right woman to do what needed doing.

"Thank you, Lord."

When was the last time he'd uttered words to God, a prayer that wasn't just a half-hearted blessing over a meal? Long enough ago that it felt strange, but at the same time it felt good. Real good.

Chapter 5

"Would you like me to help you with breakfast?" It wasn't even light out yet, but Carly found Mary Jo pumping water into a pan when she entered the kitchen the next morning.

"No."

Well, that was subtle. "All right. I'm sure whatever you make will be wonderful. Mind if I make some coffee?"

Mary Jo shrugged as she carried water to the stove, so Carly picked up the coffee pot, rinsed it out, and refilled it from the pump. "Does your uncle like his coffee strong or watered down a little?" Might as well make it the way Rand liked it.

The girl shrugged again. She certainly wasn't very talkative. Then suddenly, Mary Jo turned to face her. "Will you show me how to make coffee?"

Carly hid her smile. "Of course, but don't you make it every morning?"

Mary Jo looked at the floor. "I tried a few times when we first came here, but Uncle Rand doesn't seem to like it. He mostly makes his own or gets it from the bunkhouse."

Poor girl. It appeared she really wanted to please her uncle. Had Rand been rude about the coffee? Carly showed Mary Jo how to measure the appropriate amount of coffee to go with the water in the pot and cautioned her not to let it boil. "Scalded coffee tastes even worse than it smells," she said with a grin. Mary Jo didn't answer, but she watched

25

every move Carly made.

The water Mary Jo had put on the stove was simmering. "Were you going to make oatmeal?" Carly pointed to the sack of ground oats on the sideboard. "The water looks about ready."

Mary Jo's surprised look told Carly she didn't know how to make oatmeal any more than she had gravy. "A soft boil is better," Carly offered. "That way there's not as much chance of it burning on the bottom. You have to keep stirring it, though, to keep it from getting too hot and scorching."

Mary Jo didn't answer right away, nor did she pour any of the waiting oatmeal into the boiling water. At last, she lifted her eyes from where they'd been fixed on the wood floor. "If you were to help me make somethin' for breakfast, what would we make?"

Well, that was a good sign. Maybe Mary Jo didn't feel comfortable making anything but oatmeal. If that were the case, they were probably tired of it by now. What would sound good to a man who'd eaten scorched oatmeal every morning for too long?

"Maybe pancakes?" Carly suggested. "I saw some molasses in the pantry. That and some of your fresh butter over the top would make them pretty tasty. And perhaps some bacon or salt pork to go alongside? If you have any, that is."

Mary Jo offered her first real smile since Carly's arrival. "You'll teach me how so I can make 'em next time?"

"You can make them this time. Just follow my directions, and you can put a breakfast on the table that you made all by yourself. Your uncle will be real proud of you."

Mary Jo's eager smile remained as Carly talked her through mixing the batter, frying the cakes until they were brown in the middle and crispy on the edges, then laying strips of thick bacon in the cold skillet before moving it to the stove. Such simple tasks, but apparently ones the girl had never learned.

Jenna and Tommy joined them in the kitchen and watched as Mary Jo struggled with the pancakes. By the time Rand came in with the pail of milk, Mary Jo had a hot breakfast on the table. He sat, looked over the meal, then shoveled in a forkful of the crispy cakes. After a couple of bites, he took a second look at the food before him. "Pancakes? And coffee?" He smiled at Carly. "Thank you."

The hopeful expression on Mary Jo's face faded into disappointment. Carly was going to have to discuss this with Rand. Maybe he didn't know how much Mary Jo needed his approval.

"It's Mary Jo you should be thanking. She made your breakfast. I've just been sitting here drinking a cup of the coffee she poured for me. You're very fortunate to have someone so handy in the kitchen." Tommy and Jenna continued to eat, barely looking up from their plates.

Rand's mouth gaped open as he stared at Carly, and eager expectation flooded back into Mary Jo's features. He turned to her and nodded. "Much obliged, Mary Jo. Wonderful breakfast." His tone was incredulous. "As always," he added as an apparent afterthought.

Rand's gaze turned back to Carly as a grin spread across Mary Jo's face. Yes, it had been worth it, patiently explaining away the girl's ineptness with the frying pan from her seat at the table. Perhaps Carly could make some headway with Mary Jo after all. But this had only been breakfast. One meal. What lay ahead in the days and weeks to come as they got used to the idea of her being Rand's wife and a mother-figure to the girls?

"Weren't no coyote what done this." Parker's words followed his low whistle as they gazed at the butchered carcass in front of them.

"Not the four-legged kind, anyway," Rand muttered. "Well, we'd best get this cleaned up, or we'll have plenty of coyotes and buzzards doing it for us." Whoever the culprits were had made a campfire nearby and probably roasted his beef over it. That was before they drove an as-yet-undetermined number of almost-ready-for-market steers through a cut in his new barbed wire fence.

"Nate, you get on to mending that fence." Rand barked his orders to the ranch hands. "Clarence, you and Parker burn this carcass before it attracts every wild animal within sniffing distance. I'm gonna ride out across this pasture and see if I can get a feel for how many head might be missing." And think on this situation for a while.

Rand rode toward the herd of red-and-white cattle in the distance, leaving his men to the cleanup. Normally he would've stayed to help them, never asking them to do something he wasn't willing to do himself, but today his head was too full of questions without answers. Who had stolen cattle, and how many had they gotten away with? Should he still buy Hawthorne's pasture? With two more mouths to feed now and cattle disappearing, it was beginning to look as if his second attempt to buy that pasture he'd had his eye on for so long would fail much the same as the first had. Anyway, he was counting on this year's sale of steers for a good chunk of the payment. He was going to have to figure out who had stolen his cattle and put a stop to it.

"Dusty, whatcha reckon we oughta do?" The quarter horse gelding perked his ears toward Rand's voice but made no answer other than a flick of his long tail.

As Rand rode the perimeter of the pasture and tried to count the head of cattle milling through the tallgrass, he kept an eye on the fence and the surrounding area. Didn't look as if anyone had bothered anything else. Maybe only two or three head missing? Didn't seem to be the work of a big-time cattle rustling gang. They wouldn't have been content with a few head and steaks for supper. Maybe just a coupla guys wanting to make a little extra money? But why Bar-S cattle? There were still a few ranchers around hadn't put up fence yet. Their beef would have been easier pickings.

Rand would report it the next time he was in town. Maybe Sheriff McConnell knew if any of the other area ranches had experienced losses. He'd have to figure that out before he took it personally, but it wouldn't be the first time someone had stolen from him. Myra ...

He shook his head to clear the memories beginning to rear their ugliness and turned Dusty back toward his men. Good thing Nate had run across the carcass while riding fence this morning. It was a lot more convenient when ranches just ran cattle in open range and then rounded up all their brands come spring. Checking fence and pond depths kept at least two men busy year-round. Did away with disputes about water rights and mavericks though, and made calving season a whole lot easier, what with being able to drive the cows about to calve into the corrals where the men could help a cow out if she needed it. Tubby was an expert at pulling a stubborn calf that didn't wanna be born.

"Whatcha think, boss? Lose many?" Clarence called as Rand approached.

"Maybe two or three head is all." But depending on how many times it happened, two or three could add up to a whole bunch, especially where his plans for the Hawthorne pasture were concerned.

Chapter 6

$\mathcal{C}$arly closed her eyes and counted to ten. A good foot stomp or two might have made her feel better, but that wouldn't help this impossible situation. She would have a talk with Rand about this, and neither of them would enjoy it.

"Mary Jo, surely you have some schoolbooks. You and your sister haven't grown up ignorant. History? Arithmetic? A primer? A slate and some chalk?"

Rand's instructions on the girls' schooling had been clear. Part of her duties as caretaker of his nieces was to give them their lessons. The ranch was too far from town for them to go to school every day. Why were they behaving as if schoolwork were a foreign idea?

The four of them sat at the kitchen table. Tommy's primer and slate she'd insisted he bring were the only supplies Carly could locate, and Mary Jo was apparently not inclined to help her.

"Uncle Rand never made us do schoolwork."

Carly tried again. "Don't you like to read? What was the last book you read? Can you tell me about it?"

Mary Jo shook her head.

Carly turned her focus to Jenna. "Can you read, honey?"

Jenna nodded, so Carly handed her Tommy's slate. "Can you write your answer?"

Jenna grabbed a piece of chalk and scrawled the word "Yes" on the slate.

Jenna knew basic words at least, but this was going to be more difficult than Carly'd thought. How did one take recitation from a child who didn't speak? How was Carly to know at what level the child could read or if she knew simple arithmetic?

"Tommy, why don't you practice your fractions while I'm working with the girls? I'll write some problems here on this slate and—"

"I ain't gonna do schoolwork if they don't have to," Tommy retorted. "I wanna go ride horses with Rand."

"You should call him Mr. Stratford," Carly corrected. "And he is busy now. It's time for schoolwork."

"Nope. He told me to call him Rand and he told me I could ride a horse." Tommy folded his arms across his chest and glared at her.

Carly wrote a simple fraction problem on the slate and pushed it in front of Tommy. "Do it. Now." She turned back to Mary Jo. "Could you tell me how far along you think Jenna is in her schooling? Has she finished the first primer?" Mary Jo shrugged, but Jenna smiled and shook her head. Fine, but they still had no primer.

"Very well, then. I'll speak to your uncle later. For now, perhaps we should concentrate on something else." She stood. "I'll put some bread to rising, and then we'll heat some water and do laundry." She wouldn't have thought it possible for Mary Jo's expression to grow even more sour.

"Tubby does the laundry and makes the bread."

"Yes, well, we will be rectifying that in short order." No way was the rotund ranch cook going to wash her underthings, not if Carly could help it.

"I ain't doing no girl work," Tommy muttered under his breath.

A tug on her skirts made Carly look down to see Jenna's hopeful upturned face smiling at her. The girl tugged again and motioned toward the stairway.

"Do you want to show me something, sweetie?"

Jenna nodded.

Carly slipped her hand into the little girl's grasp and, leaving Tommy and Mary Jo frowning at each other, let Jenna lead her up the stairs and then up some more to the open attic above the sleeping rooms. Carly hadn't been up here yet.

The loft was surprisingly light thanks to windows on three sides, but it was dusty and crowded with things. A sofa, various trunks and wooden crates, even a beautiful carved rocking chair. Jenna pulled her through the array of items cluttering the attic floor as if she had been up here often and knew what she was looking for. Sure enough, tucked away in a far corner of the attic on the side with no windows were two matching crates made of wooden slats. They were full of … books.

Carly wrapped Jenna in a hug, breathing a "thank you" in the girl's ear, then sank beside the crates, eager to see the titles this treasure would yield. Fiction classics, poetry, children's stories, and yes, schoolbooks.

Amidst her joy at the discovery of the books, something else caught Carly's eye. What were those tall tablet things? Could they be … sketchbooks? A leather portfolio? Here in the Stratford attic?

Carly pulled one out and let it fall open in her hands. What she saw made her gasp. A remarkable sketch of the Kansas prairie with a winding tree-lined creek running through it. Gorgeous. Whoever had drawn this was exceptionally talented. Staring at the pencil drawing made her want to paint, fill it with life and color. But no. That part of her life was behind her, and, thanks to Lester McGraw, she couldn't go back to it ever again.

She deposited a few of the schoolbooks into Jenna's waiting arms, then grabbed as many more as she could carry along with one of the sketch pads. She followed Jenna back down the stairs, where they found Mary Jo still seated at the kitchen table, her chin cupped in her hands, her elbows resting on the table. She appeared dejected and resigned to the inevitable. Obviously, Mary Jo wasn't eager to continue her schooling. Carly would have to be careful how she handled this situation, or Mary Jo might refuse to cooperate at all.

She stacked the books on the table, leaving the sketch pad on top of the pile. Mary Jo's eyes darted to the sketchbook, then to her sister.

"Why did you show her?" she hissed. "You know my drawings are private."

The pleasure at having helped disappeared from Jenna's face, and tiny tears rolled out of her eyes. She gave her sister a pleading glance.

It took Carly a moment to register what Mary Jo had said. "The sketches are yours?" Carly eyed Mary Jo while she drew Jenna closer to her and dropped an arm around her shoulders. "They're very good."

Mary Jo didn't answer, so Carly tried again. "Do you paint?"

Mary Jo stared at the table. Her words were faint but held a spark of interest. "I've never had any paint."

"Then we'll need to see about getting you some. Talent such as yours should not go to waste." Did Mary Jo actually smile? The girl turned a page in the sketchbook and indeed let a yearning sort of smile flit over her face. Perhaps this was the way to persuade her to do some schoolwork. "But first we must see to your lessons."

"Yes, ma'am." Without further argument, Mary Jo pulled a history book from the pile, thumbed through it for a moment, then pointed to a dog-eared page. "I think this is where we left off before ..." Her lower lip quivered.

No wonder Mary Jo resisted getting back into her studies. The memories of her mother must be strong in these books. Carly eased Jenna into a chair then walked behind Mary Jo to lay a hand on her shoulder. "Study the next few pages then. It would make your mama proud that you're continuing to learn."

Mary Jo nodded and turned her attention to the book in front of her. Now, what to do about Jenna?

"I've got an idea." Carly wrote on one of the slates several words she thought might be at the seven-year-old's reading level. She handed it to her. "You sit here beside your sister and study those words. After you've had time to learn them, I'll clean the slate and dictate the words to you. You can write them down and see how many you can spell correctly. After that, you can pick something out of your primer to read, right about here, I think." She turned to a dog-eared page near the back of the first primer. Either it was a favorite story or the place she had left off under her mother's teaching.

Carly was surprised by the exuberance on Jenna's face as she took the slate and bent her head over it. Had she been afraid she couldn't have school lessons without her voice? Well, it would take some creativity, but Carly would figure out a way not only to continue Jenna's schooling but also to help her find her words again. Poor sweet child.

"Tommy, I'll hear your reading now. You may start here." Carly used her index finger to point to the place in Tommy's second primer but only half listened as her brother stumbled through the passage. It would be good for these children to learn together. Jenna and Tommy were close in age, both of them seven, but Tommy was obviously ahead of Jenna in his studies. At twelve, Mary Jo might enjoy helping plan her own schooling. History, algebra, grammar, and literature would be on the agenda. Maybe Carly could recall enough of her French studies to give the girl some basic knowledge in the language.

And what of Mary Jo's drawings? Could Carly continue to stifle her own love of art while nurturing Mary Jo's? With the girl's talent, it seemed Carly didn't have a choice. It would be wrong not to encourage talent like that.

That evening, the family was relaxing in the sitting room, Mary Jo drawing in her sketchbook. Carly's Bible was open in her lap, but her eyes were drawn away from the words as she gazed at Rand and Tommy playing a game of checkers. They sat on the floor, Jenna curled into the circle of Rand's arm, sometimes pointing out a move he pretended to not see so that his niece could feel involved in the game. Tommy chortled with laughter as Rand made jokes and feigned silly moves, before changing his mind and doing something else.

"I win!" Tommy cried. "I jumped your last king!"

"So you did." Rand stroked his chin where the day's growth of beard appeared a shade darker than his tanned face. "Jenna, how in the world did we let that happen?"

Jenna looked up at him and grinned, probably fully aware that Rand had let Tommy win on purpose.

Rand snapped his fingers. "Say, I've got an idea. How about this next game we let Jenna challenge Tommy, the reigning champion, and see if she can triumph over him. What do you say, Jenna? Tommy?"

Both children nodded eagerly and began setting up the board again. Rand looked up at Carly watching them and flashed her a smile that resonated deep in her heart. This man was so good with the children, and it was easy to see he loved them dearly. Carly dropped the fortresses around her heart enough to let her husband in for just that moment. Trouble was, he seemed to stay there no matter how much she tried to make him leave.

Carly and Tommy had been here ten days now. Not that he was counting. Rand glanced at Carly sitting in a hard-backed chair reading that black leather Bible she'd brought with her. The family was gathered in the sitting room, as was their habit in the evenings. Why was she looking at him like that? All of a sudden, she jumped up and shoved the Bible toward him.

"I think perhaps you should read Scriptures to us before we go to bed. Don't you think so, children?"

Three heads looked up, then nodded dutifully. She turned that smile on him that made him think about her lips, disarming him enough that he took the Bible from her without argument.

"What should I read?" Rand mumbled.

"Psalms, I think. Perhaps the twenty-third." Carly sat back down, and four pairs of eyes watched him. His nieces' eyes danced as though they were enjoying his discomfort.

Rand fumbled with the Bible until he located the proper Psalm and read it aloud, the words familiar in his head but sounding foreign on his tongue. He couldn't remember ever reading the Bible out loud before.

When he'd finished, Carly announced bedtime. As she'd done every night for a week when the children went to bed, she knelt with each of them in turn beside their bed and prayed with them. Rand often watched from the doorway. He'd taken to kneeling by his bed and praying too. Odd, he'd never done that before, even as a child, but he liked it. If he ever got up enough nerve, he might even ask Carly to join him.

It was a few days later when Carly came back downstairs after putting the children to bed. She usually went to bed herself after seeing to the children, but tonight she stood in front of him with an outstretched hand. In it, she held Mary Jo's drawing book.

"I'd like you to look at this, please." She smiled as he took it from her and thumbed through the book of pencil drawings. "It's time you saw how talented your niece is. We should think about getting her some art supplies."

Rand didn't know much about art, but he supposed the drawings were pretty good. He could recognize some of the places the scenes depicted. "Mary Jo did these?" That was the surprising part. Maggie had loved to draw, but she'd never said anything about Mary Jo being interested.

"Yes, Mary Jo. It is her sketchbook." Carly sounded plumb exasperated. Well, she probably was. About all he could keep his mind on these days was those missing steers, and here Carly was trying to get him all excited about some pencil drawings. He obviously wasn't giving her the reaction she'd hoped for. And why was she staring at him like that? Those big green eyes of hers could sure make him turn his thoughts to something besides pretty pictures and cattle rustlers.

"What do you think?"

"About what?"

Carly actually stomped her foot. Mercy, but that woman was beautiful when she was angry.

"About getting Mary Jo some paints. I think we should encourage her talent." Carly's voice suddenly went quieter as she turned her eyes to the floor. "I could show her how to use them."

"Oh, well, sure. Probably have to order something in, but I'll check at Keller's next time I'm in town. He's usually got a catalog or two that might have something like paint in it."

"And brushes. Some canvases and maybe even an easel."

"If you think—"

"I do." She flushed a beautiful shade of pink. Was she remembering when she'd last uttered those words in Pastor Philbrick's front room? Rand stifled his laughter but couldn't erase the smile from his face. Her blush went deeper.

"Tommy getting along all right?" Maybe she didn't think it was any of his business, but since the kid was living under his roof, Rand would make it his business. He'd grown quite fond of the child, and Tommy seemed to like trailing Rand around the ranch when he wasn't busy with his schooling.

"I think so. He and Jenna seem to have found a way to communicate. They enjoy studying and playing together. Tubby has befriended him too. He's taken time to show Tommy all over the ranch and introduce him to the animals."

"Good to hear."

While they were talking about the children, Rand might as well ask the question that had plagued him since Carly's first night here. "How did you know how to comfort Jenna when she had the nightmare that first night? I've never known what to do for her and you just—"

"I've lived it," Carly answered before he could finish. "I lost my mother when she gave birth to Tommy, my father soon after. I've been both mother and father to Tommy most of his life. We lived with our neighbor, Leo, and his wife, Anna, after that, but they were elderly, more like grandparents than parents. I was older than Jenna when my mama died, but I imagine the hurt and fear is pretty much the same. I would love to have had someone hold me when I woke in the night crying, someone to reassure me that she would always be with me ..."

Her voice broke, and Rand wished he'd never brought up the subject. He cleared his throat. "If that's all—"

"Actually, it's not."

Of course, it wasn't. "Something else then?"

"Just ... well, thank you for complimenting Mary Jo's efforts at cooking. She really is trying, and your approval means a great deal to her." Carly was staring at the floor again.

"I know, but I reckon I should be thanking you. That girl couldn't even make a cup of coffee before you showed up." Rand should have mentioned it to Carly before now. The fried chicken Mary Jo had made for supper tasted pert'near as good as Rand's mama's.

"She made that fried chicken we ate tonight all by herself."

"Under your direction, I imagine, and I appreciate it." True statement. Cooking was something he couldn't teach the girls. Fact was, there were lots of things he didn't know how to teach them. That was why Carly was here.

He held her gaze with his. She was more than simply here. She loved his nieces, and that was something they needed far more desperately than schoolwork or cooking lessons. Carly had brought love into this home, and he couldn't help but feel it—and want to feel it even more. He shook his head slightly to rid himself of the thought, but it wouldn't go away.

She peered at him from under her eyelashes, and a slight smile touched her lips. Rand moved a step closer to her just as Carly did the same, reaching for the sketchbook. Their hands collided, and it was as if sparks flew from her fingers into his. Almost as though she'd been burned, she jerked her hand away and looked at him, her eyes wide, her cheeks adorably pink.

With an effort, Rand stepped back. He had to, or he might give into the temptation to kiss those lips. No, he couldn't let himself look at her lips. He'd be wishing she were here for some other reasons that might involve those lips, and he couldn't let that happen.

Maybe the attic would be a good place. A week after her conversation with Rand, Carly stared at the stairs leading to the attic loft. Until she'd been up there with Jenna to retrieve the missing school books, Carly hadn't thought about the uppermost story of the ranch house as being a good hiding place, but it didn't appear that the space was used for anything but storage. She had to move the contents of her satchel out from under her bed. She had trouble sleeping at night just knowing it was there. She cast a glance over her shoulder to make sure no one was watching, then climbed the attic stairs with the satchel clutched tightly in her hand.

Where to put it? An old three-drawer dresser stood in one corner. Carly traced her finger across the surface leaving a line in the thick dust. The top drawer was empty, as was the second. The bottom drawer held only a few items of clothing that appeared to have been discarded long ago, an old reticule, and a small cardboard box without a lid. The box held a brooch missing some stones and a few other pieces of jewelry, obviously long forgotten.

After pulling the metal pieces from her satchel, still wrapped in the folds of an old muslin sheet, Carly jammed them into the bottom drawer beneath a moth-eaten pair of trousers. With a deep breath, she pushed the drawer closed. She hurried down the staircase, eager to put the offending items out of her sight—and hopefully her thoughts. Someday, when all this was over and Lester McGraw was behind bars where he belonged, she could get rid of them for good. Maybe hire a blacksmith to melt them down or some such thing.

The three children were still seated at the kitchen table, their noses buried in their schoolbooks. Carly focused on Jenna. The girl's brown eyes followed the words in the open primer before her, and it appeared she was reading without trouble. Now and then, she stopped to point her finger at a word, and Mary Jo or Carly would pronounce it for her.

Though it wasn't as easy as taking recitations from Mary Jo or even Tommy, Carly tried to think of questions she could ask Jenna that could be answered with either a nod or a shake of her head. Sometimes she asked her to write one-word answers on her slate. Based on her answers, Carly could be fairly certain the child was grasping most of the lesson. But was she learning? Or simply reviewing something she'd already learned? Or maybe she was just a good guesser.

A glance at the clock told her the same thing as the growl in her stomach. Almost dinner time. In the three weeks Carly had been at the ranch, she and Mary Jo had fallen into a pattern regarding the cooking of meals. Mary Jo, though still reluctant, let Carly help her prepare breakfast and supper, and Carly allowed the girl to do as much as she could, always offering instruction and direction. Mary Jo had learned much. As Carly had prompted him, Rand was lavish with his praise for Mary Jo's efforts, though sometimes it took a meaningful look in his direction or even a loud clearing of her throat to remind him.

The very thought of her husband brought heat to Carly's cheeks. She couldn't deny he was handsome, and his grin caused her stomach to tickle, but she was here for the children. She turned away from her busy students and busied herself with the meal preparation. How did the man have such an effect on her? Watching him with the children in the evening endeared him to her heart in a way she didn't quite understand.

The kitchen door squeaked, and Carly whirled around. Rand stood in the doorway, and she nearly dropped her spoon. The irrational fear that he could read her thoughts left her flustered.

"What are you doing here?" Her voice was too high-pitched. Time to get control of herself.

"I think I live here." Rand's smirk made her want to hit him with the wooden spoon.

"I just … I wasn't expecting you. Would you like to join us for dinner? It's only soup and cornbread, but—"

"No, thank you. I ate at the bunkhouse. Just thought I'd stop in and see if you wanted to ride into town with me this afternoon."

All three children gave up any pretense of studying and looked at Rand, eyes shining. "Us too?" Mary Jo asked.

"Yes, everyone." Rand turned his gaze to Carly. "If it's all right with you, of course."

Maybe he should have consulted her before mentioning it to the children, but she wouldn't bring it up just now. "That would be lovely. The children have been working hard, and we could all use a break." She hadn't been to town since the day she'd married Rand. A glance out the window confirmed that the sun still shone on this mid-September day. Why had Rand decided to spend the afternoon on a trip to town instead of his usual ranch work? She eyed him curiously, but he offered no explanation.

"Be ready in about an hour," Rand said. "I'll hitch up the wagon. Bring along your shopping list."

Chapter 7

In the horse barn, Rand harnessed the farm horses to the wagon with reluctance. He had so much to accomplish. Too bad he had to waste the whole afternoon going into town, but what else was he to do? The cut fence Clarence found this morning meant someone was still herding cattle off his place right under their noses. Rand had to get this business reported to Sheriff McConnell. Not that Jeb could do anything about it, but at least he'd be aware. Rand had already informed his hands that starting tonight, they'd be taking turns riding a night shift. The only way to get this foolishness stopped was to catch these rascals with their hands full of fence cutters and their mouths full of beef steak.

It'd be good for the children to get away from those blamed schoolbooks for a while. They'd neglected their learning before Carly got here, and that was mostly his fault, but she sure did work 'em hard. He had to admit, though, Mary Jo seemed like a different girl from the sullen, listless child she'd been since her folks died. Of an evening she'd pick up that tablet and draw with the pencils Carly had given her.

If Mary Jo liked drawing so much, why hadn't she done it before Carly arrived and discovered her sketches? And why in the Sam Hills did Carly travel all the way to Kansas with a set of fancy drawing pencils that had to be expensive when the only clothes he'd seen her wear were faded and worn?

Rand needed to talk her into buying yard goods at Keller's and making some new clothes. She could sew. At least she'd told him she could. The girls needed new things. Mary Jo's dresses were getting tight, and Jenna's hems were too short. And what did an old cowboy like him know about things like that? That's why he'd sent off for a wife. That's why Carly was here. She'd best be doing her job, or … What would he do about it if she didn't?

No need to worry. She'd done everything he'd asked of her and more. The girls loved her, even if Mary Jo was reluctant to show it most of the time. He could tell by the momentary sparkle in her sad eyes when Carly helped her with the cooking or exclaimed over one of her sketches. One of these days, Mary Jo would let go of her stubbornness and let people love her. At least he prayed she would.

And that was another thing. When had he started praying again? That was Carly's fault too. Only he couldn't find fault with the rather contagious faith of his new wife. Fact was, he and the girls had been sorely in need of a heavy dose of that faith, and he hadn't realized it. Now, they had taken up the habit of reading Scriptures most nights before bed. Carly said it helped them sleep better.

Could be she was right about that. Jenna's nightmares were less violent now and occurred less frequently. When she did wake from one of those awful things, Carly was always right there, comforting her and singing that lullaby. No wonder he'd never been much comfort to Jenna. His singing voice sounded like tom cats fighting in the barn loft. He only sang if he was alone, no one to hear but Dusty or Bo. Maybe if he started singing on his night watch, it'd scare those cattle-thieving varmints off for good.

Rand pulled the wagon around to the front of the house and opened his mouth to holler for them to come out and load up. Just in time, he thought better of it. Grumbling to himself about wasting more time, he climbed down, threw the reins around the hitching rail a few times, and went inside.

"Everybody ready?" he called, a little less loudly than he'd planned to from outside.

The three children descended on him immediately, Tommy and Jenna jumping up and down in their excitement. Where was Carly?

She came down the staircase in the dress she'd worn the day she arrived in town. It must have been what she considered her best dress. Even though she'd look attractive in a gunny sack, this *best dress* appeared rather worn and shabby.

"Get in the wagon, children. Let's don't waste time now." Carly followed the children out the door, and Rand closed it behind them. Too bad he couldn't be as happy about this trip as they were.

The children climbed into the back of the wagon, and Rand remembered just in time to help Carly up into the seat. He swung up beside her, moved over as far as he could to avoid touching her, and slapped the reins.

The September day was warm and still. The horses' tails swatted flies, and their hair glistened with sweat. So why was it the only thing he could smell was that confounded lavender? He breathed in deep to catch the scent of the woman beside him, then wished he hadn't. His mama used that lavender water too, and it reminded him of her, but only for a moment. His wife's scent made him think things he shouldn't be thinking, like what it would feel like to hold her close to him, nuzzle her neck, and breathe that enticing aroma as his lips found hers. They had a long drive to town for him to be wrestling these thoughts. Heaven help him.

If only she had some money of her own. Carly fingered the worn fabric of her dress. It had taken every last cent she had to get Tommy to Kansas, even though Rand had sent her enough for her own train ticket. Today, she didn't dare ask him for any more. She'd ask for material to make new clothes for the girls. Lord knew they needed them, but she and Tommy would have to make do until … until what? Until she got brave enough to ask her husband?

It wasn't as if she had anywhere to go or anything to dress up for since her days were spent in the ranch house. They didn't even drive into town for church services, opting for their own little service, which consisted of reading a few verses of Scripture and a short prayer. Last Sunday, Carly had insisted they sing a hymn and was sure she'd surprised Rand with her ability to play the old piano that had belonged to his mother.

She'd started giving the girls piano lessons after Rand asked her and continued with Tommy's, much to his dismay. Mary Jo had agreed to learn, and Jenna was picking it up especially fast. Perhaps music would be a way the girl could express herself until she was able to speak again. Carly did hope Jenna would speak again someday. How sad for such a bright mind as Jenna's to remain locked in silence.

Would the store in Walnut Point have a selection of yard goods, or did they only carry basics like muslin and broadcloth? She'd soon find out. The tip of the church steeple was just showing over the ridge. Oh, how she missed church.

"How many general stores are in Walnut Point?" They were the first words Carly had uttered since they'd left the farmyard.

"Just Keller's. Good store, though. We don't need another one."

"I see. Is it a large store?"

"Pretty good-sized."

What did that mean? Did Rand have any means for comparison? He'd likely never seen stores like the ones she'd been accustomed to in Baltimore.

"The girls need new clothes." Where had those words come from? Carly had planned to wait until they were in the store to ask Rand about it.

"You can pick out some yard goods while I run another errand. Sure do appreciate you taking care of that for them."

Kind of him to say. Did he have any idea how much work went into sewing dresses? Did the girls know how to sew a seam, or was Mary Jo as inept with a needle as she had been in the kitchen? Likely the girls' mother had thought she'd have plenty of time to teach the girls the skills they'd need to manage their own homes someday.

The houses and businesses of Walnut Point came into view. Somehow the town looked less fearsome than it had when Carly viewed it from the train window on the day of her marriage. Most buildings were painted and well kept, the dusty streets busy with wagons, carts, and buggies pulled by farm teams, driving horses, or the occasional mule. The three-story hotel rose even higher than the false fronts of the businesses along the main street. She caught the aroma of some frying food from the hotel dining room, which mixed with the more pungent aromas of horses, chimney soot, and train smoke. Rather flamboyant piano music drifted on the air from the direction of the open-doored saloon.

Rand drove along the main street and turned up the narrow road behind the west side stores, pulling the horses to a stop at the rear of an unpainted building. Its windows were covered in pink mosquito netting, and a screen door hung rather loosely from its hinges.

"That there's the back door to Keller's." He pointed to the screen door. "You and the children go on in and start gathering the things you need. I'll be back later to pay the bill and load it in the wagon."

"You're not going in with me?" And why did that bother Carly? She was perfectly capable of ordering supplies. But what if she spent too much? What if she forgot something important? What if …

"I'll be right back," he assured her. "Mary Jo can introduce you to Mrs. Keller." Rand seemed impatient. The children had already climbed out of the wagon box and stood looking at her expectantly. Might as well do what needed doing.

"Take your time," she answered. "We'll be fine." Her voice didn't sound as self-confident as she'd hoped. Carly jumped down from the wagon seat and followed the children toward the store. Rand jumped down after her and tied the team to the hitching rail, raising a hand to them as he walked away. Why didn't he say where he was going?

Rand's abandonment was forgotten a moment later when the scents, sights, and sounds of Keller's General Store claimed her senses. A bell jangled over the front door when another customer entered from the front. Carly took a deep breath, then let it out in delight. Pickle brine, freshly ground coffee, and cakes of scented soap wafted their aromas toward her at the same moment as bolts of cloth, both brightly colored and plain, greeted her searching eyes. Yes, Keller's was perfect. She could find all she needed here.

Mary Jo tugged at her sleeve. "You think they got any paint?"

"I reckon I'm short maybe five or six head altogether." Rand kicked the toe of his boot against the bottom of the battered wooden desk where Sheriff Jeb McConnell sat taking notes with a graphite pencil. "Blasted scoundrels keep cutting apart my fence too."

Jeb looked up. "Only six?"

"Well, it's a lot to me." Rand hoped he communicated his indignation at the sheriff's comment.

"Sure it is. I just meant that it must not be a big operation. Maybe just one or two people." Jeb jotted something else down. The sheriff had only been in town a few years, but he was friendly, and most folks liked him. He was way better at sheriffing than that old man before him.

"That's one or two too many." Rand gave the desk another kick.

"You seen anybody?"

"Nah. Got the boys taking turns on night riding, but it's tough to be in the right place at the right time to catch somebody in the act." Giving voice to the problem made it seem even worse. "My guess is whoever these varmints are, they're filling their own smokehouses rather than driving them into town to be sold."

"You got any enemies?"

Did Myra count? "Nah. Don't think so, anyway. Leastways nobody who'd wanna run off my herd."

Jeb cleared his throat. "What about your wife?"

"Carly?"

"Got any other wives?" Jeb's grin turned to a smirk.

"If Carly has any enemies, they're back in Baltimore. She hasn't been here long enough to make anyone mad." Except maybe Mary Jo on occasion when Carly made her do more schoolwork than she was of a mind to accomplish.

"How's it going?" Jeb wanted to know. "She gettin' along good with the youngins and all?"

"Fine. Just fine." None of Jeb's business.

He wrote something else on his pad, then set the pencil down. "Be sure and let me know if you have any more trouble." Jeb leaned back in his chair and crossed his arms. "Got time for a cup of coffee over to the hotel?"

Rand jammed his battered hat onto his head. "Best not. Got the womenfolk and the boy waitin' on me down at Keller's." He exited the sheriff's office with a wave at Jeb. "Fat lot of good that did me," he muttered as his boot heels clunked down the wooden steps to the dusty street.

He walked down the street to Keller's and entered through the front door. Carly oughta be about ready by now. If he could make it home before sundown, maybe he could get in a few licks on the new fence. The thought of Hawthorne's pasture plagued him. Providing for a family was a lot different than taking care of just himself, but he'd almost saved enough to buy that land he wanted. Again. How much would the bill be at Keller's this time?

"Uncle Rand." Mary Jo scurried toward him as soon as he stepped inside, followed by Jenna. Both of them had shining eyes and huge smiles. "Carly let us pick out some material for new dresses. She's gonna teach us to sew 'em too." Mary Jo's words pulled at his heart. They'd been deprived of nice things for too long. But now Carly was here.

He glanced at Jenna who gripped his hand in delight. "And did

Carly pick out anything for herself?" Jenna shook her head.

"She said she was just buying things for us like you told her to do." Mary Jo seemed impatient. "Come and see, Uncle Rand. My new pink calico dress is gonna have cream colored buttons and a collar that matches. Carly says we can crochet some lace to put on it too. See, there's the thread." She pointed excitedly at a ball of something that looked like string lying atop a pile of material on the store counter.

"You'll look real pretty, honey." Rand disentangled himself from the girls and made his way to where Carly stood next to the counter. Somehow, he'd have to broach the subject of new clothes for her and the boy.

"You and Tommy need new clothes too." That was subtle. Rand chanced a sideways look at his wife. Her big green eyes were open wide. Why did it feel like he could fall into them and lose himself there?

"I ... I don't have any money." Her voice was little more than a whisper, and that adorable blush heightening her cheeks made him want to touch them. He swallowed hard and gripped the edge of the counter in front of him with both hands.

"That's ridiculous. You're my wife. Now pick out some material so we can get out of here." His voice sounded terse, even to his own ears. "Please," he added in a softer tone.

Carly inched toward the bolts of material. Rand followed. "This is pretty." His own impatience caused him to reach out to the nearest bolt of fabric and hold a length of it out. He dropped it like a horseshoe from the blacksmith's fire when he realized it was sheer enough to see the scar on his forefinger through the thin fabric. "Pick out something you like. I need to go see if they have any saddle soap." Rand was walking away before the words made it all the way out of his mouth. He felt about as awkward as a bow-legged buffalo in a tulip patch. And he didn't need any saddle soap.

He made his way to where Matthew Keller had displayed a saddle on a sawhorse. There were various reins, bridles, and bits hanging nearby. Hardware lined the shelves on the far wall. He might need some more U-nails if he were to put up some barbed wire fences around the Hawthorne pasture once it was his.

"Uncle Rand?" The voice at his elbow startled him.

"What?" He couldn't seem to get that edge of impatience out of his voice. Mary Jo probably wanted to ask him about the promised paints, and he didn't know the answer. Carly was supposed to take care of that.

"I was just wondering how Carly is going to have time to do all this sewing. She needs a sewing machine like the one Mama used to have."

Of course. The girl was right, but what could he do? "I gave your mama's machine to the church sewing circle. They were pleased to get it." He'd thought it was a great idea at the time.

Mary Jo didn't answer. She just walked away, staring at the floor. It was a wonder the girl wasn't running into things with her eyes on her shoes like that. And she really did need some longer hems on her skirts to cover up those shoes a little better. When had she grown so much?

Rand sighed. He moved to the counter where Matthew stood transferring items from Carly's pile to his ledger book. He gave a fleeting thought to the pasture he wanted so badly, but it faded when he imagined Carly's expression when he presented her with this gift. "Say, Matt, I reckon Mrs. Stratford needs one of them sewing machine contraptions."

He glanced at Carly. Her green eyes were wide, and those adorable lips had opened to form a perfect little O. Yup, totally worth it.

"I've got the wagon out back. Load up the best one you've got."

Chapter 8

A few days after their trip to town, Carly stared at the envelope Rand held out to her. "Sent Nate into town for new fencing supplies today," he said. "He picked up the mail."

Carly heard the question in his voice. "It must be from Mrs. Cooper since it's postmarked from Baltimore." She stuck it in her apron pocket, hoping she was right about who'd sent it. No one in Baltimore but the Coopers knew the name of the town she'd come to, and she'd asked them to not tell anyone. "I'll read it later."

That evening, alone in her room, she gazed again at the envelope. It was addressed to Carly Blair in Walnut Point, Kansas. She slit the seal with a hairpin. Sure enough, a newsy letter from Mrs. Cooper was enclosed. She and Leo had moved from the farm to town and were getting along well but missed her. It was the last paragraph that caught her attention.

Your friend Mr. McGraw stopped by a few days ago. He asked me if I knew where you were. I promised you I wouldn't tell him, and I didn't, but he is such a nice, kind man, and I do fear you have broken his heart. He asked me to tell you next time I wrote that you have unwittingly taken some of his property that he is in dire need of. He assured me you would have found it by now and know what he is referring to. Is it that lovely gold engagement ring he gave you? In my opinion, you should just keep that even though you no longer plan to marry the man. After all, he did buy it for you, and I can't imagine why he would need it. At any rate, would you kindly send it back to him? He will be anxiously waiting to receive it and has vowed not to bother you again once it is in his possession.

A shiver of apprehension went through Carly. It wasn't the ring Lester wanted back. She'd left that for him when she'd run away. It was the items she'd hidden in the attic. As much as she wished to be rid of them, sending the plates back to Lester was out of the question. He would use them for his criminal purposes, and that would make Carly an accomplice. He didn't know where she was, and Carly trusted the Coopers enough to not inform him, but the veiled threat frightened her. Bother her? What would Lester stoop to in order to "bother her" again? Surely he wouldn't threaten Leo and Anna.

Best just turn this over to the Lord and let Him deal with Lester. Besides, she was safe here with Rand. Lester would never find her in Walnut Point, Kansas. Carly folded the letter and crawled into bed. She wouldn't lose sleep over the likes of Lester McGraw.

By mid-October, Carly had become quite adept at using her new treadle sewing machine, though it was still hard to believe it belonged to her. She'd never been able to afford one back in Baltimore and had sewed her dresses by hand. She turned out new clothes for the girls, along with shirts and trousers for Tommy, at a rate she wouldn't have dreamed possible. And now as she sat at her machine, the long seams of her new jade green skirt were coming together in a matter of minutes. It would have taken her hours with only her needle and thread.

As usually happened during these afternoons of sewing while the children studied their lessons, her thoughts turned to Rand. His gift of the sewing machine touched her heart in a way she couldn't describe. It was a thoughtful thing to do, of course, to buy her the sewing machine, but it was more than that. The machine—not to mention the fabric he'd insisted on for her and Tommy—made her feel as if she belonged here on this ranch in the beautiful Flint Hills. Her purpose was wrapped in the children she'd come to love. A sewing machine was simply a tool she used in her care of them, but it meant Rand recognized and appreciated her efforts and contributions to their family.

Family. Yes, that's what it was all about. Rand considered her a part of his family now. His wife? Not exactly, but family all the same. Someone he would take care of, buy things for, appreciate for her contributions, and ... love? No, not love. They had an agreement. She provided care and schooling for his nieces, he provided her and Tommy with a home. Nothing further was required or expected. Rand had been forthright about that from the beginning, and she needed to quit thinking about him in any way beyond friendship.

Carly put down the green fabric. Rand had made an offhand comment about the material being the same color as her eyes. Was that good or bad? A simple observation most likely. Or did it mean more? And if so, then what?

She shook her head free of the thought. She was having trouble keeping her mind on the task before her. Maybe she just needed to get out of here for a while.

The children looked up from their books as she neared the table. "I need some fresh air on this beautiful autumn day. Anyone want to take a walk with me?" The thud of three books closing at the same time made Carly smile. "Come along then."

As they strolled through the farmyards, the beautiful colors of the wildflowers and prairie sumac seemed to call out to her. If only she could walk among them, but Rand had told her to stay near the ranch buildings unless he or one of the men was with them. Good advice, she supposed, with any number of wild animals around, but still ...

Tommy raced ahead of them with the puppy Rand had brought home a few weeks back. Vinnie stayed close by Jenna's side. The girl rested her hand on the dog's thick yellow coat. A beautiful yellow flower with a brown center rose out of the tall prairie grasses, just out of Carly's reach. Oh, one of those fragrant blossoms on the supper table would be wonderful.

"Wait here," she said to the children. "I want to pick that flower." Could she make it over the split rail fence in her long skirts without an embarrassing fall?

Jenna left Vinnie and clutched Carly's hand with both of hers, a pleading look in her brown eyes. Mary Jo stepped in front of her.

"Uncle Rand says we're not to go past the fence," Mary Jo warned. "I think there's some cattle in there, and he says it's not safe for us to be around them."

Carly scanned the surrounding landscape. Indeed, some red-and-white cattle grazed in the distance, but they were so far away, they couldn't be bothered by her picking a pretty flower.

"It'll be fine." Carly tried to sound reassuring. "I'll just pluck the flower and get right back over the fence. See how beautiful it is." She pointed at the lovely blossom.

Mary Jo shrugged, which Carly decided was agreement.

She gathered her skirts in one hand and awkwardly mounted the fence, then dropped into a heap on the other side. So much for being graceful about it. At least no one but the children had seen. She dusted off her red calico work dress and gently broke off the yellow bloom, keeping the stem long enough to reach the bottom of an empty canning jar. Oh, but wouldn't that jar be even prettier with an entire bouquet of these? She sniffed the flower. What a pleasant aroma.

Another of the flowers—she'd have to ask Rand what they were called—grew just a few feet away. She stepped over to it, then to another until she held a handful of stems sporting a gorgeous array of gold and brown blossoms like a jeweled crown. Carly buried her nose in the bouquet and inhaled the pungent fragrance.

A flash of red out of the corner of her eye made her gasp at the same time as Mary Jo's scream rent the air and faded on the stiff Kansas breeze. The cattle were almost close enough to touch. She had to get out of here. Carly glanced at the fence, which was much more distant than she'd expected. She'd wandered too far, forgetting the danger.

Carly dashed toward the fence, but her toe jammed against a rock, and she stumbled. She caught herself before falling headlong into the prairie grass. She dropped the bouquet, but as a gust of wind carried the flowers away, it also puffed out her skirts. When they settled against her, they entangled around her legs, and she fell.

Carly squeezed her eyes shut, not daring to look behind her at the herd of cattle, praying they weren't as close as she thought they were. She struggled to her feet and tried to run again, but something held her back. Strong hands picked her up, flung her across broad shoulders, and carried her to safety.

Just in the nick of time. When Carly opened her eyes, the big red-and-white bull, along with his curved gray horns and snorting nose, pawed the ground on the other side of the fence, a herd of placid cows calmly watching from behind him. She would have fallen to the ground in her relief but for the sun-browned arms holding her upright. She turned to face the man who held her, knowing instinctively it was her husband, allowing herself to melt into his arms. She could hear Rand's rapid heartbeat pounding in his chest, his panting breaths coming in short spurts.

She tried to speak but couldn't, finding it was all she could do to breathe. She folded herself into the safety of Rand's arms, never caring to be anywhere else for the rest of her days. What a relief to allow someone to take care of her, even just this once. His hand shook ever so slightly as he touched her hair, then trailed his finger down her cheek, wiping away a tear she hadn't realized was there.

"Are you all right?" His voice held the faintest trace of a tremble.

Carly nodded, sure he could feel the movement against his chest as he continued to hold her.

Then he pushed her away. She stumbled back, but he kept her from falling with a strong grip on each shoulder.

His angry glare bored into her like a needle jammed in a ball of yarn.

"What in blue blazes do you think you were doing in there?" The harsh words poured out of his mouth. The pain of no longer feeling him against her hit Carly at the same time as the sting of his words. It was all she could do not to crumple into a heap and burst into tears.

She forced herself to hold his gaze, hoping her eyes held the same fire as his. "Picking flowers." Her voice trailed off into an agonizing whisper, her hopes at standing her ground, obviously futile. Her eyes burned with tears she prayed would not fall while a lump she could not swallow settled into her throat.

"I told you to stay out of there." Did she imagine it, or was there just a little less ire in his tone, the slightest bit of kindness in his eyes?

"I tried to tell her," Mary Jo interjected, reminding Carly they were not alone. The children should not have to witness this display of Rand's anger. Still, she probably deserved it.

"Yes, you did." Carly turned to Mary Jo, still aware of Rand's hands cupping her shoulders. "I'm sorry I didn't listen."

Tommy slipped his arms around her elbow while Jenna buried her head in Carly's skirt.

Rand released his grip and stepped back. He turned and circled his arm around Mary Jo's thin shoulders. Perhaps he was making an effort to curb his harshness. "All's well that ends well." He spoke the words as he eyed the bull on the other side of the fence. It was now grazing, occasionally stopping to sniff at the yellow blooms lying scattered where the breeze had dropped them.

"Old Cow Boy there doesn't take too kindly to ladies in his pasture unless they're the four-legged kind that moo. I reckon he was just defending his territory." Rand's words held the hint of a smile.

"Lesson learned," Carly murmured. "I'm sorry, Rand. It won't happen again. And thank you. I'm sure you saved my life."

"Oh, I doubt it would have been that drastic," Rand replied as they turned toward the house. "I'm just glad I wasn't too far away."

"Cow Boy?" Carly smiled at the name. "It suits him, I guess."

"Jenna named him back when he was a calf," Mary Jo offered. "Someone told her he was a boy cow and she got it kind of mixed up." She nodded toward the scattered blooms on the far side of the fence. "Those are sunflowers. You can pick them all over. No need to go into the pasture."

Rand shifted to walk beside Carly, then took her hand. His was warm and calloused and enveloped hers in a way that made her feel safe and cared for. He walked along casually as if it were the most normal thing in the world.

She tried not to react. He'd never reached for her before, certainly never done anything so intimate as holding her hand. Nor should he have. But she didn't pull away. She couldn't. The sparks traveling from his hand to hers ran up and down her spine irresistibly, whispering the truth she had to face. The man who'd just rescued her from the big red bull had also just stolen her heart, and there wasn't a thing she could do about it.

"Thank you, God." Rand whispered the words to himself as he eased into the big brown overstuffed chair after supper and evening chores. If anything had happened to Carly, he wasn't sure what he would have done. He couldn't allow her to get hurt was all. He needed her for the children, but something niggling his gut said it was more than that. This was new territory. Maybe it'd be best to put it aside and try to figure it out later when he was alone.

She was upstairs helping the children get ready for bed, seemingly none the worse for her experience. Tomorrow night it would be his turn to patrol the fields. At least there hadn't been any more missing cattle since they'd started the night watches. Maybe he should think about giving his guys a break. Whoever rode the shift wasn't worth a plug nickel the next day, including him.

Light footsteps on the staircase brought him out of his reverie. He glanced up and caught her eyeing him as she descended the stairs. Maybe she'd forgotten to take a glass of water up with her. She usually did that in case Jenna had a nightmare and needed a sip after her screaming and sobbing. But Jenna hadn't had a nightmare in almost three weeks.

"Forget something?" he asked as she joined him in the sitting room.

"I was almost done with the hem on this dress and thought I'd finish it before I went to bed, if that's all right."

"Sure."

She didn't need his permission. It was awkward though, without the children. Funny. They'd been married almost two months and had rarely been alone together.

Carly picked up some of that green material she was working on and ran her needle through it.

Heaven help him, but the fabric highlighted the green of her eyes in a way that made Rand wish she was looking at him instead of the needle.

"Can't you do that with the sewing machine?" It was a dumb question. Guess he felt the need to say something before the quiet between them got too loud.

"I suppose I could, but a skirt hem looks much nicer when it's done by hand." Her pause was long and thoughtful. "I do appreciate the sewing machine, though. It has saved me so much time, and I've been able to finish things faster than I ever dreamed." Carly continued wielding her needle.

He hadn't meant to make her feel defensive, if that's what had happened. Just being a dimwit about one of those female things he didn't understand.

"I see." No, he didn't. His response was more stupid than the question. Maybe he'd just shut up. Too bad he didn't have a newspaper or something. Anything to keep from sitting there, twiddling his thumbs like an old galoot.

"Thank you again for rescuing me from the bull today."

Her words were quiet, but no doubt sincere. Rand had wondered if she truly realized the danger she'd been in, even though Cow Boy was one of his tamer bulls. Must have been her red dress that set the old guy off.

"You're welcome."

"And I'm so sorry I didn't do as you told me to and stay on this side of the fence."

Her needle had stopped. She had those green eyes turned on him, and Lord have mercy, a tear was rolling out of one of them.

"You didn't promise to obey me, remember?" Where did that come from? Poor excuse for a joke. And hadn't his thoughts wandered down that very road ever since the incident? If she'd just done as he said, it wouldn't have happened.

"But if I'd paid attention, it wouldn't have happened." It was as if she'd slapped him with his own thoughts.

"It's over and done now. Best just forget about it." But how could he forget? He'd held her in his arms. She'd clung to him. He'd seen the look in her eyes when she gazed at him, memorized it. He just didn't know what it meant. And that gnawing thing deep in his gut that said he wanted to hold her again. Feel her against him. Maybe even kiss those ridiculously pink lips—how could he fight that? He couldn't let himself think this way. He had to get this subject changed and fast.

"Tell me about your life in Baltimore." So much he didn't know about her. So much he wished he knew, though he didn't know why.

Looking back down at her work, Carly said, "There's not much to tell."

Seems he'd have to help her. "Let's see. You told me your parents died several years back and you had lived with an elderly couple on their farm. I didn't know you had a brother before you came here, but I suppose you've been raising Tommy by yourself since then."

"Leo Cooper and his wife, Anna, were neighbors and friends of my father. They took us in. They helped me with him, watching him during the day while I was at work. Leo's health was failing, and he wanted to sell the farm and move to town, so Tommy and I left at just the right time. Tommy hated leaving the Coopers and his dog Riley, but I think he's adjusting well and likes living here, don't you?"

"He's doing great." But Rand wasn't going to let her change the subject that easily. "You worked for a newspaper. What did you do, exactly?"

"Set type mostly." Her needle stopped moving, but she didn't look up.

No further words were forthcoming. Was something about this conversation making her nervous? It was making him a little anxious too. Maybe he should try a different topic.

"Did you have any beaus?" Apparently, that was the dumbest question yet. Now, her face was all red, and she cast a look at the stairway as if she were trying to figure out a way to escape. If he could have kicked himself in the backside, Rand would have done it then and there. He figured he'd better try to pull his boot out of his mouth before he got it wedged in any farther.

"Sorry, that ain't nothin' I need to know about."

She said nothing for a long time, and he was about to ask another, safer question. But then she looked at him and nearly smiled. "Actually, I was engaged to be married."

Rand's jaw dropped, and for the life of him, he couldn't get his mouth back closed. Carly started sewing again. And talking.

"I probably should have told you that before now. I was engaged to my boss at the paper. His name was Lester McGraw. Obviously, it didn't work out, or I wouldn't be here."

Rand just nodded. No response came to mind, appropriate or otherwise.

"I wanted a new life for Tommy and me, somewhere far from Baltimore, so when I saw your advertisement in the paper I worked for, I answered it. When you replied, I quit my job, broke my engagement, and made plans to travel to Kansas."

There was a moment, during which he tried again to think of an appropriate response.

Then she added, "Lester didn't love me, nor I him, in case you're wondering."

Sounded to Rand as if she'd traded one situation for another about the same. Except here she didn't have to work for a newspaper. She just had to cook and sew and clean and teach and give piano lessons and manage difficult children and …

"And you?"

Her innocent question sent apprehension clear down to his toenails. Should he tell her about Myra? As his wife, she probably did have a right to know. Anyway, she was bound to find out someday. Too many people knew about Myra and her deception.

He drew a deep breath and tried to get any unruly tremors from his voice. "I was engaged myself. Her name was Myra. It didn't work out and she left." Carly didn't need to know about the money Myra stole or the way she'd humiliated him. That was all history now. Over and done.

Carly's momentary surprise at his words didn't escape him, though she hid it well after a moment. "I'm sorry."

"No need," he replied.

"Goodnight, Rand." Carly rose from her chair abruptly, put down the hemming, and went upstairs.

The void left by her absence and all the words he didn't say but should have wrenched his gut. Deep down inside that feeling grabbed at him again. The same feeling as when he'd held her in his arms after her encounter with the Hereford bull. He'd never felt this way about Myra. No matter how much he didn't want to admit it, the meaning was clear. Myra may have stolen his money, but Carly Blair Stratford had just walked off with his heart.

Chapter 9

Tommy helped Tubby with the barn chores while the girls were busy sewing crocheted lace onto their new dresses. Someday, Carly would teach them to crochet, but she had all she could do right now just to teach them sewing. Mary Jo had to practically be forced to sew. Or study, or cook, or do house chores, or even practice piano. Now that her paint supplies had arrived, all she wanted to do was sketch drawings and paint them into beautiful pictures that made Carly yearn to join her. Carly wouldn't though. She would never let on to Rand that she and Mary Jo shared this love of art. She had a family to care for, and that had to come first. Besides, she wanted to leave no clues as to her past misdeeds involving drawing and those pieces of metal in the attic.

Rand dutifully made frames for the work Mary Jo brought him and hung them for her anywhere a bit of wall space was available. Some even made their way to the bunkhouse for the ranch hands to enjoy. She really was quite talented, but the girl had to learn other things too. Carly forced her to adhere to limits on painting time, which pained Carly nearly as much as it did Mary Jo.

Each time Carly asked Mary Jo to put down her sketchbook in favor of school work, piano lessons, or sewing, a battle ensued. Just this morning, Carly caught her drawing instead of parsing the sentences she'd given her for her grammar lesson.

"Why do I have to know how to parse sentences if I'm not going to be a writer or a teacher?" Mary Jo asked defiantly.

"Everyone needs to know how to write and speak correctly," Carly responded.

"Not me. I'm going to own a ranch someday like Uncle Rand. I can ride horses and paint pictures of horses, and I won't have to talk to anybody." Mary Jo's eyes flashed her anger at Carly as if she didn't realize how ridiculous her statement sounded. "My mama never made me parse sentences. We didn't have a piano, and she had all our dresses made at Mrs. Goldman's seamstress shop in town."

The afternoon wasn't going any better than the morning had on that unseasonably warm November day. Mary Jo couldn't recite her history lesson. Tommy stumbled through his reading as if he wasn't even trying to get it right. Even Jenna had misspelled three of the ten spelling words Carly assigned her.

"I'm going to step outside to get the laundry off the line," Carly told them when she'd reached the limits of her patience. "Close your books for now. Tommy, you practice on the piano while the girls work on their sewing."

"Does he have to?" Mary Jo complained. "He plays all the wrong notes, and we have to sit here and listen to it, and then I make mistakes."

"Do not," Tommy retorted. "I play better than you."

After the long day of listening to Mary Jo's sullen remarks and Tommy's childish defense, Carly was about to lose her temper. "Fine. Tommy, go outside and play with the dog. You can practice your music later while Mary Jo is making supper." Mary Jo didn't speak the words behind her glare, but Carly heard them anyway. Tommy stuck his tongue out at Mary Jo and ran out the front door before Carly could reprimand him. She picked up her laundry basket and hurried out the back, eager to spend a few minutes alone. She yanked items from the line and tossed them into her basket.

"My britches do something to make you mad?"

Carly whirled to find Rand behind her. She eyed the top button on his shirt and the tiny black hairs from his chest peeking from the gap below his throat. She bit her lip more from the shock of what that sight did to her than at being caught taking her impatience out on the innocent laundry.

She dropped the pair of Rand's trousers she had been attempting to fold and covered her face with her hands. She was frustrated after a difficult day of dealing with Mary Jo and didn't care if Rand knew it. The next thing she knew, his arms were around her, drawing her closer to him. She sighed, choosing to ignore the fact that she ought not to allow him to do this, and settled her cheek against the rough texture of his chambray shirt. He smelled like fresh hay and saddle soap, a hint of autumn breeze filling her senses with his nearness.

"I'm sorry," she managed in little more than a whisper. "It's been a trying day."

"Come sit down and tell me what's gone wrong. Maybe I can help." She let him lead her to the back porch steps and pull her down beside him, though Carly couldn't help wishing she could stay in the circle of his arms. She shouldn't be having those kinds of feelings toward … her husband? She sighed again. This was all so complicated.

"I'm curious, I suppose." Did the breathlessness in her voice betray her inner turmoil? "How did Mary Jo get to be twelve years old with absolutely no training in things like cooking and sewing? Most girls her age—"

"Maggie couldn't sew worth a lick," Rand said. "That's why Dan bought her a sewing machine. He thought that'd help. It didn't. God rest her soul, my sister wasn't much of a cook either. Don't get me wrong. She worked hard and took good care of her family, but her real calling was with the horses. When she wasn't training or riding or helping a mare foal, she was drawing them."

"And Mary Jo takes after her mother." The situation with Mary Jo was starting to make more sense to Carly.

"Yeah, pretty much. Jenna seems to act more like Dan, but in appearance, they both look like their mama."

"I think they both look like you." And she did. Both girls had the same glittery pale blue eyes and light brown hair as their uncle, not to mention that adorable little tilt to the chin when they smiled.

"You want to tell me what's bothering you?" Rand surely meant well, but could he possibly help her get through to Mary Jo?

"Oh, it's nothing really. I just wish she wouldn't be so against me. Unless it's drawing or painting, Mary Jo fights me on whatever else I ask her to do. She doesn't want to do her schoolwork or sew or practice the music. Most of the time I can't even interest her in cooking anymore."

"She's got really good at making pancakes and biscuits. That fruit thing she made the other night was downright delicious." As if on cue, Rand's stomach growled.

Carly grinned. "That's because all those apples Tubby brings us from the trees need to be put to use. It's called Brown Betty. Kind of like baked apples with a crunchy coating of oatmeal and spices on the top."

"And you're teaching her how to put them in jars so we can have them this winter." Rand's tone indicated he was appreciative of her efforts, but he didn't say so.

"Both girls are making applesauce, pie filling, and apple butter until we're all so tired of it it's hard to imagine wanting to eat it later, but they're good apples. I don't want to see them go to waste."

Rand shifted so that he was looking at her. Oh my, she couldn't think when she looked into those eyes.

"I don't know what you'll think of this idea, and it's up to you of course, but why don't you give her a few days off?"

"Why?"

"We all need that now and then. Put away the schoolbooks and the sewing and let her draw all day if she wants. Might be she'd get it out of her system and be ready to take on the other things again after a time."

"But her schoolwork ..." Why was this sounding like a good idea? It just might work.

"Might be something in it for you too. The girls need to see you as someone who cares about them and understands their needs, not just as a taskmaster."

He was right, even if she didn't want to admit it. She'd been so concerned with carrying out all her responsibilities, Carly had almost lost track of her main role. These girls needed a mama more than a teacher. Tommy too.

"I'll think about it."

"You do that then." Rand stood and offered her a hand to pull her up.

Carly pretended as if she didn't notice the hand and awkwardly hoisted herself to her feet, making sure she didn't touch him.

"Mind if I come in for a cup of coffee? Fire went out in the bunkhouse, and Tubby's pot was cold."

Oh, so that's why he was at the house in the middle of the day. "Of course, help yourself."

And if he wanted a cup of coffee, why was he just standing there looking at her? Those pale blue eyes held hers as if by force. She couldn't look away.

His head lowered, and Carly raised hers at the same moment. A fleeting thought of what it might be like if he kissed her made shivers run down her spine. In the next instant, his lips were pressed against hers, and she was experiencing her first kiss. As his lips moved over hers, Carly lost all sense of normalcy and dissolved into his embrace.

When did wishing his lips would touch hers become more than a wish and actually happen? How did her arms crawl around him? How did her fingers get interlaced behind his neck? How did his arms encircle her in a grip so fierce she couldn't have moved if she'd wanted to?

She didn't want to.

Was she dreaming?

The screen door slammed. Carly jumped, and they pulled apart, painfully, regretfully. Who had just witnessed their ... whatever it was? Carly didn't dare look at Rand. Was he looking at her? Her face was hot. She resisted the urge to smooth her hair.

"I think that was Mary Jo ..." Even Rand seemed to be at a loss for words. "Maybe I better get on back to the barn." He turned and walked off, leaving Carly feeling empty, alone, and more than a little angry.

"What about the coffee?" Carly's words trailed after him, but Rand pretended not to hear. He didn't need coffee bad enough to face whatever it was he'd just left Carly to face all alone. What a coward. What an idiot. What a ... He couldn't even think of the word he wanted to call himself just now.

What had made him kiss her? Those big green eyes that looked like shiny emeralds under that mass of auburn hair just staring at him, begging him ... No, he couldn't blame her. He'd wanted to kiss her, and he'd done it. Plain and simple. Not even a moment's hesitation to give him time to back out of it. Not that he would have. He'd enjoyed it too much. He already wanted to do it again. And again.

What was wrong with him, anyway? Their agreement was about the girls and nothing else. He'd promised that was all that would be expected of her in this marriage.

"Lord, have mercy." His whispered words sounded like an explosion in the quiet of the barn where he'd made his hasty retreat. Dusty looked up from his bin of oats and blinked before continuing to eat.

Rand punched the stall door with his fist, then immediately regretted it. That wouldn't accomplish anything. He stared at his scraped knuckles wondering how beating on the wood door made this situation any better. And now what? Should he apologize? If he did, it'd be an outright lie. No way was he sorry he'd kissed Carly. Sorry he lost his control for a moment, yes, but not sorry for that kiss. He'd kissed women before, but it had never felt like that.

What then, if not an apology? To start with, he could talk to Mary Jo. What had Carly said to her? And what kind of low-down varmint was he to just walk off and leave her to it? Carly had been telling him about her problems with his oldest niece, and this latest development wasn't going to help anything. Mary Jo had been dead set against him marrying Myra and also against the idea of advertising for a wife. Poor kid. She desperately needed a mother, but she'd do anything else before she admitted it or let Carly step into that role.

Rand had been wondering if Mary Jo was jealous of Carly in some off-kilter way. Jealous that Carly had stepped into her position as "woman-of-the-house," or maybe jealous that Rand had taken a wife at all, preferring that he give all of his attention to his nieces. If the latter were the case, seeing Rand kiss Carly, wife or not, would put an even deeper wedge between the two of them.

He needed to talk to Mary Jo. He'd talk some sense into her while he was at it. That drawing stuff was all well and good, but she needed to pay heed to her studies and learning woman things, not to mention giving proper respect to Carly. Too bad Carly had to go and get in the way of old Cow Boy a few weeks back. Kind of lowered the bar on the respect thing. Even Jenna knew better than to get inside the pasture fence, and to pick a stupid flower, of all things.

"Whatcha doing?"

How long had Tommy been standing there?

He turned toward his horse. "Just checking on Dusty. What are you up to? Shouldn't you be inside with your nose in one of them schoolbooks?"

"Carly said I had to stay outside while she was having a 'cussion with Mary Jo."

"A discussion, huh?" Rand kicked at a pile of dirt on the barn floor, sending dust clouds into the air. "What kind of discussion?"

Tommy shrugged. "I dunno. She told both me and Jenna to come outside, only Jenna stayed up by the house with Vinnie. I like Mucklededun better than Vinnie, don't you?"

Mucklededun. What a ridiculous name for the puppy. Served Rand right for telling the boy he could name the pup whatever he wanted.

"Mucklededun is a fine hound dog for sure." So Carly and Mary Jo were having a private conversation. Was Carly trying to explain away an errant kiss? Lecturing her on allowing people their privacy? Maybe she was telling her the kiss meant nothing.

Was that true?

"Hey, Rand, when are you gonna let me ride Dusty?"

They'd had this discussion many times. "You have to learn to ride on a less spirited horse," Rand told him. "I told you, Mr. Krisson has a Shetland pony he's gonna bring over for you one of these days. We just have to wait until her colt is weaned." Rand had meant to put the boy on Old Polly for some lessons before the pony got here, but he'd been so distracted with the missing steers and all. Maybe he should have Tubby do it. He eyed the line of stalls in the barn. Most of the horses were out with his men. He oughta be doing that too instead of standing here talking to the kid and kicking himself in the backside for kissing his own wife.

Rand forced himself to focus on the conversation at hand. "Maybe in a day or two, we'll let you ride Polly. Polly is bigger than the Shetland but a good one to learn on." Polly was too old to ride range anymore. In her day she could throw a great colt. She'd given Rand some of his best mounts.

"Really?" Tommy's eyes shone. Maybe he didn't know how docile Old Polly was, or maybe he didn't care. To him, a horse was a horse. "Can I ride him now?"

"Her. And no, I've got things to do now. In a day or so we'll—"

"I don't wanna ride no girl horse. That's for sissies. I want a boy horse that goes fast." No more shine to his eyes.

"It doesn't make any difference whether it's a boy or a girl horse, Tommy." Yeah, pretty much unsuccessful at hiding his frustration. "A girl horse can move just as fast as a boy horse. Anyhow, you can't go fast until you learn how to go slow. It's too dangerous."

"I wanna ride a boy horse like you do." Tommy stomped his foot in the dust, gave Rand a wretched, miserable sort of glare, then turned and ran out of the barn.

"Yeah, kid. I know what frustration feels like," Rand muttered under his breath as he strode out of the barn.

"Do you love Uncle Rand?"

How was Carly supposed to answer that? She wasn't about to tell this girl any of her secrets. "Mary Jo, that's not an appropriate question."

"Well, do you? Because I know my mama loved my daddy, and they're the only people I ever saw kissing like that." Mary Jo looked down at the fingers twiddling in her lap. "I didn't see it very often, though."

"Sometimes people kiss because they love each other, but not always. Kissing is usually a private thing. It's something that happens between two people, not for someone else who might chance to see it."

"It's my fault that I saw you kissing? Because I didn't mean to. I actually came out to tell you I was done with the lace." She eyed Carly with a defiant smirk. "So, can I paint now?"

Carly hesitated. "Sure. Go ahead." Mary Jo ran to get her paints.

Carly heaved a sigh. Fine with her. She could use a few minutes alone while the younger children were outside. She'd allowed Mary Jo to paint just to get her to stop asking questions for which there were no answers. At least not answers she could give to the girl. She had the same questions.

Why had Rand kissed her?

Why did Carly want him to do it again?

The only reason she'd agreed to come to Kansas was that Rand had promised her an in-name-only marriage. So far, he'd kept up his end of the bargain. She couldn't change things around now just to suit her unruly emotions.

She had to think about something else.

What to make for supper?

But the thought flitted away when she thought of him coming in to eat. How was she going to sit across the table from Rand over the meal and not look at him? How could she keep him from looking at her as the telltale flush crawled up her neck and into her cheeks?

Now that Mary Jo had her paints out and a piece of drawing paper on the three-legged easel Rand had made for her, Carly would never tear the girl away to help with cooking the meal. For that matter, Carly would consider herself fortunate if Mary joined the family at the supper table without a fuss.

Carly understood, though. That feeling of losing yourself in the creativity, forgetting what time it was, never mind things like eating and sleeping. Once that brush was in a person's hand and the vibrant colors at her command, the rest of the world drifted away. Oh, to paint again. But she couldn't let herself think in that direction either. She was Mrs. Stratford now, and with that title, she must deny herself two things she most genuinely desired, her husband and her art. Rand must never know about her former life and the awful thing that had resulted from her own vanity about her artwork. And he certainly could not be allowed to discover she'd fallen in love with him. One more kiss like the one he'd given her today, and she might not be able to keep that secret. All the more reason to keep her distance.

The screen door slammed, and someone ran across the kitchen floor. Good. Carly had been about to call Jenna and Tommy inside. The air was getting chilly.

"Tommy, is that you?" No answer. Jenna, trailed by Vinnie and Mucklededun, came around the corner. "Jenna, honey, take the dogs back outside. Is Tommy with you?"

Jenna shook her head and turned back toward the kitchen, shooing the dogs with her outstretched hands. Odd that Mucklededun wasn't with Tommy. Carly distinctly remembered sending her brother out to play with the dog. Romping with the puppy helped burn off some of that excess energy he always seemed to have.

Carly followed them to the kitchen and made sure the dogs went out the back door. She focused on the little girl. "Have you seen Tommy? Do you know where he is?" Again, Jenna shook her head.

"I'm going to look for him, then. Mary Jo is painting. Do you think you could find some potatoes in the bin and get them ready for frying? It'll be suppertime soon."

Jenna nodded.

Stepping out the back door, Carly was met by the dogs jumping and chasing each other so that had she tried to walk, she probably would have tripped over one of them. She cast a disapproving glance at them, for all the good that did.

"Tommy," she called, "time to come inside."

No answer was forthcoming, nor did a little boy come darting around the side of the house to answer her command. Come to think of it, if Tommy were somewhere nearby, the dogs would likely be with him.

"Tommy, where are you?" She heard the note of fear in her own voice. She gazed at the western horizon. Dusk had set in, and darkness wouldn't be far behind it.

"Getting colder by the minute," she muttered, hugging herself around the middle and rubbing her arms to suppress a shiver. Where was that boy? Perhaps she should go back in and get a shawl before she looked any further.

"Something wrong?" Rand's voice brought a measure of relief and, at the same time, sent a tremor of trepidation down her spine. The memory of their kiss produced a tingle of excitement. She'd wondered what she would say to him. Now, Tommy had solved that dilemma for her. Best tell him so he could help her look. He was leading a horse toward the barn.

"Tommy is missing."

"Missing? What do you mean? Have you called him? He's probably just around front playing with the dogs ... Oh." He eyed the animals still dancing around her skirt hems.

"Of course I called him. Didn't you hear me?"

"I was putting Dusty here back in the barn and ..." As if a realization struck him, Rand turned his gaze to the horse. Even in the duskiness of the evening, Carly could make out the expression of dismay that came over his features. Then he seemed to force his expression back to calm. Couldn't the man even finish a sentence?

"Tell you what then." Was there a trace of unease in his voice? "Why don't you go on back inside, and I'll see if I can round up the youngster. Don't worry now. I'll find him, and we'll both be in for supper in two shakes of a lamb's tail."

Carly started to protest, but her teeth were chattering in the chill now, and Mucklededun had nearly knocked her over with a jolt to the back of her knees. "Stop that," she hissed at the dog. "All right then. Thank you." She gave Rand a crisp nod and ducked back into the kitchen. She needed to start supper anyway. For some reason, Rand's too-bright smile gave her a sinking feeling deep down in her stomach that something was terribly wrong.

Chapter 10

Rand waited until the back door closed behind Carly, then took out for the barn at a run, Dusty trotting along beside him. News that Tommy was missing solved the mystery of why he'd found Dusty wandering through the barnyard a few minutes ago. He'd thought maybe he hadn't latched the stall gate properly, but ten-to-one Tommy had let the gelding out of the barn. Rand could only hope Tommy hadn't tried to ride Dusty, fallen off, and was now lying hurt somewhere—or worse. No saddle, not even a bridle. What could the boy have been thinking?

Better yet, what could Rand have been thinking? He knew Tommy was upset about Rand's refusal to let him ride Dusty. Maybe he should have just taken the time right then and there to put Tommy on Polly and give the kid his first riding lesson without waiting for the Shetland. He could kick himself in the hind end later on. Right now, he had to find Tommy and make sure the boy was all right before Carly figured out something was wrong. He didn't need her getting herself lost—or into the bull pasture—because she was out looking for her ornery little scamp of a brother.

Saddling the horse would use up valuable time, and Tommy had to be somewhere nearby. Best look for him on foot. Shoving Dusty back into his stall, Rand bit back a curse word that would have made his mother wash his mouth out with soap. The confounded puppy had followed him into the barn and now yipped at his feet. He pushed the dog away with the end of his boot. It didn't faze the dog at all, which continued to jump and bark, just like it had when Carly was outside.

Wait a minute. Maybe the pup wasn't so stupid after all. Was Rand imagining that pleading look in its little brown eyes?

"All right, fella. I'll follow you."

Mucklededun ran out the barn door, then checked to see if Rand was behind him. They were soon joined by Vinnie, though it seemed to Rand as if Jenna's dog was just hanging around to see what all the excitement was about. There could be no doubt Mucklededun had a mission.

It would be dark soon. Did this pup really know where Tommy was, or did he just think it was a lark to lead Rand off on a wild goose chase? Carly was worried, and coyotes would be howling soon. Rand needed to find the boy before it got any darker or colder.

Something kept Rand following the yellow dog. At least until he had a better idea of where to look, it was all he knew to do. If anyone knew where Tommy was, it would be this mutt. Rand prayed as he stumbled after the dog in the semi-darkness. If Tommy was hurt, Rand needed to find him sooner rather than later. The thought of Tommy lying hurt, perhaps unconscious, spurred him onward. It wasn't but a few minutes later, near the gate to the west pasture, when Rand heard a muffled moan. He breathed a deep sigh of relief. Rand didn't see the boy, but it had to be him.

He peered into the fading light, finally catching sight of a small booted foot sticking out from under the cedar tree just to the right of the gate. Mucklededun sniffed at it between anxious little yips. Rand knelt down and gently pulled the child from beneath the branches, gathering him into his arms.

"Are you hurt?"

Tommy's head wagged back and forth against his chest, but his voice was little more than a whimper. "Are you awful mad at me?"

He was, but Rand had best keep that to himself just now. "Are you all right? Did you bump your head or your elbow or anything else when you fell off?"

Again, the shake of the head. "I didn't fall off." The lad pulled his head back and wiped a fist over his eyes.

What? Had the child actually ridden Dusty without a saddle or bridle? Dusty wouldn't try to hurt the little guy, but then he probably wouldn't try not to either. "What happened, then?"

Tommy buried his head in Rand's shoulder. "I couldn't never figure out how to get on 'im," the little boy admitted. "And then he runned away from me, and I couldn't catch him."

Rand stifled the laugh that rose from his throat. "Next time, I'll help you, but it's important that you pay real close attention to what I tell you. You need some riding lessons first, and somebody has to be with you whenever you're around the horses."

"I know. I'm sorry."

Rand lifted the boy to his shoulders. "Let's get you on inside before your sister gets any more worried about you. And if you aren't hurt, why were you under the tree? Didn't you hear her call you?"

"When I couldn't get the horse to go back in the barn, I figgered you'd be real mad at me, so I was hiding. I was starting to get kind of cold, though, and Muckledun wouldn't stay with me. He kept running off."

"He came to find us because he knew you needed help." Rand stooped and gave the dog an appreciative pat. "He's gonna be a real good ranch dog one of these days."

"You really think so?"

"I do," Rand answered, though it struck him as mighty strange that he really did. *Thank you, Lord.*

The bond between Rand and Tommy had definitely grown stronger. Carly watched out the window as Tommy had his first riding lesson on Old Polly a few days after the attempted riding fiasco. She'd been horrified when Rand told her what Tommy had done, but he'd been swift to stop her from berating the boy or punishing him for his disobedience. He'd convinced her to let him handle it.

Now, Rand and her brother were closer than ever. Tommy had grown up without a father in his life. Leo had served the purpose for a time, but Rand, it seemed, was taking the responsibility to heart. At least the chaos of the moment had saved them the embarrassment of what they would say to one another after the kiss they'd shared in the backyard that day. As of yet, neither of them had brought the subject up, and Carly hoped Rand never would. She certainly wouldn't mention it. However, she was dying to know if Mary Jo had confronted Rand as she had Carly. She wouldn't ask though. It was too embarrassing.

Carly turned from the window and gazed at the girl who was now the object of her thoughts. Rand's idea actually seemed to be working. Carly had released Mary Jo from her responsibilities one day a week, not including Sundays when they did only the necessary work. In return, Mary Jo spent the other days diligently working on her lessons and household chores. Mary Jo learned her lessons better, practiced the piano longer, and made her seams more even than ever before. Her new dress had been finished, and now she sat at the table helping Jenna with her spelling words, the older girl's lessons for the day already completed. Tomorrow would be Mary Jo's promised day off, and Carly was anticipating it almost as much as Mary Jo.

A light rap on the back door made Carly step away from the window and open it. On the other side of the screen door was Nate, hat in his hands, looking red-faced and uncomfortable.

"Letter for you, ma'am." He held out an envelope.

Carly opened the screen door and took the missive from his outstretched hand. "Thank you, Nate. Would you like to come in? I just made some oatmeal cookies, and the coffee's hot."

Nate shook his head. "Thank you kindly, Mrs. Stratford, but I just got back from the feed store in town and got some unloading to do. Clarence is waiting on me."

Carly gave him her best smile. Most of the ranch hands were still nervous around her. Only Tubby seemed to take her presence in stride. "I'll send some over to the bunkhouse for you and the men to enjoy later. Thank you again for delivering the mail."

"Yes, ma'am." Nate jammed his hat back on his head and practically ran toward the barn.

Carly glanced at the envelope in her hand. Odd. A Baltimore postmark, but it wasn't Anna Cooper's usual handwriting, just block manuscript letters. Maybe Leo had addressed it. She pulled a pin from her hair and slit the envelope.

As the paper unfolded, Carly sank into a chair and stared at it. The entire page contained only two sentences.

Send the plates to me at the newspaper office. If I do not have them within the next two weeks, I will come there to retrieve them.

As if it were a snake, Carly wadded the paper and threw it into the stove, fear settling in her mid-section. How had Lester learned where she was? He may not know she was on the Bar-S and married to Rand, but he knew she'd come to Walnut Point, Kansas.

Maybe she should just send back the counterfeit plates and be done with them. But if she did, he would use them for his own ill-gotten gain, and it would be her fault. Carly dropped her head into her hands and prayed with all her being. *Lord, take this burden. I can't bear it alone.*

The family had gone to bed, but Rand stood staring out the sitting room window into the blackness of the night, mulling over the day's events. Nate had gone to town for feed today, but he might have to go back tomorrow for more barbed wire.

Right under their noses, apparently in broad daylight, someone had snipped his pasture fence again, and more steers were gone. Granted, it wouldn't be hard to lure cattle out of their pasture with fresh hay or some such thing. The grass was getting pretty thin, and he needed to start thinking about moving the breeding stock to their winter ranges, closer to home and the haystacks. Once the snow was flying, it'd be too late.

But that wouldn't help the situation any. Who could be doing this and why? If he kept having to replace barbed wire, he'd never get enough saved to buy that Hawthorne pasture.

"Must be a real coward to take out his mad on some cattle. Dumber than a doorknob." Rand muttered the words to himself as he turned to stoke the coals in the stove. Nights were getting chilly. Still, he'd just as soon have the guy driving off his cattle as hurt Carly or the children.

"Uncle Rand?"

He turned to find Mary Jo standing behind him, her flannel wrapper covering her cotton nightdress.

"I thought you'd gone to bed." He tried to keep the harshness out of his voice, but he didn't like being surprised like that. Had she heard him talking to himself about cowards and doorknobs?

"I did." She didn't elaborate any further.

"Can't sleep?"

Mary Jo shrugged. "I guess." She stared at her bare toes peeping out from beneath her wrapper. "Carly's in her room crying. Just thought you might want to know."

Rand slid into a chair. "Oh."

"Do you know why she's upset?" Mary Jo sat as well. She wasn't going to let him off easy on this one.

He'd told her about the fence and cattle. Could that be the problem?

"I'm not sure." Noncommittal but honest.

Mary Jo was silent for a few moments. When she spoke again, her voice had a slight tremor to it.

"Do you think it might be because tomorrow is my painting day and she wishes she could paint too?"

He studied his niece. What an odd thing to say. Rand doubted Carly's crying had anything at all to do with Mary Jo, but maybe he'd better find out why she suspected it did.

"Why do you think Carly wants to paint? Has she said anything about it?"

"Well, no." Mary Jo seemed to search for her words. "It's just that she stands and watches me sometimes and gets this look on her face. I can't explain it exactly, but sometimes I feel like she's going to grab the brush right out of my hand."

"Have you ever seen her paint?" Was Carly an artist? How come she'd never said anything?

"Sometimes she makes suggestions that make me think she's done it before. A lot of it."

"Like what?" Rand leaned forward.

"Put some more shading here or add a touch of brown to that grass to bring out the green. Maybe that kind of thing doesn't make any sense to you. Sometimes it doesn't to me either, but if I do like she says, it always looks better, and then I understand. It's kind of like she's an art teacher or something, except I didn't know anyone could really be a painting teacher. Do you think someone could teach painting, like maybe in a big city or someplace where they have those special kinds of schools for artists?"

That was quite a long speech for Mary Jo. And Rand was definitely out of his realm here. He didn't know good painting from the backside of his barn.

"I reckon so, maybe, but I don't think Carly ever did that. She worked for a newspaper before she came here. Anyway, I've never seen her draw or paint anything. Maybe she just has an eye for it, kind of like your mama did."

"Yeah, maybe." Mary Jo looked thoughtful. "I guess I'll go back upstairs. Do you think I should knock on her door? Ask if she's all right?"

Sure as shootin', he couldn't do that, and somebody should see if there was something they could do to help. But would Carly want the intrusion?

"Better not. Let her have some time alone."

Mary Jo headed for the stairs.

"Let me know if you figure anything out," he said, "about the painting or otherwise."

"I will. Night, Uncle Rand."

"Goodnight."

A yen to paint? He'd never have guessed that.

Rand stoked the fire again, blew out the lamps, and headed upstairs. Muffled sobs filtered from underneath Carly's door when he walked past. If only he could go in there, take her in his arms, and comfort her. He shook his head. Yeah, she'd probably really carry on if he tried that.

Chapter 11

$\mathcal{J}$ust put Lester's note out of her mind and pretend like everything was all right, Carly kept telling herself. It meant nothing, and she needed to get past it.

She didn't believe her own lies.

Should she tell Rand? If Carly was in danger from a devious plan crafted by Lester McGraw, that was one thing, but what about the children? She had to think about the children. Would Lester really come to Walnut Point, or was that an empty threat? Surely he wouldn't hurt the girls. They had nothing to do with this. But what about Tommy? Maybe Lester wanted the counterfeit plates and would think that Tommy might know where they were.

There wasn't any *maybe* about it. Lester wanted those plates, and if he sent her the letter, he might just follow through with his threats. Carly dabbed the cold water around her red-rimmed eyes, praying no one would notice the telltale marks of her tears from last night. She'd tried so hard to control them, but Lester's leering face kept popping into her mind. Carly took a deep breath and left her room in the dim light of early morning. Today was to be Mary Jo's day off, and it was time to fix breakfast without the older girl's help.

When the family had gathered around the breakfast table, they were treated to eggs scrambled with fresh milk, bacon, toasted bread, and fried potatoes. Apple butter flavored the toast and honey sweetened the tea for the children. The blue enamelware pot was full of steaming, aromatic coffee, and Carly sipped it for whatever stamina she could take from the strong brown liquid.

"Good breakfast. Real good." Rand scooted his chair back from the table. "Need my help with anything or got anything we should talk about?"

What an odd question. Oh, how she wanted to open her heart to him, but she couldn't. What if he found out about the plates and turned her in to the law? Instead, she shook her head. "No." She hadn't meant for the little word to come out quite so terse, but Rand only shoved his hat on his head and let the back door slam behind him on his way to the barn. He didn't even look back. Well then, that was that.

Carly dumped the water boiling on the stove into the wash pan and shaved in some soap. She'd have to see to making some more soap soon. The supply on the pantry shelves was nearly gone.

"Jenna, honey, would you bring some of the dishes from the table over to the sideboard? I'll wash and you can dry, then you can practice piano for a while. Tommy, put on your coat and hat and go help Rand with the morning chores." She purposely gave no directions to Mary Jo. The girl's eyes were shining, and she'd been fidgety all during breakfast.

Mary Jo's joy as she anticipated painting only caused Carly's heart to sink further. Oh, how she did miss letting her creativity express itself onto a blank page. Maybe just one time wouldn't hurt, if Mary Jo would let her borrow some of the supplies? Carly's heart raced at the prospect of once again holding the brush in her hands.

But no, she couldn't and she wouldn't. Daddy hadn't let her mama paint even though Mama had been very good at it in her younger days. Daddy said a good wife tended her home and family. She didn't waste time painting. Maybe that was why Lester had appealed to her so. He always encouraged her artwork. She swallowed a snort. Of course, he did. He'd had an ulterior motive. But so had she. She'd needed a place for her and Tommy to go when the Coopers sold the farm. She'd told herself she would eventually grow to love him. She swallowed the humiliation of her own foolishness, finding it tasted even more bitter than before.

Jenna dried the last dish as Carly gave another swipe to the already spotless sideboard. Tommy came in the back door after hanging his chore coat and hat on the hooks in the lean-to. It was time for lessons. Time for them to join Mary Jo in the big front room, where they'd taken to doing their schoolwork. Carly heaved a sigh and stepped into the room. She stopped mid-step when she caught sight of Mary Jo sitting at the table, her history book propped open in front of her.

Carly glanced quickly at the area by the window where Mary Jo liked to paint. The easel was set up, the paint bottles on the table next to pencils, a palette, and brushes. The page on the easel was clean and white. Mary Jo had not even drawn a sketch as yet. The girl didn't look up from her book when Carly entered, but a smile played about her mouth. Maybe Carly should just ignore the situation? She had told Mary Jo the day was hers to do whatever she liked. Maybe she just wanted to go over tomorrow's history lesson before she started painting. No, it wasn't possible. Mary Jo would never choose studying over painting. What was she up to?

"Mary Jo?" Her voice faltered, full of doubt.

"Yes?" Mary Jo looked up and met her eyes, an almost defiant expression on her face. But Carly had seen plenty of defiance from Mary Jo, and something else was going on here. All right then. She would play along.

"It's nice to see you studying, but have your forgotten this was to be your day off?"

"You did say I might do as I pleased."

"Yes. It pleases you to study?"

Mary Jo put down her book, rose from the chair, and came to stand in front of Carly. The girl was almost as tall as Carly, and she looked so … what? Determined? Yes, that was it. Determined to have her way, no doubt. But at what?

"What would please me today is to give you my painting time." Mary Jo let a smile slip into her stern countenance, then quickly wiped it away.

Carly stared at her for a moment. "What? I don't understand."

Mary Jo took her hand and led Carly to the easel. "You draw, you paint, whatever you like."

Carly could not keep the surprise and pleasure out of her voice. "Oh, Mary Jo, what a delightful thought, and how I would love to do that. But I can't."

"Of course you can." The deep, gruff voice from the kitchen doorway made her jump. When had Rand come back in, and what did he know about this? "I insist."

Carly stared at the two of them, searching for the words to express just why she couldn't take advantage of this lovely gift, but she couldn't find them.

Rand sipped at a cup of coffee. "This was Mary Jo's idea. She told me about it this morning while you were fixing breakfast. I'm real proud of her for it, and I won't allow you to spoil it. We all know you've been pining to paint, but none of us knows why you haven't done it yet. Tommy tells me you used to paint all the time back in Baltimore."

"But the children, their lessons, I can't just ..." Carly stammered.

"Yes, you can," Mary Jo interrupted. "You deserve a day off more than I do. While you paint, I will see to lessons for Tommy and Jenna. Jenna will help me make dinner when it's time, and we'll do whatever chores you want."

Rand added, "Tubby is making enough supper for the hands and us. He said he'd add another potato to the stew pot and another biscuit to the oven, so there'll be plenty." Rand's grin was so contagious, Carly almost wanted to grin back at him. She managed to suppress her own smile, still not at all convinced this was something she should do.

When she didn't move or respond, Rand picked up one of the pencils from the table near the easel and put it in her hand. It had too bold of a tip for sketching, but Carly didn't lay it back down. He whispered in her ear, low enough that only she could hear.

"Paint me something really nice. I can't wait to see what you can do." His lips may have brushed her neck when he moved away from her ear, but it was surely an accident. The tingles that ran down her spine were all too real.

"All right then." The words were out of her mouth before she could force them back. The feel of the pencil in her hand was more tempting than she had strength to refuse. If Rand and Mary Jo already suspected she could paint, then what good did it do her to refrain?

Mary Jo went back to the big table and perused Tommy's primer, assigning him a lesson. She then proceeded to write Jenna's spelling words on the slate and handed it to her to study for later recitation. Rand continued to stand beside her.

"Aren't you going to draw something?" Curious, expectant, anticipatory, his words made her ache to touch the pencil to the paper.

"Not while you're watching."

He grinned. "I'd best get back outside anyway. Dusty is tied to the hitching post with an empty saddle on his back, and Bo is like to wander away to chase a rabbit if I don't get out there and put him to work." He lowered his voice. "I'm looking forward to seeing it." Without another word, he was gone.

Carly drew a deep breath. Unable to resist a moment longer, she sketched, letting the scene in her head express itself onto the paper. All the fear of being found by Lester McGraw, all the hurt, anger, and frustration in being forced to marry someone she didn't know and raise another woman's children, all the guilt and pain in knowing she'd committed a criminal act in making the drawings for the plates, wound together into a churning tornado in her mind. The storm spilled out through her fingertips and onto the paper as she drew and then added raging bits of color and texture to the work before her.

Seeing her chaotic emotions transformed into beauty in front of her, Carly lost herself in the wonder of it. The deep craving to paint again satisfied at last, nothing else intruded on her thoughts. She was painting for Rand.

The hands gathered round him and waited for their orders. They seemed nervous and fidgety. "Just be alert and cover as much range as you can today. Tubby'll stay near home and keep guard over things here. That way there'll be something in the grub pot when you all come back with your belly button rubbing against your backbone tonight. Now ride out and keep sharp."

Parker and Clarence went one way, Rand and Nate went the other. Rand purposely chose the direction where the fence had been cut yesterday. Maybe they'd come across something he'd missed in his initial examination in the dim light of dusk.

Carly sure did seem happy about the painting thing Mary Jo had planned, once she got over thinking she couldn't do it. Rand had been totally honest when he'd told her he couldn't wait to see what she would paint. Even now, his mind drifted to that blank piece of paper and Carly's eager expression. Could she paint as well as Mary Jo thought she could?

And whatever had gotten into his oldest niece to devise this sort of thing, Rand couldn't fathom. To give up her own painting day for Carly was something he couldn't have imagined would even cross her mind. Maybe Carly was getting to her. Maybe he wasn't the only poor sap that had gone and fallen in love with her. Jenna had, practically on sight, but Mary Jo was stubborn like her mama. She didn't give in easy and wouldn't open her heart to just anyone. Poor Carly had been at her wit's end with the girl not so long ago. The day he'd kissed her in the backyard.

Rand didn't know anymore whether he was glad he kissed her or just plain embarrassed, but he sure thought about it a lot. He couldn't risk doing it again, but heaven help him, he wanted to. He wanted to so badly it twisted a knot in his gut just to be near her.

"Say, boss, I've been thinking." Nate's words startled Rand out of his reverie.

"Yeah?" Normally Rand would have made some smart remark about how unusual it was for Nate to think, but his heart wasn't in the mood to joke around today.

"What if whoever cut that fence doesn't really want the cattle but just wants to get back at you for something?"

Rand considered this, then shook his head. "Can't think of anyone who would have a grumble with me that would make 'em do something like that. Steer rustling can get a fella arrested and worse if the sheriff's boys catch him at it."

"Spose you're right." Nate looked uncomfortable, but then Nate pretty much always looked uncomfortable.

"You got something to say, then say it," Rand barked at the younger man.

"What about Miss Cunningham?"

Rand pulled up on the reins so hard Dusty nearly reared onto his hind legs. Now that was something he hadn't thought of before.

Myra. The name barged into his head like a freight train then out as fast as a jackrabbit being chased by a coyote. No. Myra didn't give a flip about him. She'd been the one to leave, the one who only pretended to want him until she could get her hands on his money.

"Well, I know it ain't my place to say," Nate continued, "but the whole county knows the story about Miss Myra and her running off with your bank account and—"

Nate stopped short at the look Rand flashed him, meant to do just that. But it wasn't Nate's fault. He was just speaking the truth.

"I'll do me some thinking on that idea. I doubt it, though. Myra's not the type to fool around with stuff like hiring someone to rustle cattle. What would that gain her?" If she wanted something, she'd come barreling in here and demand it of whoever could give it to her.

"Maybe she's jealous." Nate's face was crimson.

"Jealous? You mean that I married Carly? Never." Rand couldn't even fathom that as a possibility.

"Sorry for bringing it up." Nate pushed his hat farther down on his head.

Rand gave Dusty a slight kick, and they started off again. "No need for sorry. Just don't mention it to the others." The red creeping up to Nate's hairline suggested he probably already had, but Rand didn't care so much. His hands were as loyal as they come. Whatever they said in the bunkhouse at night wouldn't go anywhere else.

He needed to think about something or someone besides traitorous Myra. Even steer rustlers was a better thought than that woman.

Chapter 12

What a relief—and a joy—to finally paint again. Carly's reasons for trying to hide this part of her life from Rand didn't make sense anymore now that she'd picked up the paintbrush again. She gazed at the colorful scene in front of her and let her mind relish the blending, shadowing and even the purposeful texturing her brush created. Oh, how she wished the paper went on and on, wished that she could continue to fill it with whatever her heart envisioned.

A movement at her side startled her. Carly pulled her gaze from the picture and looked into Mary Jo's pale blue eyes, so like her uncle's.

"It's beautiful. I knew you could do it." Mary Jo's quick smile and sincere compliment touched Carly's heart. "I know Uncle Rand will like it."

"What will I like?" Rand's voice boomed from across the room as he came in from the kitchen. Carly tensed. She wasn't ready for him to see it. A few more touch-ups and just a little more shadow over the pasture fence ... But before she could think how to stop him, he was looking over her shoulder.

Carly held her breath. She'd never painted an animal before, let alone a living breathing human, but her heart had won out despite the questioning of her abilities to do it justice. There was no doubt about it. Rand sat, his back to the viewer—mostly because she didn't dare try to paint his face—high in the saddle, Dusty carrying him as man and horse stared over the horizon of the ranch, red-and-white cattle in the background milling over the Flint Hills pasture. The yellowish rock outcroppings, the brown-and-gold sunflowers, even a far-off glimpse of Cow Boy watching over his cow herd, made the spot easy to identify.

The moments dragged while Rand stared at her creation. Why didn't he say anything?

Her nervousness took over as Rand continued to gaze at the painting, totally silent.

"I could probably make the likeness truer if I did some touch-up work and a little more texturing in the grass. And I really need to work on the sunset. The sunsets are so beautiful out here, I can't do them justice, but maybe I could—"

"Don't change a thing." Rand's voice was gruff and firm, but it softened somewhat as he added, "It's perfect just the way it is."

Mary Jo nudged her elbow as if to say *I told you so.*

Rand's arm dropped over her shoulders and gave her a slight squeeze. "Supper's on the table."

Refusing to bask in his brief compliment as her heart yearned to do, Carly cleaned up the paints, washed her hands under the hydrant in the kitchen, then sat to enjoy a bowl of beef stew courtesy of Tubby. The stew was good, but it was more the fact that someone else made it that allowed her to enjoy it so much. That and the exhilaration the day of painting had instilled in her spirit.

When she stood to begin clearing the supper dishes, Rand pushed firmly on her arm, forcing her back to her chair. "It's still officially your day off. Let the girls do that."

"Oh, but I—"

"Tommy will help"—Rand gave the boy a pointed look—"won't you Tommy?"

He stood and snatched his bowl, none too happy but not arguing.

"And it's a beautiful moon tonight, almost full. Let's you and me go for a little walk. Grab your coat, though. It's chilly." Rand's tone left no room for argument. A walk? In the moonlight? Odd Rand would suggest such a thing. Perhaps he didn't realize how romantic it sounded.

As she thought back on the day's painting spree, Carly pulled her woolen shawl around her shoulders. She needed a new coat. The one she'd brought from Baltimore was tattered, even threadbare in places. Was she talented enough as a seamstress to make a coat? In any event, the shawl would have to do for now.

Rand held the back door open for her and then let it fall shut behind him as he followed her outside. The air was definitely chilly, the moon a golden orb low in the sky. So beautiful.

"Wanna walk over that way?" Rand pointed toward the pasture she had used as the setting for her painting today, the same one where he'd rescued her from a close call with Cow Boy.

"Sure, but on this side of the fence," she replied with a chuckle.

"We'll be moving Cow Boy and the rest of the breeding stock in a few weeks. We put them in the pastures with the windmills for the winter so we don't have to worry about the ponds freezing over."

As if he could read her thoughts and wishes, Rand reached down and took her hand in his. Something about her small hand grasped in his larger one made her feel so safe, so protected. And though the moonlight lit their path with a sparkling radiance, it wasn't light enough that he could see the blush that must surely be coloring her face at the moment.

"The picture you painted was beautiful." Rand gave a slight squeeze to her hand.

"You liked it, then?" She wasn't really hoping for more compliments by asking the question. Then again, maybe she was, but coming from Rand, it meant so much.

"I did. Will you allow me to frame it? I know just the place I want to hang it."

"Of course. I painted it for you." This admission brought more color to her face. Maybe he wouldn't notice.

"Thank you. I'm hoping you'll do more painting. Next time I'm in town, I'll order some more paint and paper. That way you don't have to use Mary Jo's."

"Oh, that would be wonderful." Carly's voice was breathy with elation. She tried to temper her enthusiasm. "I'm thinking of giving her a day off tomorrow since she gave hers up for me today. What do you think?"

"I think Mary Jo's gift to you would mean more if you didn't toss it back to her tomorrow. She can wait until next week. That way her sacrifice has a bigger purpose. Know what I mean?"

"I suppose so," Carly mused. "I just don't know how to adequately thank her for such an unselfish act."

"You miss the point," Rand chided, though he squeezed her hand again. "Her gift of the day for you to paint was meant to thank you."

"I haven't done anything."

"Oh, but you have," he said. "It's her way of saying she appreciates you teaching her to cook and sew and play the piano. She knows that all her studying she dislikes so much will be worth it in the end. She just wants to say thank you for loving her and her sister."

"Oh." Carly had no response adequate for that statement.

"I thank you too. Our agreement was that you would come here to take care of my house and my nieces and see that they were educated. I never asked you to love them, but you do. That means the world to me."

Carly wanted to say something, but her voice seemed caught in her throat. Her prayer was silent. *Thank You, God.*

What a lovely evening for a walk. What a handsome man at her side. What a great ending to an absolutely beautiful day of surrendering her heart to a paintbrush.

Two weeks had passed since Carly's painting day, and Rand smiled at her as he hung the painting in a prominent position in the sitting room. "You wanna tell me how come you didn't tell us before now that you were a painter? By the looks of this painting, you've been doing it for a while, and it's easy to see that you love it. If I'd known, I would have insisted on buying you some supplies back when we got things for Mary Jo."

"That's probably why I didn't," Carly replied.

"Oh." Nice answer, cowboy. Better try again.

But Carly continued. "My mother was an artist, but she gave it up when she married my father. He believed a woman should be a wife and mother and that painting was a waste of time. I don't agree with him about the wasting time part, but I do think my responsibilities to you and the children should come before other pursuits."

She didn't want him to spend money on her for something he might have considered a frivolous expense. He got that, and she may have even been right about that if she'd asked him for paints when she'd asked that he buy them for MaryJo. But now, he could see her heart in this and wanted to encourage it.

"You're very good. I hope you'll do some more painting soon. Also, I'm much obliged to you for teaching Mary Jo about this artist stuff. It seems to be in her blood, same as yours." Rand gave her a quick squeeze with his arm around her shoulders he hoped showed her that he meant what he said.

"Thank you." Her voice was soft but full of meaning.

"I'd best be getting on outside. The boys'll be waiting on me." Rand left the house suddenly feeling just the least bit embarrassed.

Another letter had come from Lester McGraw yesterday, this one dated ten days prior. Carly was relieved to see the postmark was still Baltimore, but Lester threatened to come after her if she didn't comply with his request to send him the plates immediately. As before, Carly disposed of the letter in the stove, watching it catch fire, shrivel, then turn black and melt into ash.

After these last few months on the Stratford ranch, her biggest fear was not Lester or getting caught with the counterfeit plates but being asked to leave this place that had become home to her. If Rand ever found out about the plates or her part in creating them, he wouldn't want her around his nieces any longer. He wouldn't want to be married to her anymore, and at this point, given their current relationship or lack thereof, an annulment would not be hard to arrange.

Where would she go and what would she do? Maybe she wouldn't have to worry about that. Maybe she'd wind up in jail. Counterfeiting was a federal crime. Maybe the marshals would be after her. True, no bills had actually been produced, because she'd run away and taken the plates with her once she realized Lester's intentions, but even making the drawings for the plates was a criminal offense.

She'd expressed her horror at Lester's intentions when he first showed her the plates. She'd threatened to take them to the police, but Lester had given her an article in the newspaper about a man named Emanuel Ninger. Mr. Ninger was an artist who had drawn intricate replications of ten- and twenty-dollar bills. When he was caught, he was sentenced to years in a penitentiary. Lester told her the same thing would happen to her.

Running away with the plates seemed like the only way to stop him without incriminating herself. How could she have been so gullible?

"What now, Carly?" She gave her head a slight shake and turned back to Tommy. He was waiting for her to check his sums. *Get your attention focused on these children.* The mental chiding did no good. All she could think about was Lester's letter and what had happened to

Emanuel Ninger.

"Your arithmetic is mostly correct," she told her brother. "Try checking this one again." She pointed to the numbers on the slate that Tommy hadn't added quite right, and he returned to the table.

"All right if I grab a few of those oatmeal cookies?" Rand's voice from the kitchen startled her.

"Of course." She left the children to their studies and entered the kitchen to find Rand, his mouth stuffed full of a cookie, and two more in his hand. "Want a cup of coffee with that?"

He nodded and pulled out one of the chairs and sat in the one beside it. Carly poured the coffee and handed him a cup just as he swallowed and was able to speak again.

"Pour yourself one too and sit with me for a bit."

She shook her head. "I'm in the middle of the children's lessons." The look of disappointment in his eyes almost made her reconsider.

"Aw, they can get along without you for a while. Please?"

She grabbed another cup from the cupboard and poured it half full. "Just for a minute then." What was she doing?

"Can you ride?"

The question surprised her.

"I rode quite a bit as a child. When I got older, all we had was the old mare, but I rode her most every day to go bring in the milk cow." She kept her gaze on her untouched cup of coffee. "Why do you want to know?"

"Did you ride sidesaddle?"

"We never had such a thing. I had some split skirts I wore when I got on the horse."

"Did you bring one with you?"

"No." Carly scooted her chair back from the table. "Really, Rand, I need to ..."

"No, you don't. You've made such pretty things for the girls. Mary Jo says you've made some things for yourself as well, though I don't think I've seen you wearing them."

"I don't need anything but my calico work dresses here on the ranch."

"Perhaps not. I should see about taking you into town more often. Maybe we could attend church a time or two if Old Man Winter doesn't show his face for a while." He gave her a hopeful grin.

That prospect was appealing. "I'd like that."

"As for riding, I don't have any sidesaddles, but if you could make yourself a riding skirt, I'd like to take you on a ride up to the top of the ridge. You can see practically the whole ranch from up there."

"We couldn't walk?"

"It's too far for that, this time of year anyway. Come summer we might try it." Rand gave her that lopsided grin that made her heart flip-flop.

"I miss riding. I'd like to do it again. You have a horse tame enough for someone who isn't used to riding?"

"You could ride Polly, if Tommy will let you."

This time she returned his grin, then sipped her coffee.

"I'll see what I can do about riding apparel. Will you be making another trip into town soon?"

"I was thinking of going this afternoon, but I was going to go alone. I need to make it a quick trip. Got to get some fencing supplies and whatever is on your list to get from Keller's. Don't know how I'd do about picking out material."

"Maybe Mrs. Keller could pick something out if you tell her what I intended to make." Carly rose and found the list she'd been keeping since their last trip to the general store. "I don't have it on there, but you might get some more coffee too." She handed it to Rand.

He rose and carried his empty cup to the sideboard. "Tubby will be nearby if you need anything while I'm gone. Just holler, and he'll come running."

She knew Rand was concerned for their safety because of the missing steers, but Carly was glad Rand was keeping someone nearby after the letter she'd received yesterday. "All right."

Rand grabbed his sheepskin coat and headed out the back door. The wind that blew in with his exit made her shiver. Good thing he hadn't planned to take her to town today or do this riding thing. The wind was downright icy.

After a simple dinner of soup and bread, Mary Jo asked to be allowed to sew the hem in her new dress, and Carly agreed. "Why don't we all close the schoolbooks for today? Jenna, you can work on your crocheted lace, and Tommy, you practice piano." It would give her a chance to do some thinking while they were busy with other things. Carly picked up her knitting needles and yarn so the children wouldn't think she was doing nothing. Good thing knitting was second nature because she couldn't concentrate on the task in front of her with thoughts of Lester invading her mind.

Carly looked up as Vinnie and Muckldededun raised a ruckus. What were those dogs barking about? Rand must have Bo out on the range with some of the hands, or he'd be in on this too. Maybe a coyote or a rabbit? Hopefully not a skunk. It had taken weeks to get the skunk smell off Vinnie the last time that silly dog had encountered one of those creatures.

The back door slammed. Rand had left for town an hour ago. Who could that be? Her heart began to race. Surely Lester hadn't …

"You all right, Mrs. Stratford?"

Tubby. Carly breathed a sigh of relief. But since when did he walk into the house without knocking and appear in her front room? Should she chide him? No, he was probably just following Rand's orders.

"Yes, we're fine. Would you like a cup of coffee or something?" From a conversation she'd overheard a few weeks ago, it had become a well-known fact that the coffee she made "up to the house" was way better than Tubby's bunkhouse coffee. Sometimes she took a cup out to whatever men might be working close by.

"No, ma'am. Thank you, but I just came in to let you know you're about to have company. I'm thinking since the boss ain't here, Ol Tubby better help you welcome her. By the looks of things, this isn't going to be pleasant." Tubby removed his hat and looked at her rather apologetically.

"What?"

A sharp rap sounded on the front door. All three children turned toward the door. Tubby made a silent motion with his finger, and Carly caught his meaning.

"You children go on upstairs until I call you." All three obeyed her instantly. Thank God for that. Apparently, she had more whats and whys than they did at this point.

After another glance at Tubby, Carly hurried to the door and opened it a crack. The young woman standing on the porch gazed back at her, curiosity apparent in her expression.

"Won't you come in? It's awfully cold and windy out there." Dark hair and dark eyes, color painted onto her lips and cheeks, the woman was exotically beautiful. Her slender figure was tall and willowy, but it was the air of confidence she carried with her that left Carly feeling somehow small and inadequate.

The woman made her way inside, shrugged off her coat and hat, and dropped them over the back of a chair as if she were familiar with the place. Then, she turned toward them. "Hello Tubby. And who is this?" She motioned toward Carly.

Carly gathered her bravery and stepped forward, her hand extended in greeting. "I'm Carly Stratford. How may I help you?"

"A relative of Rand's I haven't yet had the pleasure of meeting? How nice." The woman ignored Carly's hand and dropped onto the long sofa without being invited.

"A hot cup of something to drink would be nice." The woman nodded at Tubby as if she expected him to do her bidding. To Carly's surprise, he disappeared into the kitchen. So much for his intention to be with her during this ... this ... whatever it was.

The woman motioned for Carly to take a seat as if this were her house and Carly the guest.

Carly remained standing until the woman spoke again.

"Tell me about yourself, Miss Stratford. Are you here to take care of Rand's nieces? I heard their parents died and they were living here with Rand. Such a sad state of affairs. But no fear, I'm here now, and you need not bother yourself with them any longer. I have the perfect boarding school picked out for them back in Virginia. I'm Myra Stratford, Rand's wife."

Carly sank into a chair, suddenly unable to hold herself upright. Her whole body trembled. "Rand's wife?" The words came out as little more than a squeak. "You must be mistaken."

"I assure you, I am not. Rand and I were married this past April, and I have the license to prove it, though I'm sure that won't be necessary. Where is Rand? I can't wait to see him. We've been apart for a few months, you know."

Feeling as if she might faint, Carly avoided the woman's condescending look, realizing it was meant to intimidate her. It was working.

"Please excuse me. I'm not feeling well." Carly, coaxing her legs to carry her, fled to her room desperate to be alone as her world collapsed around her.

Chapter 13

$\mathcal{R}$and couldn't wait to get home. Carly would be so pleased with the things he'd bought at Keller's. Mrs. Keller had talked him into some calicoes besides the broadcloth for the riding skirt. Carly was still wearing those old threadbare things she'd brought from Baltimore. Now there would be no excuses for not making some new work dresses, though he couldn't imagine her as anything but stunning, no matter what she wore.

Mrs. Keller ordered more art supplies at his request, so now both Carly and Mary Jo would have plenty of items to keep them at the easels. He'd make another easel for Carly just as soon as he could get to it. But he was still hornswoggled as to why she hadn't said anything about wanting to paint before she was coerced into it by Mary Jo. Smart girl, his niece. He'd always thought Maggie's obsession with her pencils was kind of odd, but he was beginning to understand it a little better. Mary Jo and Carly took to painting the same way he took to things like pastureland and cattle.

Myra mostly took to money. Rand pulled on the reins enough to slow the horses when that sudden thought surprised him. He hadn't even spared a passing thought toward Myra in so long, the idea of her didn't cause even a niggling bit of the heartbreak he'd endured when she left. Or maybe it wasn't heartbreak at all. At this point all he could feel toward the woman he'd almost married was irritation.

Snow swirled around him as Rand pulled his sheepskin coat tighter.

The gray skies looked ominous. He hoped the men had gotten all the cattle moved today. Rand grinned as he slapped the reins on the horses' backs. "Almost home boys. Giddyup." Wonder what Carly was cooking up for supper? Hot soup on this cold, snowy night sounded mighty good.

As Rand pulled into the farmyard, Vinnie and Mucklededun ran to greet him. They sure seemed excited to see him. He whoaed the team and threw the reins around the hitching post. It'd be easier to unload the wagon before he went onto the barn with it. Or was that just being lazy? The wind was picking up so he'd best get these things to the house. He grabbed the crate with the grocery items from Carly's list and hefted it through the back door, the dogs underfoot. Snow was coming down harder now.

Expecting to find Carly tending to supper preparations in the kitchen, he was surprised to see Tubby bending over the stove. That was odd.

"Hey, Tubbs," he called out. "What's cookin'?"

Tubby turned to face him, his usual grin replaced by a deep frown. "Um, we got us a situation here."

"A situation? What are you talking about? Where are Carly and the kids?" Rand dropped the crate onto the floor and began unloading items onto the sideboard. Tubby was taking a long time with his answer.

"I reckon Miss Mary Jo would be in the front room fiddling with her painting things. The little ones, they're upstairs with Mrs. Stratford." Tubby shuffled his feet and stared at the floor. "Miss Carly, she weren't feeling too good and took to her room." Tubby wiped his forehead on his sleeve and turned back to the stove. "Uh, boss, we got company, and you ain't gonna like it."

"Rand!"

The voice cut through him like a knife to his soul. It couldn't be. Impossible. Myra Cunningham would never show her face around here again. He whirled around to stare into the deceptively innocent ebony eyes that still haunted him.

"Home at last. I'm so glad to see you, darling."

Standing there with a smug grin was the person whose face went with that husky, sensual voice that lived in his dreams. Or his nightmares. The bag of coffee in his hands fell to the floor and split open, leaving him standing in a black heap of aromatic grounds. Served him right for paying the extra nickel to have Mrs. Keller grind it for him. What in the land of the living was Myra doing here, and what was that she'd just called him? It took all his effort not to cross the room and grab her shoulders to shake the smirk off her face. Only that'd mean touching her, and he wasn't about to do that.

"Surprised to see me? Surely you didn't expect your lawfully wedded wife to stay away too long. I would have been here sooner, but I was … detained." A slight crack in her otherwise stoic armor. She recovered quickly. She sent him that alluring smile. She knew all too well how it used to make him weak in the knees, willing to give her anything she wanted. Not anymore.

"What are you doing here, Myra?" His voice was firm, none of the tremors he was feeling inside. For that he was grateful.

"Don't be silly, darling. I'm here for our honeymoon. Better late than never, don't you think?" Myra sashayed toward him, her skirts rippling, her big black eyes seeking his.

Rand stepped backward. "What are you talking about? What honeymoon?"

The pout on her lips meant to sting his heart sprouted no such reaction. Myra reached for his hands, but he firmly pinned them behind his back. "Get out of here, Myra. You're not welcome."

The pout smoothed into a sneering smile. "Oh, Rand, darling, surely you don't mean that. I had some business to tend to, but now I'm ready to take on my role as your adoring wife. That snip of a niece of yours tried to tell me you were married to that freckle-faced woman with that atrociously dyed red hair, but I know that's not true. The preacher man in Walnut Point wouldn't have married you to someone else when he signed our marriage license not so long ago. Now isn't that right, Rand, dear?"

"I'm not your darling or your dear, and I am definitely not married to you." The words came out terse, harsh, perhaps even cruel, but Rand didn't care. "I'm going to tell you one more time. Get out of my house."

"She showed me the marriage license." Carly's quiet words came from the doorway. How long had she been standing there? Tears trickled down her pale cheeks.

Rand turned his gaze from Carly back to Myra. "There is no marriage license because I'm not married to this woman." He spoke the words to Carly, pleading with her to trust him.

Tubby began sweeping up the spilled coffee, so Rand moved toward the doorway. He was desperate to get to Carly, reassure her somehow.

"Myra, you need to leave. Now."

He gripped Myra's shoulders, moving her out of the way, and reached for Carly's hand. She pulled it back.

"You two can discuss this all you want. I'll be upstairs packing." Carly's words squeaked around what must be a huge lump in her throat. She turned and retreated up the staircase. Myra stood in front of him again, leaving Rand unable to stop or follow his wife. His real wife.

Mary Jo, who now stood in the kitchen doorway watching the exchange, followed Carly up the stairs. The look his niece shot him as she left spoke volumes.

"Doggone it, Myra. What have you done?" He was angry now. And there was this awful wall of hurt around his heart that said it might just be breaking at Carly's words. Myra may have given him his first heartbreak, if that's what one would call it, but he wasn't about to let her be the instigator of this one too. He shoved past Myra into the sitting room. Tubby didn't need to hear this altercation. Myra followed.

He focused on her. "I don't know what kind of a fake marriage document you've got or why you'd think now is a good time to produce it, and frankly, I don't care. I want you out of my house and gone. Carly is my wife, and you have no right to be here."

His irate words only broadened the smugness in Myra's smile. She reached into the pocket of her dress and pulled out a folded piece of paper.

"Remember this? I believe that's your signature on there." She handed him the paper.

Rand could hardly unfold the page of thick paper with his fingers trembling as they were. From anger, he told himself. Not fear. Never fear. *God help me.*

Sure enough, it was the marriage license he and Myra had signed the morning of their supposed-to-be wedding. He couldn't deny he'd signed it. Unlike her, he'd planned to promise this woman a lifetime together in just a few hours. His signature didn't matter. Hers either. What was important was the preacher. And Pastor Philbrick's name was scrawled across the line marked for clergy.

"As you can see, it's quite legal." Oh, how he wanted to erase that confident smirk off her face. If Mama hadn't raised him to be a gentleman he'd … "Right down to the two witnesses." Signatures of two witnesses were there but unintelligible. Anyone could have signed those lines. Even Myra. Probably was Myra. She could have even signed

Pastor Philbrick's name for that matter.

"I'll take this to town tomorrow and find out if this is really Pastor Philbrick's signature, and who these supposed witnesses are." Rand shoved the so-called license in his pocket. "You know as well as I do we are not married."

Myra's smile dropped for an instant, then reappeared. "Check it out all you want. It's a marriage in the eyes of the law whether or not we ever stood before a preacher and recited a bunch of meaningless words. My lawyer agrees."

Rand's knees felt like jelly. He would not give in to the despair rising in his chest, nor would he curb the anger that wanted to lash out at Myra. He sank onto the couch. Big mistake. Myra sat down beside him. Close. Too close. Way too close.

She leaned her head against his chest. He scooted over, but so did she.

He stood abruptly and headed for the stairs. He needed to go see to Carly.

"Can we eat now, Rand, darling? I'm starving. Haven't eaten a bite since breakfast at the hotel. An appalling plate of cold eggs and burnt bacon. I do hope your Tubby's cooking has improved."

Rand stopped on the second stair and turned to face her. "You are not invited for supper. I asked you to leave, and I'm going to make sure you do. How did you get out here, anyway?"

Tubby appeared in the doorway, and Rand met his eyes. "She got a wagon or something?"

"Buggy and a horse. Nate put them in the barn 'cause it was too cold to let him stand outside." Yes, that much was true. By now the ranch hands would have done the same with the team he took to town today. He'd meant to be right back out to get the rest of the things from the wagon and see to the horses. Well, Carly wasn't likely to be exclaiming over his fabric purchases tonight. It'd just have to wait till he could get rid of Myra and settle this mess.

"I got some soup on the stove," Tubby continued. "If'n it's all right with you, I got to get back to the bunkhouse. Boys'll want something to eat too."

Rand nodded. "Go on and make sure someone's seen to my horses and wagon. Tell Nate to bring Miss Cunningham's buggy back around front. She'll be leaving."

But Tubby didn't move. Instead, he stood there looking uncomfortable.

"Well? What is it?"

"Rand, darling," Myra interrupted. She needed to quit with that darling thing. "It's dark. Surely you don't expect me to find my way back to town in the dark."

"I don't care if it's midnight. You found your way out here, now find your way back." Even as he said the words, Rand knew he shouldn't send her back now. What if she got lost and froze to death? He wasn't sure he cared.

He looked from Tubby to Myra, determined to show he was the one in charge here. "Get your coat, Myra." He left the stairway and made a show of stomping over to the front door. "You can wait outside for Nate to bring your buggy around." He threw open the door to a cold blast of air and looked into the black night made even blacker by the thick swirls of snow blown about by a biting north wind. A blizzard had arrived.

Carly turned from her window, from the blackness and blizzard outside, when a light tap sounded on her door. "Go away."

"It's Mary Jo. I've brought you some supper."

Food was the farthest thing from her mind, but Carly couldn't bring herself to turn away Mary Jo or the girl's thoughtfulness. She reminded herself that even if Rand wanted this Myra person to be here, Mary Jo did not. Nor did Jenna, for that matter, if the horrified expression, on the younger girl's face at her appearance were any indication.

"Come in." Her voice cracked on a sob.

Mary Jo opened the door and set a bowl of soup and a mug of steaming chamomile tea on top of the four-drawer dresser in her room.

Carly didn't ask, but Mary Jo answered anyway. "She's still here. It's snowing, and Uncle Rand thought it was too dangerous to send her back to town tonight. I overheard him talking to Tubby in the kitchen, and I think he's going to go sleep in the bunkhouse so she can have his bed for tonight."

Carly's trembling increased. She'd be alone in the house with the children and that awful woman. Would Myra wonder why she and Rand had separate bedrooms? But didn't that just prove Myra's point? Carly wasn't really married to Rand. Not if their sleeping arrangements were any indication.

"Thank you," Carly managed to answer Mary Jo's expectant look. "Are Jenna and Tommy all right? I can ..."

"They're fine," Mary Jo interrupted. "Tubby made us supper, and I cleaned up the dishes. They went to bed soon after. I checked, and they're both asleep. Uncle Rand told me to bring you some soup and ask if he could come up and talk to you."

Carly turned back to the window so Mary Jo wouldn't see the new batch of tears welling up in her eyes.

"Tell him no."

"Too late." Rand's voice from the open doorway sounded so dismal and forlorn, Carly almost felt sorry for him. "You can leave now, Mary Jo. Go on to bed." The girl left the room after a brief touch on Carly's shoulder.

"Go away, Rand."

"We have to talk about this." Rand's words were pleading.

"No, we don't."

"Carly ..."

The door clicked shut. He'd gone then. Carly sniffed and turned only to see Rand still in the room. He closed the space between them and stood close enough to touch her. Thank God he didn't. Could he see her trembling?

"Eat your soup, then we're going to bed."

"Go ahead. I'm sure you'll be very comfortable in the bunkhouse." Carly couldn't smooth the wrinkles the tears put into her voice.

Rand acted as if he hadn't heard her. He settled his hands on her shoulders and didn't move them even when Carly tried to shrug them off.

"I'm sleeping in here."

Carly jumped, horrified. "And just where do you expect me to sleep? Are you relegating me to the bunkhouse?"

"Of course not." Rand kept his voice low. "Don't you see? If Myra thinks we share a bedroom, that makes her story weaker. I don't know what she's after here, but she's scheming something, and I'm not about to let her follow through with it."

"If you think I'm going to invite you into my bed ..." Carly couldn't even finish the sentence. It helped to know Rand wasn't admitting to Myra's claims about them being married, but to sleep with him? Now? What if they weren't really married?

A hint of red tinged Rand's cheeks. "Of course I don't expect that. If you would loan me one of your blankets, I'll sleep over here on the floor. I promise I won't touch you or look at you or do anything to go back on our agreement. It's just one night. Tomorrow when this blizzard is over, I intend to send Myra packing, then we can get back to normal."

Horrified by the slight twinge of disappointment she experienced at Rand's words, Carly backed up until her shoulders were pressed against the wall.

Rand moved closer.

"No. I couldn't."

"Please," Rand begged. "I had nothing to do with this. Myra showing up here is a complete surprise to me. I am most definitely not married to her, and a quick conversation with Pastor Philbrick will clear that up. I'll see to it tomorrow." He paused for a second as he stared at her. "I'm married to you. No one else. As your husband, I'm not violating any rules of impropriety by sleeping in the same room as you."

Unless their marriage was nullified by a prior marriage. Surely the pastor wouldn't have married them if he'd married Rand to Myra. Carly had no reason to disbelieve Rand's claims. What could it hurt? She had only to call out, and three children along with an undoubtedly furious Myra would be in her room in an instant. She had nothing to be afraid of, and if it would help the situation, well, she didn't want to be alone in the house with Myra anyway.

When it was all said and done, she did trust this man ... her husband. "You promise you'll stay on the other side of the room?"

"Yes." Rand's blue eyes looked hopeful. "Anyway, Tubby snores something awful." He smiled, and, unable to help herself, Carly smiled back. Trust Rand to bring a bit of levity to a trying situation.

"All right then. One night."

He nodded. "One night. I'll go back downstairs and see to things. You eat your supper and get ready for bed. I'll be back up in an hour or so and bed down there on the floor." He pointed to the side of the room farthest away from Carly's bed. "You can be asleep before I get here, and likely I'll be up and gone by the time you wake." He wiped a tear from her cheek. "Everything is going to work out. I promise."

Carly nodded, not trusting herself to speak. Rand turned to leave. "Soup's getting cold." The door shut behind him.

She swallowed some of the soup and let the warm tea give her some semblance of peace. As quickly as she could manage it so she wouldn't be caught undressing when Rand arrived, Carly changed into a floor-length flannel nightgown with a high neckline and long sleeves, pulled woolen stockings onto her feet, and wrapped herself in a heavy robe. She made a pallet on the floor out of a blanket and one of the feather pillows from her bed, blew out the lamp, and climbed beneath her quilts.

Would Rand be comfortable enough sleeping on the hard floor? It was such a cold night. Would the one blanket keep him warm? Would Myra be fooled by their pretense? The only thing Carly knew for sure at the moment was that she would not sleep a wink with a man in her room—even if he was her husband.

Chapter 14

 as she asleep? Rand wasn't convinced this was the right thing to do, but he didn't have any better ideas at the moment. He crept into Carly's room as quietly as he could and shut the door behind him. It was pitch dark, but he hoped she'd put a blanket somewhere in the vicinity of where he intended to sleep. It was gonna be a long night on the cold hard floor, but with Myra here, it would have been a long cold night just about anywhere on the ranch.

Sure enough, a blanket was spread across the floor for him, and she'd even spared him a pillow. He'd have slept on the crook of his arm before he asked for one, but he was mighty grateful she'd been mindful of his comfort.

Rand shucked his boots and suspenders, but he'd have to keep the rest of his clothes on tonight. Anyway, they'd help him stay warm. He rolled the blanket around him and tried to get comfortable. Carly hadn't made even the slightest of noises. Was she asleep or cowering there in her bed? Quite possibly the latter.

Unable to stand the thick but silent tension in the room any longer, Rand finally whispered into the darkness. "You awake?"

"Yes." The answer came in a whisper even quieter than his own.

"You don't have to be afraid. I made you a promise, and I'm a man of my word." Besides, he was too tired to think about much of anything except getting some sleep.

"I know." A long silence ensued. Maybe she had gone to sleep. But then her whisper found him in the darkness once more. "What's going to happen?"

Rand sighed. If only he had a better answer. "I don't know. What I do know is that I'll do everything in my power to disprove her claim of marriage and get her out of this house."

"I could leave. If you'd rather, that is." Her words might have contained a whimper had she been willing to speak above a whisper.

"No, Carly. Please don't leave. The girls need you." *I need you.* Whatever he did, he couldn't let her leave. Dadburn it all, anyway. Why did Myra have to go and show up just when he and Carly were beginning to get closer? Or had he imagined that? Wishful thinking maybe?

"Why does Myra want to be married to you now?"

Good question. "I don't have the slightest idea. She ran off with my bank account once. I've fixed things so she can't do that again, but knowing Myra, it's got something to do with money."

"Maybe we should pray about it."

"I've been doing that ever since I saw her in the kitchen earlier."

"Oh."

That was it. The whispered conversation ended abruptly. Rand did his best to get comfortable, but it was difficult. His constant turning and rearranging of the blanket and the pillow had to be keeping her awake. At last she spoke again.

"Do you snore?"

She couldn't see his smile, but Rand smiled nonetheless. "Don't guess I rightly know. Why?"

"Just wondered if I'd be able to tell when you went to sleep." So it would be safe for her to go to sleep too. Yeah, he had that one figured out.

"Do you snore?" he asked in turn.

She gasped, then chuckled. "I'll ask you in the morning."

And even if she kept him up all night with snoring, he'd never admit it to her.

Just enough light crept in through the windows of her room to let Carly peek at the place she had made the pallet on the floor. The blanket was folded, the pillow on top, and the neat bundle set in the corner. Rand was already gone. Her sigh turned into a yawn. She hadn't meant to fall asleep but couldn't remember much past their teasing conversation about snoring. She still had no idea if Rand snored, not that it mattered, of course.

Today she would have to face Myra again. Another glance through the window at the gray light of morning told her the snow continued to fall. She couldn't shirk the children's lessons just because an unwelcome guest was in the house. Letting them close their books early yesterday because of Myra's arrival was one thing, but today she'd have to go about things as normally as possible. Oh, dear. Would she be expected to cook meals for this woman claiming her position as Rand's wife? Would Myra be invited to sit at the table with her family?

Her family. That was the answer. This was not Myra's family, and Myra wasn't Mrs. Stratford. Carly had every right to cook in her kitchen, teach the children's lessons, and carry on as though nothing out of the ordinary had taken place. Rand had said he would fix this, and he would. He was probably getting ready to head to town as soon as it was light enough. He'd deposit Myra at the hotel, visit Pastor Philbrick, and set this mess to rights. It'd all be over by sundown, and there would be no need of the blanket and pillow in the corner tonight. Carly left it there anyway.

A freshly washed face, clean clothes, and most of a good night's sleep gave Carly confidence. She held her head high as she left her room and tiptoed down the hallway. The door to Rand's bedroom was closed. Perhaps Myra wasn't awake yet.

Carly followed the aroma of fresh coffee to find Mary Jo in the kitchen frying bacon and mixing pancake batter. The table was set for four. Maybe Rand and Myra had already left? Carly took a deep breath, trying to relax.

"What can I help you with?"

"I've got everything under control," Mary Jo answered. "Pour yourself a cup of coffee if you'd like. Uncle Rand already drank a few cups, but there should be plenty left."

"Thank you." Carly poured the hot liquid into a cup. The trembling in her hands had almost stopped. "Your uncle has left for town then?"

Mary Jo turned away from the stove and stared at her. Her expression was incredulous.

"Have you not looked outside? There's a foot of snow on the ground, and it's still coming down. Nobody will be going to town today."

Carly sank into a chair as her heart sank to the floor. Myra was still here, would be here for … for how much longer? Carly's gaze traveled to the window. Mary Jo was right. Swirling whiteness was all she could see.

"You're right, of course." Carly agreed. "Where is your uncle?" Maybe he would be in soon.

"He said he had to go help the men bring the heifers into the corral so they can watch them. If one of them would try to calve in this storm, the calf probably wouldn't make it. He was kind of mad they hadn't brought them in yesterday, but I guess nobody expected a storm like this to come up so suddenly."

How could anyone anticipate this? And did that mean she was stuck in here with Myra all day without Rand around to buffer whatever storms blew up right here in the house?

Tommy ran into the kitchen, followed by Jenna. "I'm hungry," he announced. "What's for breakfast?"

Jenna rubbed her tummy, eyeing the food behind Mary Jo.

"Sit down," Mary Jo answered calmly. "Breakfast is almost ready."

Tommy and Jenna sat at two of the empty places. Carly forced herself to get up and pour them milk. Her hands were shaking again.

"Hey, ain't that mad lady that got here yesterday gonna eat with us?" Tommy wanted to know. "You only got four plates on the table."

"Tommy," Carly chided, "you mustn't refer to her that way. Her name is Miss Cunningham." Carly turned a questioning look at Mary Jo. Where was Myra?

Mary Jo flipped pancakes in the skillet. "You won't be seeing her for a while. She'll probably sleep right through breakfast and then some." Her words held a note of derision. "Once when she was staying at our old house, she slept right up until dinner time."

Dinner time? Carly had never heard of anyone staying in bed until noon unless they were sick. Still, Mary Jo's words brought her a small bit of relief. At least they wouldn't have to abide her company at the breakfast table. Carly let Mary Jo slide a pancake onto her plate.

"Why did Miss Cunningham stay at your house?" She probably shouldn't have asked that question, but Carly was more than a little surprised by Mary Jo's statement.

"Sometimes she would come to visit Uncle Rand, but he wouldn't let her stay here. He said it wasn't proper for an unmarried couple to sleep in the same house without a chaperone. She'd stay at our house, and I'd have to give up my room for her. Mama didn't like having her there because she would complain about things like the food or the smells from the barn."

"I see." No wonder Rand had been so adamant about the sleeping arrangements. "Tommy, would you say grace, please?"

Breakfast proceeded, but Carly had no appetite. How long would Myra be here? The snow showed no signs of letting up. Would she complain about food and smells here? Would Rand spend another night on the floor in her room?

She sipped her coffee, glad for the warmth. She must try to be polite to Myra and behave worthy of the title of Mrs. Stratford. Like it or not, she was on trial here. But who was the judge? Maybe Rand would decide he'd prefer Myra to her. Why wouldn't he? Myra was gorgeous with her jet-black hair and eyes. Too much rouge on her cheeks couldn't disguise the beauty of her fair skin, and even her sneering smile showed perfect white teeth. She was a beautiful woman, especially standing next to Carly with her red hair and freckles.

Why hadn't Rand prayed with Carly last night? It had taken all the bravery she could muster to ask him, but he'd acted almost offended as if she thought he wasn't praying. Didn't he understand she wanted to pray *with* him? Together? Maybe this wasn't the right time or the right subject for them to pray about together. Had he ever prayed with Myra? Did Myra even know how to pray?

"Um … Carly?"

"I'm sorry." Carly forced herself to focus. "What did you say?"

Mary Jo turned her eyes to the empty plate in front of her. "Do we have to have lessons if she's in the room with us? Maybe I could just paint today and …"

"Nonsense. Of course we'll have our lessons. Don't pay any attention to Miss Cunningham. I'm sure she won't bother us. Let's get the dishes done, girls. Tommy, put your coat on and bring in some more wood from the lean-to, but do not step outside."

"What about Mucklededun and Vinnie?" Tommy asked. "Can I let them in? I bet they're cold."

Rand had let them in to sleep by the stove last night, but the dogs hadn't ever stayed in the house all day. Tommy was right, though. It wasn't a good idea to leave them out in the storm.

"Uncle Rand said he'd put them in the barn for the day," Mary Jo said.

"They'll be nice and warm there," Carly assured Tommy. The look of resignation in Mary Jo's eyes said she would have liked to have them inside today too. It was clear the girls had no love for Myra. Even Jenna wore a pout.

Carly stood and began clearing the table. The children rose as well to do as she had asked them. This might turn into a long day for all of them. She'd have to do her best to keep the children busy, but she wouldn't take any pains to make Myra comfortable or entertain her. *Is that wrong, God?* No answer was forthcoming.

Chapter 15

Rand squinted into the flying snow trying to see if he'd missed any of the bred heifers that had been on the north range. If it were possible, he'd give himself a kick in the backside for putting off moving them in because the weather had been so unseasonably warm. Up to now. This was Kansas, and a man had to be prepared for the unexpected here. Now he and his men were out in this blasted storm trying to round up the cattle. Probably it was too early for any of them to calve, but he wasn't taking the risk.

"See anything?" Nate hollered to him above the roaring wind.

"I 'spect we got 'em," Rand answered, riding closer to his ranch hand. "Let's get these last two pointed toward home and see if we can catch up." Clarence, Parker, and Tubby had gone ahead with the majority of the herd. With Bo's help they'd been able to get most of them on the first go-round.

"Regular old she-blizzard," Nate remarked. "How long d'you suppose it'll last?"

Rand didn't answer. He didn't much like the response he'd have to give, and it was too cold to talk anyway. By the looks of things, it would probably keep snowing and blowing all day. What a time for Myra to show up. If he didn't know any better, he'd think she'd planned it that way. On second thought, maybe she did.

Another fit of coughing made him pull up on the reins and pause while he tried to stop the annoying hacking. This had been going on all morning, and he was downright irritated about it.

"You coming down with something, boss?" Nate had stopped beside him.

"Nah, just the cold wind, I reckon." Rand hoped he was right.

"Well, all the same, might be best if you go on in once we get back. Clarence and I can see to getting some hay pitched in the corral for the heifers. Parker will get the ice chopped out of the tank while Tubby's puttin' on some hot coffee and cooking up some dinner. We'll see to your horse, too."

It wasn't that Rand didn't appreciate Nate's concern, but he wasn't the head of this outfit. Nate ought not be giving him orders.

"Don't make no nevermind about me," Rand barked. "We'll work till the job's done."

Nate gave him a sideways look and nodded. Could it be his observant ranch hand knew that Rand didn't particularly want to go back to the ranch house just yet? Had he figured out what an impossible situation this was with Myra here sticking her nose into everything and Carly all upset over it? The hands would have to be imbeciles to not realize the conundrum Rand faced at the moment.

"Confounded snow." Rand's muttering may or may not have reached Nate's ears, but he made no reaction. "I reckon we're about there," he said a little louder. "I can hear the rest of 'em bawling."

"Yep. Not used to being penned up and close quarters and all. They'll be happier once we get some hay forked into the corral."

Nate's remark was almost swallowed up by the howling wind. Mercy, but it might be blowing even harder. Good thing they'd started early this morning. Pretty soon it'd be too rough to have sent any of his men out in this. Nothing safe about not being able to see where a man was heading.

Another bout of coughing forced Rand to stop and try to get his breath again. A hot cup of coffee would feel good on his scratchy throat. "Open the gate," he called. His voice was hoarse enough, he wasn't sure if he could be heard. Nevertheless, Parker opened the corral gate, and the last two heifers they'd been herding ran in to join the rest of them.

"Ice is broke and snow's piled high so they got water." Parker sent him a meaningful look. "Clarence is up in the hayloft about to fork down a good pile. We got this, boss."

Great. Now Parker was trying to get him to go inside. Rand coughed again and winced at the pain in his throat. Maybe he'd just take him up on that. He dismounted, handed the reins to Parker, and called over his shoulder, "Make sure to put Bo in the barn with the other mutts and see that they've got water. All of you stay inside this afternoon. I'll be at the house if anyone needs me."

Too tired and too cold to care about the look Parker and Nate exchanged, Rand stomped away from the corral and made the trek to the house. He tried to cut a path as he went, but the snow was swirling so fast and coming down so hard, his footsteps seemed to fill up behind him. This was a mean storm for sure.

Rand let the back door slam behind him. Still plenty of wood in the lean-to and more piled right outside the door. That was good. The bunkhouse was well supplied too. He shucked his snowy boots, hat, and coat in the lean-to and opened the kitchen door. He wanted a cup of that coffee he could smell clear out here. He stepped inside only to see Myra sitting alone in the kitchen, a steaming cup in front of her.

"Rand, darling," she called in that irritating drawl of hers. "I've been so worried about you, out in this terrible storm. You should have let your men take care of the cows. No sense in you being out in this."

Rand coughed again, not bothering to explain to her how his ranch worked. He grabbed a mug from the top shelf and crossed to the stove. The coffee pot held only enough to pour a few drips into his waiting cup.

"Oh, I'm sorry. Did I take the last of the coffee? Carly should have made some more." Myra rose from her chair. "I'll see if I can find her."

"It's not necessary." Or maybe it was. Rand sat in the chair next to the one Myra had vacated. His knees didn't seem to want to hold him up.

"You poor dear. You must be freezing."

Myra stood behind him and rubbed his shoulders and the back of his neck. He should tell her to stop, but it felt so good. He was achy and cold. He did want a drink, though. Rand swallowed the drops in his cup.

"Where's Carly?" he asked.

"I'm right here."

Her voice was hard and cold. Myra's hands fell to her side.

"Oh, good," Myra exclaimed. "The coffee's gone, and Rand needs a cup. Would you be a dear and make another pot?"

Carly moved toward the stove and grabbed the empty pot. She didn't speak. Yeah, he shouldn't have let Myra do that rubbing thing, and now

Carly was upset. Why was it so hard for him to care? All he wanted was for someone to make some coffee.

"Thanks," he managed to say as Carly walked past to put the pot back on the stove.

She turned to look at him. His voice was hoarse, but Myra hadn't seemed to notice.

"Are you feeling all right?" Carly's voice was tinged with concern, but her terseness hadn't faded.

"I'm fine." The words were punctuated by another coughing spell. It seemed his body wouldn't quit betraying him today.

Carly stoked the fire in the cook stove as Myra sat and sipped her coffee. Rand watched as she spooned more sugar from the bowl on the table and stirred it into the liquid.

A hand slapped across his forehead. A nice cool hand. Carly?

"You're running a fever," she snapped. "You should be in bed."

Rand nodded. He could agree with her on both points. And he might even do as she suggested—if he had a bed.

The nerve of him. How dare Rand sit in her kitchen and let Myra go all goo-goo eyes over him? The woman had no right to touch Carly's husband, and Rand shouldn't have allowed it. She'd been tempted to tell him to make his own coffee, but a distant expression in his eyes warned her that something might not be quite right. He confirmed it when he spoke, and then that hacking cough made its presence known.

If Rand was sick, she had to take care of him. The compassion inside her for how he must be feeling grated at the angry countenance she'd tried to wear. Feeling the heat of his skin when she touched his forehead left her with no choice. This man was her husband, and even if he had an affinity for this other woman in her kitchen, it would be up to Carly to nurse him back to health.

Her voice turned gentle. "Come with me, Rand. Let's get you upstairs and in bed. I'll bring you a cup of coffee when it's ready, or tea if you'd rather. Some tea and honey might feel good on your throat."

She expected him to protest, but he didn't. He simply stood and let her take his hand. Carly led him out of the kitchen, Myra staring after them.

The children looked up from their books as she and Rand crossed the room and headed for the staircase.

"Uncle Rand?" Mary Jo ventured. "Is something wrong?"

You mean like his ex-fiancée being snowed in with us? "Your uncle isn't feeling very well," Carly answered. "You children go back to your studying. I'll be down once I get him settled in bed."

Mary Jo started to protest, but seeing Myra standing in the doorway watching them, she closed her mouth and turned her eyes back to her history book. Was Myra watching to see what Carly would do next? Did she suspect that last night's sleeping arrangements had been a farce?

"Come, dear, I'll tuck you into bed, and you can have a nice nap." Did she really just say that? Carly glanced at the children. All three were staring at her, Jenna's mouth opened in a big round O.

Feeling the color rush to her cheeks, Carly turned back toward the stairway and pulled Rand with her. He offered no resistance, just followed along complacently. His grip on her hand was solid, though. Let Myra think what she would.

At the top of the stairs, Carly eased into Rand's room. The bed was unmade, articles of clothing were strewn on the floor and over the chairs, and Myra's perfume wafted through the air. Carly grabbed a clean pair of Rand's long johns from the dresser and closed the door behind her. Apparently, Myra wasn't much of a housekeeper.

She thrust the clothing into Rand's hands and pushed him into her room. "Change into something clean then get in bed. I'll go down and make you some tea. You want me to send Tommy up to give you a hand?" Whatever he said, she wasn't going to help him change.

Rand shook his head. "I can manage. Would you bring a glass of water, too?" he croaked. "Please."

"Sure." She turned away. She could use some cold water herself. Her hands were shaking again.

Rand shut the door behind him, and Carly winced as more coughing ensued. To think that man had been out chasing cattle in a snowstorm. Served him right for leaving her here alone with Myra.

That wasn't really how the situation had come about, but it felt good to put the blame somewhere, even if just for a few seconds. None of this was anyone's fault, except Myra's, and it would do no good to try to blame her. Carly had never met a more selfish person in her life. On second thought, maybe Lester McGraw would rival her in that category. Those two would make an insufferable pair.

"I've been supervising the children for you, Carly."

Myra's smug expression was the only clue that Myra was insinuating Carly's job was not a difficult one. Carly clenched her fists at her side, determined not to take the bait Myra offered.

Myra continued. "The school I have chosen for the girls will give them a much better education than they can get out here on the Kansas prairie, of course. Just as soon as Rand is feeling better, I must talk to him about sending them as soon as possible."

Carly glanced at Jenna. The girl wore a horrified expression, much the same as her sister's. Great. "Your uncle would never send you to a boarding school," Carly assured them. She prayed she was right.

Ignoring Myra, Carly continued to speak to the children. "Close your books for today. I think we need to concentrate on keeping warm and keeping well. Tommy, we need some wood brought in again, please. Mary Jo and Jenna, please help me in the kitchen. We'd best make a big pot of soup so that your uncle and anyone else who might come down with this can have something to eat that won't hurt the throat so much. I'm thinking maybe noodle soup with some of that chicken stock we made a few days ago. Doesn't that sound good?"

She was rambling. Anything to keep from looking at Myra, then saying or doing something she might regret later. At this moment it'd be pretty tough to regret anything that might obliterate that smug grin from the other woman's face.

The children followed her into the kitchen. Looking back, Carly drew a sigh of relief that Myra wasn't tagging along. Fine. She could sit in the front room by herself and watch it snow for all Carly cared.

She set Mary Jo and Jenna to making the noodles for the soup while Tommy carried in wood from the lean-to. Carly brewed some tea and stirred in a generous teaspoon of honey. Remembering Rand's request, she filled a glass with water from the pump and left the kitchen.

Myra wasn't sitting in the front room. Where had she gotten to? Perhaps she had gone upstairs to take a nap? But why would she need a nap as late as she'd stayed in bed this morning?

Carly climbed the stairs, careful not to spill either of the drinks as she made her way to her bedroom. As she entered, she stopped short at the sight of Myra, sitting on her bed, her hand across Rand's forehead. Some of the water sloshed to the floor.

"I think it's just a nasty cold," Myra said when she saw Carly. "He should be up and about soon." She gave Carly an evil sort of smile.

"I'll thank you to leave my bedroom this instant," Carly spoke the words through clenched teeth.

Myra shot her a surprised look.

"And stop touching my husband."

Myra stood, albeit it slowly. "Pardon me, I meant no harm. I just wanted to see how Rand was doing."

"Best to leave, Myra." Rand's words came out with a cough.

He'd been lying there with his eyes closed, but apparently he wasn't asleep. Did that mean he'd welcomed Myra's intrusion? Had he invited her to sit on the bed? Maybe even asked her to soothe what must be an aching head with the cool touch of her fingers?

Carly's anger fell away. It wouldn't help a thing. All she wanted now was to get back downstairs to the kitchen. Myra tossed a meaningful glance over to the corner where the pillow and blanket sat neatly bundled. "Looks like somebody had a little tiff last night," she muttered under her breath, then brushed past Carly with a slight huff and left the room.

Carly set the mug of tea and the glass, still mostly full, on the small table beside the bed. She tucked the quilt around her husband, though his eyes remained closed. It was all she could do to hold back the tears threatening to fall. She left the room without speaking and closed the door behind her.

Chapter 16

*I*f it didn't hurt so much to talk, Rand might have said one of those words his mama wouldn't tolerate. With an effort he sat up in the bed, Carly's bed, and swallowed in a few gulps most of the glass of water she'd left. His throat did hurt.

He grabbed the teacup and sipped at it a little. It did feel kind of good going down, but he'd still rather have had the coffee. Confound it all. Why did Myra have to sneak up here and go upsetting Carly again? Maybe his wife would have stayed and kept him company for a few minutes. Or at least talked to him. A word or two would have been nice as opposed to icy silence. She was good at that. What other poor coot did she practice that silent stuff on?

A knock sounded at the door. Who bothered knocking around here? He tried to say, "Come in," but only a hoarse grunt came out. The door opened anyway. Jenna? His youngest niece stood in the doorway wearing a smile that sank into his heart like a tired head on a goose down pillow. Rand waved her into the room.

After pulling the only chair in the room to the side of the bed, Jenna sat beside him and picked up his hand to hold in hers. Her gentle touch was like sweet music to a troubled soul. Neither one of them said anything, and it was so nice that they didn't have to talk.

After a while, Jenna got up, picked up his empty teacup and water glass, and left again, her slipper-clad feet shuffling down the wooden staircase like a gentle whisper. A few minutes later she returned, the water glass refilled and a mug of fresh steaming coffee to replace the teacup. He would have hugged her if he'd had the energy to do it. She left again and came back with a stack of his handkerchiefs and set them on the bedside table. He would make use of those, for sure.

After sitting with him a little longer, Jenna turned his hand upward and used her index finger to etch the words "Get well" into his palm. That simple gesture probably did more toward that end than the sweet girl would ever know. She departed the room soon after, closing the door behind her.

The coffee tasted so good. Had Carly encouraged Jenna to come visit him, or had Jenna taken that initiative? Somehow, he wanted Carly to have suggested it. Maybe because it would mean she was still mindful of him even if she was mad. She deserved to be mad. He hadn't invited Myra in here or asked her to sit on his bed, but Carly didn't know that.

He was about to doze off when his door opened again. No knock this time.

"How are you feeling?"

Carly's voice was a balm to his soul, even if it was a little terse. She rested her fingers across his forehead.

"Not too good," Rand managed. Might as well be truthful.

"Still a little warm, too. You better plan on staying in bed the rest of the day, at least."

Rand wanted to protest, but Carly kept talking. "The girls made some noodle soup that ought to be easy on your throat. I'll have one of them bring a bowl up for you closer to dinner time."

It wasn't even noon yet? No way a man could tell by looking out the window. All he could see was flying snow. He really wanted to ask what Myra was doing. Was she pestering Carly over every little thing, or had she found a way to entertain herself and stay out of the way of the household routine? He wouldn't ask, but he was curious.

On an impulse, he caught Carly's hand in his as she pulled the covers up closer to his chin. "Thank you," he rasped.

"For what?" She looked a little perturbed but didn't pull her hand away.

"This." He motioned at the bed, hoping she could figure out he meant taking care of him. He was usually fairly healthy, but the few times he had been sick enough to take to his bed, he'd had to fend for himself. No one to bring him drinks or make him soup or …

"Yes, I suppose I'll be the one sleeping on the floor tonight." Carly sighed. "I'm not sure it's worth it, though. My guess is Myra's on to this charade."

"I meant for taking care of me." Rand resorted to a whisper to get the words out. "No one has been this kind to me since my mama died."

Carly smiled at him and withdrew her hand. "No need to thank me. That's what a *wife* does."

Did he imagine that emphasis on the word wife? He really had to get this mess straightened out with Myra. He wouldn't, couldn't, believe her claim of them being legally married, but Carly must have her doubts, and understandably so.

"Wood?" That had been bothering him. Would she understand his meaning?

"We've got plenty. Parker brought another whole load into the lean-to a few minutes ago. I had to get downright angry with him to make him see reason and go back to the bunkhouse. He was planning on chopping some more."

If not for his pounding headache, Rand might have chuckled. Not so much at Parker chopping wood in a snowstorm as at the thought of Carly acting angry. Yeah, Parker was probably really scared. Hightailed it back to the bunkhouse in fear, no doubt.

"I'd best be getting back downstairs and see to the children before ..." Carly left her sentence unfinished as she exited the room, but Rand would have bet money the unsaid words had something to do with Myra.

God Almighty, get me out of this mess.

He'd never have thought it, but he might have enjoyed all this pampering and attention a little if Myra weren't around. But lying here alone watching the snow and knowing Myra was in his house doing the damage that only she could do, well, it was enough to make a man sick. And he didn't need any help with that.

What a day. Carly resisted the urge to rub her aching temples with her dishwater-soaked hands. Night had finally come, and it appeared, though she couldn't tell for sure, that the snow might have stopped. Supper had been nothing more than the leftover soup from dinner, though she had managed to bake a fresh loaf of bread that afternoon. Still, most of the day had been spent trying to avoid Myra—entirely without success.

At this moment Myra was exclaiming loud enough for the men over in the bunkhouse to hear about how utterly beautiful Mary Jo's painting was. Myra had gone on and on about the boarding school she planned to send the girls to and how they had professional artists on their staff who could nurture and develop Mary Jo's talent. For all Carly knew, Myra might actually have Mary Jo wanting to get to that boarding school by now, even though she'd had to take both girls aside today and assure them they were staying right here.

Doubts were slamming her from every direction. Carly was even uncertain as to whether Rand really would consider sending his nieces away. More than that, if Rand found out he was legally married to Myra, would he send Carly and Tommy away? Most likely. But even if he didn't, Carly would never stay in the same house as Myra. Even now, running into the snowstorm seemed like a better option than having to tolerate Myra's exaggerated and obnoxiously loud gushing.

Carly had asked the girls to do the dishes after supper. Myra immediately vetoed that by saying how she wanted to watch Mary Jo paint some more, then put an arm around Jenna, effectively leading her out of the room along with her. Mary Jo followed, grabbing the opportunity to paint. Carly didn't blame her. Was Myra winning this battle, worming her way into the Stratford family at Carly's expense?

The door to the kitchen opened revealing Jenna and Tommy. Both children grabbed a dishtowel and set to drying the clean dishes on the sideboard. "We'd rather be in here with you than out there with them even if we gotta do dishes," Tommy muttered.

Jenna nodded vigorously. It appeared these two might still be on her side.

"Thank you." Carly was glad for their company, even more so than for the help with her chore. "As soon as you're done here you can put Vinnie and Mucklededun in the lean-to for the night, then head on to bed." The dogs had been underfoot ever since they'd been let out of the barn and allowed to return to the house. It would be a relief to have everyone settled down for the night.

"Is Rand gonna sleep in your room again?" Leave it to Tommy to ask the question the girls had stayed away from all day.

"Yes. He's sick, you know, and as long as Myra is here, she's using his bedroom." Carly wouldn't even try to answer the additional questions she could see swarming in the children's eyes. It was all Carly could do to keep a smile on her face.

"Go on, now, you two. I appreciate all your help today. Tiptoe quietly when you walk past the bedroom upstairs in case Rand is asleep. He needs his rest." The two children obeyed, and Carly sank into one of the chairs at the kitchen table and let her head fall into her hands.

Heaven help her, but she didn't feel well. Her head throbbed, her shoulders ached, and her throat was sore. She would not, could not, succumb to whatever sickness Rand was experiencing. Someone had to save this house, these children, even the dogs and ranch hands, from the ruination Myra could roll out as if on a whim. Rest. Yes, that would be best. If only she had a bed to sleep in, but the floor would have to do.

After making sure the dogs were warm and comfortable in the lean-to, Carly blew out the kitchen lamp. Taking a deep breath, she entered the front room to find Mary Jo still painting, Myra looking over her shoulder. Both were smiling.

"Time to call it a night, Mary Jo," she called to the girl, hoping they couldn't hear the rasping in her voice.

"Oh, but she's just getting started on the horse," Myra protested. "Such beautiful work this child does. She will be the star painter in her new class at the school I've chosen."

Carly didn't feel like fighting. All she wanted was to lie down and close her eyes against her pounding head. She turned toward the stairs.

"I'll get things put away and be up directly," Mary Jo called after her.

Whose side was Mary Jo on? Why did there have to be sides? Maybe it was all in Carly's mind. Maybe nobody but she had drawn lines in the dust. Whatever the case, she couldn't take it anymore. She trekked up the stairs and closed the door of her room behind her.

The room was dark, and Rand was snoring. That settled that, then. Hurrying lest he awaken, Carly shucked her calico work dress and threw her flannel nightgown over her head. Feeling worse by the minute, she rolled out the blanket Rand had used the night before and slid beneath it, her back against the hard, cold floor.

She closed her eyes but could find no relief from her shivering, nor could she stifle the one cough that led to another and still another. Rand's snoring stopped.

Carly held her breath, willing herself not to cough until the snoring began again. The shivering grew worse, and she felt frozen from the inside out. They'd kept the house toasty warm all day with the wood Parker brought in, both stoves and the fireplace burning hot. The logs had been replenished for the night, the fires stoked before she came upstairs. Why was she so cold?

Probably running a fever. The thought surprised her at first, then settled into her foggy brain with a sinking feeling of despair. Oh, how could she have gone and caught this thing too? It was the worst possible timing.

Another spell of coughing was almost like waving the white flag of surrender. She couldn't do this. She was married to Rand. He was her husband. They were both sick. She didn't care about anything beyond that as she rose from her uncomfortable position on the floor and eased into the bed beside Rand, careful to keep from touching him.

The quilts and down comforter felt so good. She snuggled into the warmth and let blessed sleep carry her away from the cares of this day.

Carly had no idea how much time had passed when her eyes flew open. The room was still dark. Her head still ached. But warmth surrounded her. Rand's arms were curved around her middle, and her back was pressed against his warm chest. Perhaps his gentle snores had awakened her. Too tired to care, too blissfully warm to move away, she let sleep overtake her once more.

Gray daylight filtered into the room as Carly opened her eyes. A sudden thought made her leap out of bed and turn to stare at the space she had just vacated. She was alone. Had she only dreamed of waking up in Rand's arms, then shamelessly snuggling closer against him as she went back to sleep?

The blanket from the floor had been tossed over her for another layer of warmth. Shaking with cold, her throat sorer than ever, Carly crawled back into the bed, still warm from her—or their—presence. She couldn't be sure she'd dreamed it all, but if she had, she wanted to be back in that dream.

Where was Rand? Had he found another place to sleep when she joined him in the bed? She couldn't very well blame him. She closed her eyes, willing the ache behind them to disappear. Just as she was falling back to sleep, a light tap at the door jerked her awake.

"Yes?" That didn't sound like her voice at all.

The door opened, and Mary Jo entered, a tray in her hands and a smile on her face. "Uncle Rand says you seem to have come down with the same thing he had yesterday. I thought you might like some tea and scrambled eggs."

Carly sat up and propped a pillow behind her back. "Thank you." A waft of steam floated off the tea and curled tantalizingly over the small plate of eggs. "That does smell good."

Mary Jo set the tray on her nightstand and handed her the cup of tea. "How are you feeling?"

"I'll be fine," Carly croaked. "I'll just drink this nice tea and sample those eggs, and then I'm sure I'll be ready to get up and face the day."

"I don't think so." A voice from the doorway as hoarse as her own made her turn and look. Rand stood there, peering into the room, a grin spread across his stubbly face. "You made me stay in bed, which was just what I needed. Now, it's my turn. You need to spend today resting."

Carly could hardly look at him, embarrassment crawling up her neck and into her face, but neither could she turn away from the look of concern and caring emanating from his blue eyes. Rand crossed the room and reached past Mary Jo to lay his hand across her forehead.

"I'm not much of a judge about these things, but I reckon you got one of them fevers like was dogging on me yesterday. Mary Jo, see that Carly stays in bed today. You and Jenna take care of her, now. You hear?"

"We'll take care of her."

"Wait." Carly couldn't clear the croak from her voice. "Where are you going?"

The grin disappeared. "Soon as I can get out, I'm heading into town to get this business with the …" He glanced at Mary Jo. "I'm fixing to get this license thing put to rights."

"But you're still sick." His raspy voice was proof enough of that.

"I'm fine. Snow's stopped, and the sun's gonna shine soon as it gets over the horizon a little farther. Best get this taken care of as soon as we can and get things back to normal around here." Rand disappeared from the room as his boot heels clunked down the hallway and then the stairs.

"You think he's all right?" Carly asked. Her voice was little more than a whisper.

Mary Jo nodded. "He was up early this morning, even before I could get coffee made. I made him let me feel his forehead, and I'm pretty sure the fever is gone."

Carly sank back against the pillows. Wasn't anything she could do about it anyway. Rand obviously had his mind made up. She wanted to ask if Myra was going with him but couldn't bring herself to do it.

"Will you be all right if I go back down and make breakfast for the others?" Mary Jo asked.

Carly nodded. "Thanks again for the tea and eggs."

"I'll be back up later to check on you and see if you need anything." Mary Jo left the room, her footsteps treading softly on the wooden staircase.

Surprised to find she had an appetite, Carly made short work of the eggs, then leaned back into her pillows to enjoy sipping the hot, fragrant tea. She felt a little better than she had last night, but, even though she wouldn't admit it, she was relieved for the chance to stay in bed.

Except for Myra. Was she still downstairs trying to get in good with Mary Jo and Jenna? At least she ignored Tommy. Or maybe Myra was with Rand riding into town beside him on the wagon seat. Could a wagon roll through snow this deep? No, Rand would be on horseback and therefore alone. Did that make her feel better that Myra wasn't with him, or worse because the woman was still in the house?

A fit of coughing almost made Carly spill her tea. With every cough, her head hurt a little more and added to the burning in her throat. She took a few more swallows of tea, then set the cup back on the tray. Burrowing under her blankets, she closed her eyes and tried to sleep.

But sleep did not come. Was there any way she could find out if, indeed, she had woken up in Rand's arms? If it really had happened, why had Rand done that? The warmth of him lying next to her had been seared into her memory. That was real enough. And even if she'd imagined that part in some kind of feverish stupor, the fact remained that she and her husband had slept in the same bed all night. Take that, Myra Cunningham.

Chapter 17

Dusty trotted through the snow as Rand made his way to town. If it hadn't been for the snow, he'd have made Myra follow him with her horse and buggy and trunks. He'd put her up in the hotel if it meant getting her away from Carly and the children. When the snow melted enough to allow the buggy wheels through, it'd be the first thing he did.

To make it worse, he was miserable. The fever might be gone, but his throat still burned, and the ache in his head felt like someone had taken a sledgehammer to it. It'd be worth it, though. Once he visited with Pastor Philbrick and got all this nonsense straightened out, he could put this behind him and focus on Carly. Funny how Myra didn't seem to get the fact that he had no feelings for her anymore. Or maybe she just didn't care.

The church bells rang as he rode into town. It couldn't be … but it was. It was Sunday morning. How had he lost track of the days? Pastor Philbrick wasn't going to be able to talk to him this morning. May as well make the best of being in town on the Lord's day.

He reined Dusty into the churchyard and tied him to one of the hitching rails. How long had it been since he'd been to a church service? Too long. He needed to make more of an effort to get Carly and the children here now and then. Once the weather cleared anyway.

Didn't appear to be a lot of folks here this morning, thanks, he was sure, to the snow. He left Dusty outside and stepped into the small building.

Many of the pews were empty, but Mrs. Kaiser was at the piano plunking out off-key notes on the old instrument. It made him appreciate Carly and her musical abilities.

Rand slid into a pew toward the back. He could easily slip out if he got a coughing fit. Try as he might, Rand couldn't concentrate on Pastor Philbrick's sermon. His mind kept jumping to the night just past. He wasn't sure when Carly had joined him in the bed, but once he'd felt the heat radiating off her, he'd understood why she had. The floor must have been utter misery if she'd climbed into bed with him. At any rate, he'd wakened enough at some point to realize she was beside him. He hadn't been able to resist gathering her close to him, and she had yielded to his embrace as if it were just where she wanted to be. Of course, she was asleep, and ill besides, but all he'd been interested in at the time was being close to her. Surely it wasn't wrong for a man to feel that way about his wife.

He'd hoped to savor the moment awhile longer but had fallen back to sleep, too comfortable to stop himself. When he woke in the morning, she was still in his arms. It was all he could do to pull himself away from her and get out of bed. Lousy as he'd still felt, his illness had taken second place to some other desires he couldn't give into just then. Maybe after he got this thing with Myra worked out and she was gone … Well, he'd see how it went.

Was it his imagination, or was Pastor Philbrick throwing glances his way? It had been a long time since he'd been here, but surely he wasn't an uncommon enough sight to have the preacher paying him nervous attention.

After the amen, people headed for the doors.

He joined the short line of folks who were waiting to shake the pastor's hand as they left the building. Wasn't it too cold for that old tradition to be in practice today?

"Rand, pleasure seeing you today." The pastor's words didn't quite agree with the expression on his face. "Did you bring Mrs. Stratford with you?"

How to answer that question? "No, sir. Carly is back at the ranch a little under the weather." Rand took a deep breath. "I was wondering if I could come by the parsonage and have a word with you, maybe before you sit down to the dinner table. Not meaning to disturb you, but I need to get something cleared up."

The pastor didn't look surprised at his question. "Of course. If you'd like to wait until I'm done here, we can go to my office." Rand stepped to the side and waited. So few people were here, it wouldn't take long.

After the last person had left, Pastor Philbrick closed the front door to the church and turned to face Rand. "I can guess why you're here. Come into my office and have a seat."

Rand followed the man into the space at the back of the entryway, little more than an alcove, and sat at the flimsy table serving as Pastor Philbrick's desk. He was at a loss to understand how Pastor Philbrick might know why he'd come until the man sat across from him and spread his fingers over the table top. His expression was troubled. "Miss Cunningham came to see me a few days ago."

Myra had already been here. No wonder she was so smug about this.

"She has a valid claim?" It was all Rand could do to get the words out. He didn't want to hear the answer.

"I'm not sure." Pastor Philbrick stared at Rand. "I've penned a letter to the church legal authority board at the seminary I attended back east. I've explained the situation and asked their opinion, but it may take a while to hear back."

"Perhaps you could explain the situation to me." Rand fought against the panic rising in his throat. Was there actually some possibility he could be married to Myra?

"Miss Cunningham showed me the marriage license I had filled out for her and you when you folks planned to be married last spring. I always fill out the license with the couple's names and the date before the ceremony takes place so that all that remains to be done is the signatures."

Here, Pastor Philbrick paused. Rand couldn't stand the hesitation. This might be difficult for the other man, but Rand had to know. "And …"

Pastor Philbrick propped his elbows on the table and dropped his head into his hands. "The day before the wedding, Miss Cunningham asked to see the license. I thought it was an odd request, but I consented. She asked about the signatures. I told her the license was not valid until the couple being married, the clergyman performing the ceremony, and two witnesses had signed."

"But you signed it? Before the ceremony?" Rand couldn't keep the accusation from his tone. "How could you do that?"

"I have asked myself the same question many times in the last few days." Pastor Philbrick lifted his head and met Rand's eyes. "Miss Cunningham was quite convincing. She told me the two of you were leaving on a wedding trip immediately after the ceremony and would barely have time to catch the train."

That much was true. At Myra's insistence, Rand had planned to take her to Kansas City for a honeymoon of sorts. He'd bought train tickets and had known even then they'd have to hurry in order to board the train on time, but he couldn't talk Myra into an earlier hour for the ceremony. She'd said she wanted to sleep in and have a leisurely morning on her wedding day.

Pastor Philbrick continued. "I knew the license wouldn't be valid without the witnesses' signatures, so I consented to letting her take the license so the two of you could sign it beforehand. That way, all that would be required in the moments after the ceremony would be the witnesses' signatures."

Maggie and Dan were to have been their witnesses. Rand would never forget the feeling of waiting in this very spot with his sister, his brother-in-law, and their two daughters for a bride who never showed. It had been the most humiliating moment of his life. Pastor Philbrick was still looking at him. What was he supposed to say?

"Myra had a room in the hotel the night before the wedding. She said she wanted to be close so she didn't have to make the trip into town. Maggie and Dan got a room too, and I slept in the back of the wagon over to the livery. Figured it would save a little money. But Myra wanted a big doings, so we all ate supper together at the hotel the night before. Myra made a show of having us sign the license. She said it should be a 'family memory' since we'd be in such a hurry after the ceremony."

"But your sister and her husband didn't sign?" the pastor asked.

"No. Myra was mad enough to throw cow pies, but Dan refused, and then so did Maggie. Said he couldn't sign his name as a witness to something he hadn't witnessed."

Pastor sighed. "Bless that man, God rest his soul." Another long pause. "But you did sign the license?"

He was no less guilty than the man across from him. "Myra said it was all right with you if we signed early, and I figured she was right since she had the license."

"For whatever it's worth, I did caution Miss Cunningham at least twice that the license would not be valid without the witness signatures, and she had to wait until after the ceremony to obtain those. I told her if she brought the license back signed by witnesses before the wedding occurred, I'd have to tear it up and start over. It seemed so important to her to have the two of you sign beforehand, I was sure it was only because she wanted to make sure to catch the train."

"I don't blame you, Pastor." To Rand's amazement, he didn't. Rand knew better than anyone how persuasive Myra could be.

"I thank you for that," Pastor said. "But I blame myself nevertheless. I admitted my part in this fiasco to the seminary board, even though it means I might not be allowed to pastor a denominational congregation under my seminary credentials, here or anywhere else in the future."

Pastor Philbrick looked about as broken as any man Rand had ever seen. Probably about the same way Rand had looked the day Myra stood him up for their wedding.

"If I were to write a letter to the seminary board asking that you be absolved of any wrongdoing, would that be helpful?" It wasn't right that Myra's deceit should be the cause of the downfall of a good man like Pastor Philbrick.

"Again, I thank you for the offer, but let's wait and see, shall we? There is still the matter of the witnesses. I don't know the folks who signed those witness lines on the license, but unless they can be found and will swear they witnessed your marriage, the license is still not valid." Pastor looked a bit hopeful.

Rand couldn't find any hope in this situation. According to what Pastor Philbrick had told him, Myra had planned this whole thing. She'd purposely left him at the altar and run off with his bank account just to show up a few months later and claim marriage to him. Why? Why would she do such a thing?

"She planned this." Might as well say what they were both thinking.

Pastor nodded. "It would appear so, but I suggest talking to her before you make accusations. Find out what her reasons were, and if you can, offer your forgiveness. It can go a long way toward mending rifts in relationships."

Rand banged his fist on the table a little harder than he intended. He stood quickly and paced. "Nothing in this scenario is about mending a rift with Myra. I don't care if I ever see her again."

A firm hand clapped over his shoulder, and Rand stopped, turning to face the pastor. "I meant a rift with your wife. Surely she hasn't reacted well to all this."

Carly. Yes, this was going to take more of a repair job than Pastor

Philbrick had any idea about.

"Am I legally married to Carly?" He had to know the answer.

Pastor Philbrick shrugged. "In my opinion, I see no other way to look at it. If you contest Miss Cunningham's claims of marriage, they will be deemed irrelevant once her supposed witnesses are located and questioned. You and Miss Blair married in good faith, and since you have been, uh, living together the past several months, she certainly has far more claim to being your lawful wife. I'm sure the seminary board will see it that way too."

"And if they don't?"

"Then I resign my pastorate duties because of a breach of ethics, we have the false marriage annulled, and I marry you again to Miss Blair. I am still recognized by the state of Kansas as clergy and can marry you even if my seminary pulls my credentials from the denominational records."

"I hope it doesn't come to that." This man had made an error in judgment, no doubt, but he'd admitted his wrong and was trying to make it right. Pastor Philbrick did not deserve to go down because of Myra's treachery.

The men shook hands, and Rand departed, wishing he could say something to raise the other man's spirits. He couldn't think of a thing. Best just go home.

Pastor had talked about forgiveness. He wasn't there yet, but if somehow opening his heart to forgiving Myra would help Carly do the same for him, he'd try it.

Had it not been for the errand Rand was on, Carly might have felt better. But the relief was only physical. Her emotions were reeling, her nerves stretched so taut it seemed they might collapse. If Rand was having a discussion with Pastor Philbrick, then she was left without a means of defending herself.

And why should she have to defend herself? She'd done nothing wrong. At least not until she'd climbed into bed with a man she might not really be married to. And even if she was, it couldn't be considered a real marriage. Not the kind she'd always dreamed of anyway.

If she had somewhere to go, she'd take Tommy and leave, even though she would probably have to ask Rand for money. If he wanted to be married to Myra, he'd probably give it to her, though. Myra was beautiful, and he'd loved her once. Probably still did. Carly was only someone to look after his orphan nieces.

Though Mary Jo was mostly capable by now, Carly still worried over the children being downstairs by themselves while she lazed in bed. All three had been up to check on her periodically and see if she needed anything, but now that afternoon had set in and Rand still hadn't returned, perhaps she should try to go downstairs. She was feeling better.

Careful not to move too fast, Carly got out of bed and dressed in a plain work calico that had been hers before coming to the Stratford ranch. The ones she'd made since then seemed off-limits somehow in light of Myra's claims. Rand had paid for them, after all.

Shrouding her cold feet in several layers of stockings, Carly skipped the shoes and trod down the stairs without making a sound. The children were all gathered in the big front room around their school table. They looked up in surprise.

Carly was also surprised. They were quietly working on their lessons. It appeared that Mary Jo was helping the younger two. What a remarkable amount of progress they'd made in the short time she'd been here.

"Are you feeling good again?" Tommy asked.

"Better," she replied, looking to make sure Myra wasn't around. "I'm just going to go to the kitchen and make some tea. You all keep on with what you're doing." Her voice was still pretty croaky, but she must have gotten her point across, as the children bent over their schoolbooks once more.

In the kitchen, Carly steeped some tea then pulled out a chair to sit and enjoy it for a moment. It did feel good to be out of bed.

The front door slammed. "How is Carly?" Rand's voice was as croaky as hers, but it did sound as if he really cared how she felt.

Mary Jo said, "She's feeling better. She's —"

"Glad to hear it. Where's Myra?"

"The lady's been upstairs in your room all day," Tommy answered.

"You children get upstairs until I tell you to come down. Mary Jo, you knock on Myra's door and tell her to come downstairs."

The quick footsteps of three children sounded on the stairway. Carly rose, meaning to try to make it upstairs before Myra came down. She had no desire to see her.

"In the parlor. Now." Rand's voice had lost its kindness. And he could only be talking to Myra. Knowing her, she had probably been on her way downstairs the moment she heard Rand's voice.

Carly sat back down. If Rand and Myra were in the parlor, she didn't want them to see her. She wouldn't be able to hear their conversation from the kitchen anyway.

But she was wrong about that. The voices were so loud, she could hear every word through the open kitchen door. "You planned this, Myra. You planned it down to the detail. You knew ahead of time you wouldn't go through with our marriage. And you went to a lot of effort to make sure you could come back later and claim to be my wife. Why?"

"Rand, darling ..."

"Stop calling me that. I want the truth."

Had Carly been on the receiving end of that demand, she'd have spilled it all.

"I love you, Rand. I loved you back when we planned our wedding. I've always wanted nothing more than to be married to you." Myra sounded as if she were crying. Were they real tears, or was she trying to garner Rand's sympathy?

"Then why. Why did you do it?" Rand's voice was a little less terse. Maybe the sympathy ploy was working.

"I owed some money to a man I met in St. Louis before I came here. He ... he set me up in a ... a business venture, and I was supposed to pay him back with the proceeds of what I earned. The project failed, and I left town one night to try to escape him."

"What sort of venture?" Yeah. Carly wanted to know that too.

"It was all above board and proper, Rand, I promise you." Myra's voice had gone a little quieter, and Carly had to strain to hear.

Shame on you, Carly chided herself. She shouldn't be listening at all.

"I was going to ship clothing and accessories in from Europe— you know, Paris, London, and the like. I thought the ladies of St. Louis would be glad to have a place where they could buy something beautiful besides the plain things that the stores there carried or ordering them weeks in advance from a dressmaker."

"But they weren't?" Rand's question didn't sound like he was too surprised.

"They might have been, but I never got the chance to get started. I found out right after I got my first shipment that the man I borrowed the money from wanted something besides being paid back promptly.

He wanted … uh … something I wasn't willing to give."

"And what was that?" Rand was giving her no way to leave anything out. Good for him.

"I had living quarters on the second story of the store building he'd purchased for me. He wanted the key and *privileges* to come and go from there as he wished." Myra was definitely crying. Carly almost felt sorry for her.

Rand didn't answer, but Myra's voice went on after a few minutes. "He was married. Had a wife and children. He was a financier. It was what he did for a living. He was wealthy and … I was too naive to figure out beforehand why he was so willing to help me get started with a business."

"So instead of reporting him to authorities, you just up and left." Now Rand sounded a little sympathetic. Carly was too if Myra's story was true.

"Yes. All I had was the loan documents. They were legal and binding. I couldn't report him for … well … for that. I would have been the laughing stock of the town, and no respectable ladies would have patronized the store."

"Probably just the way he planned it," Rand mused.

"I felt so foolish and gullible. I left and ended up in Walnut Point. I thought no one would ever find me here. When I met you, I was too embarrassed to tell you what had happened in St. Louis."

"That doesn't answer my question, though," Rand said. "I need to know why you planned to run out on our wedding day and come back later pretending to be my wife." Rand sounded more matter-of-fact now.

"I wanted to marry you. I didn't want to run away, but I knew I couldn't marry you with my debt still outstanding. If Lowell Hornbaker ever found me, he could make you responsible for all the money I owed. He could take your cattle and your ranch and everything you own. I couldn't let that happen. I … I found out about the money you had saved to buy the pasture land, and I decided that if I used it to pay off the loan instead, we could be free to marry and live without my mistakes haunting us."

Even Rand's sigh was audible. "Did it never dawn on you to simply ask me for the money? Why all the deception? Why the whole thing with the marriage license?"

"For one thing I needed the license to convince the bank they could give me what was in your account. But the real reason was, I was afraid you didn't love me enough to give me the money. I thought you wouldn't marry me if you knew about the mess I was in. I took the money, left to pay my debt, and thought if I gave you a few months to get over being angry at me, then I could come back and show you the marriage license. You'd remember that you loved me and maybe even understand about the money. I knew you'd want to go stand before the preacher again and say vows, but I didn't mind. We could do that. We can still do that. Do you still love me, Rand? I know you do."

Though Carly strained to hear, no answer from Rand was forthcoming. She should have gone upstairs before she heard any of this. Rand wouldn't take kindly to catching her eavesdropping.

The silence from the other room taunted her. She imagined Rand taking Myra in his arms, kissing her passionately, and forgiving her for everything. She imagined him whispering I-loves-yous into Myra's ears.

Carly couldn't bear to hear … or not hear … anything more. She ran out of the kitchen and rushed past the now silent parlor. That door was slightly ajar. Noiselessly, she ran up the stairs in her stocking feet, collapsed on her bed, and sobbed.

Chapter 18

$\mathcal{R}$and stared at Myra. The woman was stark raving mad. Still love her? After all this? Looking back, he probably never did love her. Just kind of thought he did because she was so beautiful. She didn't look beautiful to him now. Just weepy and annoying. Yep, he'd dodged a real bullet with this one.

He sank on the red velvet love seat his mother had ordered from New York City many years ago. The parlor was so seldom used, it still looked brand new. What should he say to Myra? How should he say it? She was looking at him with such regret, so much sorrow, and yet hope still shone in her eyes. She always had a flair for the dramatic. Was she truly repentant or just saying what she thought he wanted to hear? The second, no doubt, because if she really cared about him, she'd leave him alone now that he was married to Carly.

A door slammed upstairs. The children needed to stay up there until this discussion was finished. He waited a few moments, but no footsteps came tromping down the staircase.

"I guess you didn't plan on coming back to find me married."

"Oh, Rand." Myra looked small and vulnerable in the big chair that used to belong to Rand's father. "I'm sorry about that. I truly am. Carly seems like a nice enough girl, but even I can see there is nothing between you. She's here to look after your nieces and nothing more. I thought they would enjoy the boarding school I have in mind, but if you'd rather they stay here and want to keep her on as their governess, I could abide that. She could be a housekeeper and cook too. I'm sure she wouldn't mind having the marriage annulled."

Rand didn't even know how to respond to that remark. Myra was giving no consideration to the fact that Rand might want to stay married to Carly. She really believed he would jump at the chance to marry her. The thing of it was, as annoying and selfish as Myra could be, Rand felt sorry for her. If what she said was true, she'd gotten herself into quite a predicament at no real fault of her own save a little naivete.

"The marriage license is null and void, Myra, unless you can produce the witnesses who signed and they are willing to swear in court they witnessed our marriage. I'm guessing those signatures are not even real since there was no ceremony to witness, which means that I am legally married to Carly. We *did* have a marriage ceremony, and we *did* have witnesses. Carly has been living here for almost four months."

Myra's dark eyes blazed. "Why would you want to be married to that little bit of nothingness when you could have me?" Myra sounded overly confident. "You can't fool me, Rand. The boy told me you sleep in the room where I'm staying. I know that's true because all your clothes are in there."

"You shouldn't be asking questions like that of Tommy." But Tommy had told her the truth.

"All right," Myra conceded. "You win for now. I'll pack my things, and tomorrow morning, I'll go back into town. I'll get a room at the hotel and wait for you to see reason."

She rose and stomped to the door. Just before she exited the parlor, she turned back to face him. "And you will see reason, Rand, darling. Just remember that I won't wait forever." She stormed out of the room.

After she'd made it to the top of the stairs and into his room, Rand called the children downstairs and asked Mary Jo to make supper. "I'm going to go check on things outside, make sure the hands have got everything under control, and see if any of those heifers in the corral decided they needed to calve during this storm. I'll eat in the bunkhouse."

"You going to leave us in here with *her*?" Rand knew Mary Jo wasn't referencing Carly. Her tone was full of disrespect, but Rand didn't admonish her.

"She's up in her room and won't be back down tonight. You can take a tray up to her if you want, but don't be surprised if she refuses to open the door." Mary Jo just smiled.

Rand shoved on his boots and coat, jammed his hat back on his head, and slammed the lean-to door behind him. Somehow, he was going to have to explain all this to Carly, and right now he had no ripping idea how to do that.

Carly welcomed the food Mary Jo brought her at supper time but told her she would stay in her room the rest of the evening. She had no desire to be in the same house as Rand or Myra. The two of them together was even worse. As soon as she could figure out where to go and how to get there, she and Tommy would leave.

Carly didn't know if Rand would sleep in her room tonight or not. They'd sort of agreed to do that while Myra was here, but did it even matter anymore? Myra was definitely still in Rand's bedroom. Carly could hear her on occasion, pacing the floor or slamming things. Once, there'd been a big crash. Myra had broken something, but Carly couldn't imagine what. The wash basin in that room was enamelware. It might crack, but it wouldn't shatter. Oh, well, what did it matter? Myra was Rand's problem now, and Carly refused to deal with it anymore.

Carly listened to the sounds of the children's laughter as they trooped up the stairs and each went to their respective rooms. None of them came to check on her since Carly had told them not to. Unfortunately, now she wished one of them would stick a head in just to say goodnight. The loneliness hung heavy around her like a weight that would not be tossed aside.

How would she ever say good-bye to Mary Jo and Jenna? She'd grown to love them, and she believed they might love her too, or at least come to someday. Now? She and Tommy would be gone soon, though try as she might, Carly couldn't come up with a place for them to go. The Stratford ranch had been her last resort. Maybe some obscure town where no one could find her. She'd start over. Find a job in a hotel or a seamstress shop. Any moral occupation that would put a roof over their head and food on the table would be acceptable. It would solve the problem of Lester McGraw coming after her too. This time, absolutely no one would know where they'd gone.

When her head ached too much to think, Carly closed her eyes and tried to sleep. The effort was futile.

It was late when Rand stepped in the room. It had to be because

Carly had been lying in the dark staring at the ceiling for hours. She'd been sure Rand had chosen to sleep in the bunkhouse, but no, his boot-clad feet made clacking noises on the wood floor, and his breathing was heavy, still feeling the effects of his illness. Why had he bothered to come? If Myra knew the truth, what was the point of sleeping in here?

She listened to the sounds of him pulling off his boots and spreading the blanket on the floor. Plop. There went the pillow. At least he didn't have it in his head to sleep in the bed again. She wouldn't have allowed it anyway.

He sank to the floor, the blanket rustling as it settled over him. "Carly? You awake?"

Carly didn't move or respond. She wasn't up to talking to him just now.

"I just wanted you to know that Myra's leaving in the morning. The marriage license is not valid. You and I are very much still legal and still married."

For now, anyway. Carly gave no answer. Maybe Rand would believe she was asleep. She'd leave without waiting to be asked. Maybe the hotel in Walnut Point would take her on until she had enough money saved to go somewhere else.

No. Staying in Walnut Point for any length of time was out of the question. She couldn't bear to see or even hear about Rand and Myra and their new life together. She couldn't give Lester time to find her here. She would miss the girls terribly, but they were young and resilient. They'd get over any sadness they experienced at her departure and begin their new lives with Myra as Rand's wife and whatever that entailed. Rand would see to it that they weren't sent away to a boarding school, and they'd grow up happy and healthy right here on the Stratford ranch. Maybe Rand would let them write to her on occasion to tell her how they were doing. Oh, she did hope dear little Jenna would find her voice soon. Carly prayed for it every day and would continue to do so until the miracle occurred.

"Carly, I know you're awake. Don't you want to know what I found out in town today?"

Rand didn't know she'd overheard his conversation with Myra. Maybe she should let him explain. "I suppose."

Rand heaved something akin to a sigh of relief. "All right, then. My voice still isn't very strong, so I'm going to sit on the other side of the bed so we can whisper."

"No!" Her voice sounded alarmed even through the hoarseness.

But Rand stood anyway and made his way around the bed. "Don't worry. I'll stay on top of the covers and clear over on this side. All I want to do is talk to you, and then I'll move back to the floor."

Carly didn't answer, but she didn't try to stop him either. For the time being, they were married, and this conversation was one they needed to have, whether or not she wanted to. Rand sat on the bed, not touching her or even turning to face her.

"Pastor Philbrick signed the marriage license between Myra and me, but it wasn't valid because the witnesses' signatures weren't real. Myra falsified them."

"Why would she do that?" Carly had heard Myra's answer, but she was curious as to Rand's take on the whole thing.

Rand didn't hesitate. "Apparently, she owed some money to someone in St. Louis and didn't want to come into a marriage with that hanging over our heads. She came as close to marrying me as she felt like she could to solidify our commitment, then ran off to pay her debt. She thought she could give me time to get over being angry with her, come back, debt-free, and we could pick up where we left off."

All true according to what she'd heard, but it did make Myra sound rather innocent. "Why didn't she just tell you the truth and let you help her?"

"Same thing I asked. You have to understand, Myra is very strong-minded. She incurred the debt and wanted to pay it off without involving the Stratford ranch."

So, Rand had chosen to overlook or forgive the part where Myra stole the money from his bank account to pay her debt. Couldn't he see how foolish that made him appear to Myra?

"Now what?"

"Myra never expected to come back and find me married. My guess is she has no prospects for the future and just thought if she married me I'd take care of her. She will stay in the hotel for a while until this mess gets straightened out, then she'll go away, and we will go on as we have been."

Did Rand even realize the longing and yearning in his voice? He was playing her for a fool. He might feel obligated to remain married to Carly, but she wouldn't put him through that. He needed to realize that she could never stay here, always knowing he wanted someone else, someone who would be a true wife to him.

"You can move back to the floor now." The abrupt statement sounded harsh. If this marriage was to be annulled, it was improper for him to be on her bed, and she couldn't abide it. No matter how much she wanted to.

Another night on the floor of Carly's bedroom had not been very conducive to sleep, especially when he still wasn't feeling well. Rand rolled up his blanket, picked up his boots, and tiptoed out of the room before Carly woke.

Looked like no one else was awake yet either. He opened the kitchen door. Except Myra. She was sitting at the kitchen table, apparently waiting for someone to make coffee. The bleary eyes and prominent frown were evidence that she'd probably just experienced a sleepless night as well.

"Good morning." He might as well try to be kind to her. Pastor Philbrick said he should forgive her. He'd best do some praying on that one.

"Mind if I have a cup of coffee before I head to town?"

"Fine by me. Soon as it's light enough, I'll have Nate or Parker hitch up your horse and buggy."

Rand crossed the room, stirred up the stove fire, and stoked it up with a few more logs. He carried the coffee pot to the sink and pumped some water in it, then set it back on the stove to heat. How could the woman not even know how to make coffee? Was she that inept in the kitchen, or did she just think other people should do these things for her?

He found a partial loaf of bread, a lump of butter, and some blackberry jam in the pantry. It'd do. He set the items on the table with two plates and cups. "If you want to wait until Mary Jo is awake, we might convince her to fry some eggs and potatoes." Yeah, he wasn't much of a cook either. Why should he be when he had Tubby, Carly, and Mary Jo around here making delicious things for him to eat? Well, Carly and Mary Jo anyway.

"What about your *wife*?" She all but spat the word at him.

"I'm not sure if she's feeling well enough to cook breakfast." Rand kept his voice steady with effort as he measured some ground coffee into the pot. "Coffee will be ready soon."

Myra sneered. "Sooner for me to be on my merry way."

"You have money enough for the hotel room?" Rand didn't want to offer to pay, but he had to ask.

"I'll be fine." Myra's words were clipped. She didn't look at him.

Rand sat across from her and buttered a piece of bread, then slathered it with blackberry jam. He made a show of biting off a big chunk. "Sure is good. You want some?"

He pushed the loaf and jam toward her. Myra looked as if she didn't want to accept the offer, but she did anyway, eyeing the bread hungrily. When he'd come in to check on them last night, Mary Jo said Myra refused all offers of food.

They ate bread with jam and sipped coffee in silence. Rand couldn't wait until she was gone. Hopefully, he'd made it clear that she need not stay long in Walnut Point. He wouldn't be chasing after her.

At last, the sky grew pink, and Rand excused himself to the barn. He'd hitch up Myra's buggy himself if it meant she'd be gone sooner. But a few steps out the door, he rethought his plan. The snow was still deep. The buggy wheels wouldn't pull through it easily. Was it safe to send Myra off on her own with nothing but her flimsy buggy and weak-withered horse?

Clarence was already in the barn shoveling manure from a stall into a wheelbarrow. Rand raised a hand in his direction.

"Mornin', boss."

None of his hands had ever spoken a word of disrespect to his face, so why did he always feel like they were second-guessing him and his decisions? Probably because they had more sense than he did when it came to women.

"Whatcha think, Clarence? Suppose I oughta drive Miss Cunningham into town in the cutter rather than sending her out in the buggy?"

"I reckon so." Clarence's cheeks went a little ruddier. "Snow's still too deep for them buggy wheels to grab any traction."

"I'd guess you're right." Rand stifled a sigh. What he'd like to do was ask Clarence to drive Myra to town. But no. The poor guy would get an earful and then some before he ever made it to the hotel. Myra wasn't selective who she complained to when she wanted to complain. His ranch hands already knew more than he wanted them to about this whole situation. At least he'd kept them from discussing it among themselves last night by sitting in the bunkhouse with them until every last one of them had fallen asleep.

"Want me to hitch up Hank?" Clarence asked.

"Much obliged," Rand answered reluctantly. "Pull him around front when you're done." The cutter was too small to haul those blasted trunks. Myra would have to make do with what she could fit in her satchel. He'd haul her trunks to town when he took the buggy and horse. For now, whatever it took to get her out of his house would be well worth it.

"Yessir." Clarence put down the pitchfork and stepped into the tack room to retrieve the harness.

He considered running upstairs to tell Carly the new plan but discarded the idea immediately. She was probably still sleeping, and he'd have plenty of time to explain everything when he returned.

Confound it all anyway. How did Myra always manage to foul up his plans and his life? He could kick himself for ever thinking he was in love with her. But his thinking had changed. That's what Carly had done for him. She'd come into his life all meek and unassuming and beautiful and made herself a solid place as his wife and the caregiver for his nieces. Somewhere along the way, he'd fallen in love with her. And now, it was going to take some real convincing to convince her his heart belonged to her and not to Myra Cunningham.

Chapter 19

$\mathscr{M}$orning had arrived, but what to do? Carly rolled over and pulled the quilt tight around her. Rand had promised Myra would leave today, but what if she wasn't gone yet? What if she slept until noon, or worse, was sitting downstairs wanting breakfast? Carly didn't want to see or talk to the woman.

Rand was a problem too. She was so confused about where she stood with him. The words he'd insisted on speaking last night said he wanted Myra to leave and for them to continue their relationship as in the past. Which wasn't much of a relationship at all. She remembered too well the silence after Myra's declaration of love the day before. Had they been locked in a passionate kiss? Even if that weren't the case, Rand didn't seem to be in a hurry to let Myra know she couldn't say those things to a married man.

Leaving was Carly's only option, and she'd best do it soon. Trouble was, how could she and Tommy leave? Could she ask her husband to drive her to town so she could get away? Even more ironic, could she ask him for money to help her get away? She couldn't think of any other way to accomplish that feat.

She was feeling pretty well after her bout with the illness. Best get up and face whatever this day held, even if it included seeing Myra. She couldn't hide out in her bedroom. There were chores to be done and children to be tended.

Carly washed, dressed, and braided her hair, gathering it into a loose bundle at her nape. Hand on the doorknob, she took a deep breath and cracked open the door. No one was in the hallway. The door to Rand's room where Myra had slept was closed.

The dogs set to barking the way they did when activity in the farmyard excited them, so Carly left the hallway and hurried back into her room. Peeking out her upstairs window, she had a perfect view of Clarence stopping Rand's cutter in front of the house. Her hopes leaped at this signal that Myra was really leaving. But as she continued to watch, the front door opened and Rand came out, Myra leaning heavily on his arm as he led her through the snow.

He helped her into the cutter, threw a satchel in the back, then settled himself in, wrapping a blanket around both him and Myra. To Carly's utter chagrin, Myra looked up and caught her watching, sending her a smug, sure smile. Clarence handed Rand the reins, and the cutter set off in the direction of Walnut Point.

Carly let the curtains fall closed and turned to lean her back against the wall. Taking deep breaths, she forced a calm back into her body, if not her heart. Myra was gone. At least that was a reason to be glad. Carly had her home back—for now.

Why was Rand driving her, though? And what about Myra's buggy? She'd arrived at the Stratford ranch with two trunks. Carly heard Rand tell Parker to carry them up to his room. Were they still here?

Carly ran to the hallway and yanked open the door to Rand's room. Yes, Myra's trunks remained, even though it looked as if she'd packed them and had them ready to go. So Myra would be back. Somehow, she would finagle her way back onto this ranch. Carly intended to be long gone when that happened.

Her gaze traveled to a smashed photo frame lying against the far wall amidst a pile of shattered glass. Carly walked over and picked up the torn photo that had once been in the frame. Her intake of breath was sharp. Myra sat on an upholstered bench, a ring on the third finger of her left hand prominently displayed. Rand stood behind her, his hand on her shoulder.

They'd had an engagement photo taken? Rand had actually bought her a ring? Carly gazed at her own ringless left hand. What did it mean, if anything? Carly dropped the photo back onto the pile of glass shards, not caring if it became more tattered than it already was. Obviously, Myra had thrown the frame and photo in a fit of pique. Not only that but she'd left it behind.

Carly exited the room and closed the door behind her. Today she would put the house back in order, make sure the children had a full day of studying, and cook a family supper that would surely please Rand. Tomorrow would be soon enough to come up with a plan for leaving. She squared her shoulders and set off for the kitchen. A good breakfast would be in order for her and the children. If Rand wanted to miss out by driving Myra to town, then so be it.

Breakfast was ready by the time the children came downstairs. Mary Jo set out plates and utensils and poured glasses of milk while Carly put a platter of pancakes and a bowl of steaming sausages on the table. The meal was eaten without a lot of conversation, but smiles were in abundance. The children were probably as happy to have Myra gone as Carly was.

"How about you children get started on your lessons, and I'll be in to help as soon as I get the dishes washed?" Carly's voice was still hoarse, but she was able to insert a bit of cheerfulness.

Tommy grumbled a little but went with the girls into the large front room. As soon as they had settled with their books, Carly returned to the kitchen and poured another cup of the hot tea she'd steeped. The coffee pot on the stove suggested Rand had made some of the brew before he left. One sniff of the murky liquid and Carly threw what remained in the pot out the back door. The man couldn't make coffee any better than Tubby. Or perhaps Myra had made it? No, the woman wouldn't have lifted her finger to a menial task like that.

Carly washed the dishes, dried them, and arranged them in the cupboards. It felt so routine, so normal, something she very much needed just now. She set bread dough to rising then joined the children.

School books, piano, crochet and sewing for the girls—the day proceeded as many before had. None of the children mentioned Myra or asked about Rand. Carly wouldn't have had an answer anyway. The noon meal was a simple one of boiled eggs with toasted bread. The simplicity of it warmed Carly's heart. After a few days of worrying over Myra's exotic behavior and tastes, the lack of sophistication was most welcome.

The children were busy with their books, so Carly excused herself to the kitchen. She put extra time into the preparation of supper. For tonight, this one night, this house would feel like a home again.

"But Rand, darling," Myra pleaded through her tears. "I love you, and I know you love me."

Rand looked away. Myra could turn those tears off and on at will. Maybe she should have been an actress. Trouble with that was, he didn't believe a word of this role she was playing. Everything was clear to him now, and he could see straight through all Myra's shenanigans.

"You don't love me, Myra. All you love is my bank account. You've proved that. If you want someone to take care of you, you need to find some rich sap that doesn't know how deceptive you can be and beguile him. If you need me to pay for the hotel room tonight, I'll do it, but that's all I'm offering." Rand glared at the woman standing by his cutter. "And furthermore, I don't love you. I am desperately in love with my wife. My real wife. Now get out of our lives and don't come back."

As if to prove his suspicions, Myra's tears dried up. Her sarcasm was back. "I can scrape together enough for a hotel room, I suppose. I can't leave town tomorrow, though. I need my trunks."

Rand sighed. "Send me your address, and I'll have the trunks sent to you." He climbed back in the cutter.

For once, Myra seemed to have nothing else to say. He left her there without another word, standing in front of the hotel, holding her satchel, and sending him an evil sort of smirk that left an uneasy feeling in Rand's stomach.

He stopped by the parsonage and told Pastor Philbrick that Myra had admitted to forging the witnesses' names. The look of relief on the pastor's face was evident.

"I'll still write that letter recommending absolution if you need me to," Rand assured the pastor. "No need to let Myra's deception affect you and your calling to preach."

"Much appreciated." Pastor Philbrick extended his hand to Rand and shook it hard. "That means a lot coming from you."

After that, Rand stopped by Keller's and bought a gift for Carly. The ivory combs would look lovely in her auburn hair. He also bought her a new pair of boots. Unbeknownst to her, he'd traced one of her shoes onto a piece of brown paper. Mrs. Keller found the pair he wanted in a size that matched the trace. Now, once she got her riding skirts made and winter backed off a bit, he and Carly could go riding together.

"Snow's melted quite a bit." Rand spoke the words to Nate as he led the horse into the barn and began unhitching him from the cutter.

"Another day or two like this one and we won't even know it snowed." Nate's cheerful conversation carried over the sound of the bawling heifers in the corral.

"Maybe you and Parker oughta turn those ladies out into the calving pasture we got ready for 'em a few weeks back. Sounds like they're not happy about being crammed into that corral, and I'd venture to say they'd prefer dropping their calves out there to that muddy muck their standing in now." That'd keep his hands busy for a while.

"We'll get on that right away, boss." Nate put down his pitchfork and grabbed his saddle. "You want me to send Clarence or Tubby in to take care of Hank for ya?"

"I'll do it. Appreciate the offer, though."

Truth was, Rand needed a little more time to plan what he would say to Carly. Myra's cantankerous mood had near put him in one of the same. He regretted that he'd told her about his love for Carly, but only because Carly should have been the first to hear it. He'd tell her when she opened these packages he'd brought her.

Nate left the barn with the two saddled horses, and Rand heard him calling for Parker as he headed for the corral. He stowed the cutter in its place in a corner. It was crowded with Myra's buggy in here and that worthless nag he had to feed while she was in his barn. He'd get them back to the livery as soon as he could, preferably without having to talk to Myra or even see her.

The horse he'd taken today got a good rubdown, an extra scoop of oats, and a stall full of clean straw. It was time to go inside and greet his wife. Would she be glad to see him? Was she still mad at him? Would his gifts make her smile?

The kitchen smelled like something akin to heaven when he opened the back door. Cinnamon and ginger mingled with the aroma of fresh bread and coffee. Rand's stomach growled. He'd bought a pickle and some crackers out of the barrels at Keller's, but otherwise, he'd skipped dinner so he didn't have to eat in the hotel where Myra was staying. He took in a deep breath, and his gaze settled on Carly.

She stood by the stove stirring a pot of something, a ruffled apron covering her dress, tendrils of hair falling loose from her braid and frizzing around her temples. A smudge of flour covered her left cheek, giving Rand the urge to kiss it. He refrained, but God in heaven help him, this woman took his breath away.

"Hello." Such a simple word, but she said it with a little half smile that made Rand want to kiss more than her cheek.

"Hello, Carly. I'm back." Dumb as a fence post. He had to talk smarter than that.

"Supper'll be ready in about an hour. I think we'll eat a little early tonight." She turned back to the stove.

"I brought you something." He placed the packages on the sideboard and stood near her. He wanted to tell her Myra was gone, but he wouldn't speak the woman's name to Carly, not if he could help it.

She turned to face him. "I think we have a good supply of most things. We might need a little more tea before long, but we can make do."

At that moment Rand wished like sixty he'd bought some tea, but of course he hadn't. He would have never even thought of it. Coffee was his brew of choice.

"Sorry. I can get it next time. How are you feeling?" Rand's voice sounded about as nervous as he felt.

"Much better. And you?"

Her question came with a polite smile. This was like having a conversation with Mrs. Keller while she tallied up his purchases.

"I'm fine. Don't you want to see what I brought you?" That sounded too eager, but then he was too eager. He couldn't wait to see Carly's expression when she opened those packages. How long since someone had given her a gift just because?

"I believe I'll wait until after supper if you don't mind. I'm about to put the chicken in the fry pan." Carly turned back to the stove, where she worked on breading chicken before dropping it into the hot skillet.

Rand made himself close his mouth and quit staring at her. All right then. He would wait. Fried chicken sounded pretty good to his hungry belly. But … he gave another glance at the brown paper packages. He'd have to wait. He headed toward the door to the sitting room.

"I'll just wash up and grab a change of clothes, then." He left the kitchen, not sure she'd heard him or even cared.

"Uncle Rand," Mary Jo called to him from across the room. "Come look at my painting."

Not exactly what he wanted to do just now with thoughts of kissing his wife still on his mind, but Rand dutifully walked over to the easel and exclaimed over Mary Jo's drawing of cattle in a snowstorm. The sketch had been done on paper already painted a gloomy shade of gray. His niece really was talented, and he was so grateful she had someone like Carly to help her.

"That's great, honey." He slung an arm around her shoulders, pulling her close for a moment. Mary Jo went back to dabbling white snowflakes over the gray background.

He rounded the table, gave Jenna a quick hug and Tommy a manlier pat on the back. He sure had gotten himself attached to the little guy. It was great to see them all back at their normal routine. He continued on up the stairs.

Entering his bedroom, Rand stood stock still. "What in the Sam Hill?" Myra's trunks took up most of the empty space in the room. The bed was unmade, and a pile of glass that might have once been a photo frame lay against the wall. Crunching through the shards and glad he'd left his boots on, Rand crossed the room and picked up the photo.

That ridiculous portrait Myra insisted they have done when they'd gotten engaged. One more thing he'd let himself be talked into despite his better judgment. He ripped the photo in half, crushed one half in his hand and stood looking at the other. Myra's engagement ring. He'd almost forgotten about it. She'd picked out what she wanted—an expensive frivolity Rand would never have spent the money on except that she'd insisted.

What had she done with the ring? Sold it most likely. If this whole thing had always been about money, no doubt the ring had done its duty by her and then some. Carly had never even mentioned a ring. Shouldn't he have given her a wedding ring? Thoughtless old coot that he was, it'd never occurred to him. An idea struck him, and he grinned. Yes, that would be perfect. He'd look in a few days, once all this business was ironed out and Carly wasn't angry at him anymore.

"Jenna," he called loudly. He didn't let the children holler from upstairs to down, preferring they make the effort to get up and find the person they were talking to. However, this time it might be warranted. "Would you bring a broom up here, please?"

Once the room was put to rights as much as possible with Myra's things still making it feel cramped, Rand changed his clothes and proceeded back down the stairs. Carly called them to supper not long afterward, and the meal was so good, Rand wanted to go back and eat it all over again. Fried chicken, mashed potatoes and thick, peppery milk gravy, fresh bread with apple butter, and green beans from one of those jars Carly had stocked the pantry with last fall just before the garden froze. For dessert, he couldn't decide between the succulent apple pie or the aromatic ginger cookies like his mama used to make, so he had both. No man deserved to have a wife who could cook like this, least of all him.

Jenna and Tommy did the dishes while Mary Jo did some more work on her painting. Not knowing what else to do, he sat in the front room across from Carly as she sewed, his face in a newspaper he wasn't reading. How did he start a conversation like the one he wanted to have? When was a proper time to bring up something like hoping theirs could be a real marriage soon, complete with a ring and words of love? He'd say it, eloquently he hoped, when she unwrapped the gifts he'd brought her.

When Jenna and Tommy joined them in the front room, Rand reveled in the feel of family. It was something that had been denied him for a long time. No more. He had a beautiful wife and three children he loved dearly. Yes, things were looking up, for sure.

"Mary Jo, it's time to clean up the painting for today." Carly's voice broke into the stillness. "Jenna and Tommy, off to bed with you. Head on upstairs, and I'll be there shortly to tuck you in and hear your prayers."

All three children obeyed her instantly. Rand's thoughts went back to the days before Carly came here. Getting Mary Jo and Jenna to go to bed at night was a never-ending battle. Jenna never wanted to leave his arms, where she cried herself to sleep in the rocking chair of an evening. Mary Jo sat sullen and silent, staring at nothing. Carly had worked a miracle with them. Or God had worked a miracle by bringing him Carly.

Yes, that was it. Rand's heart was full of gratitude for this miracle that was the lovely woman sitting in his front room tonight. And surely God would help him be a real husband to Carly, to bless her and cherish her for the rest of their lives.

Mary Jo finished with her paints, and Carly followed her upstairs. It had been a long day. Rand might as well go to bed too. He stoked the fires and let the dogs into the lean-to. The temperatures would dip down below freezing again with nightfall. Bo could handle it, but Vinnie and Mucklededun were pretty well spoiled.

Just as he was about to blow out the lamp in the kitchen, he glanced at the sideboard, and his heart sank. The packages he'd brought for Carly were stacked there. Unopened.

Chapter 20

$\mathcal{C}$arly couldn't believe it.

Rand was acting as if nothing had happened out of the ordinary. He never told Carly what transpired with Myra, never explained her trunks in his room, and never so much as mentioned her name. Didn't he think she deserved some answers? Carly was tempted to slam the door to her bedroom but thought better of it. This was her own fault.

If she hadn't gone and fallen in love with her in-name-only husband, it would be easy to leave. She and Tommy could just pack up their belongings and go away. Only now it wasn't that simple. Now it was going to tear her heart out, and likely Tommy's as well. He looked up to Rand like a father.

In fact, she should prepare her brother as best she could for what had to happen. Maybe if she told him now, he'd be better able to deal with it in a day or two once Carly had figured out a way to leave and the means to do so. It was only fair.

With a heavy sigh, she stepped across the hallway to Tommy's room and tapped lightly on the door. Maybe he was already asleep.

"Come in." His little voice invited her into the room where the lamp was turned down low. His red hair and freckles, so like hers, stood out in contrast to the white pillowcase he laid on, one arm stretched out over the layers of quilts covering his bed.

"Carly?" He sounded sleepy.

"I wanted to talk to you a moment if you're still awake." She sat on the side of his bed and held his hand in hers.

"I'm awake."

Carly wasn't so sure, but she'd better finish what she'd started. He'd be awake enough once she uttered the words she dreaded to say.

"Tommy, I know you like it here on the Stratford ranch—"

"Oh, I do." Tommy interrupted. "It's just like you said it would be. There's cows and horses, and I get to ride, even if it's just Old Polly or the Shetland."

"You're doing great with Polly. Rand said so." Carly couldn't think of what to say to get this conversation turned around.

"He did?" Tommy beamed. "Rand is the best cowboy ever. I want to live with him always."

Carly looked down at her brother's trusting face. The words would come hard, but they had to be said.

"I'm afraid we might have to leave." Carly watched in the dim light as confusion crossed his expression. "Soon."

"You mean like to go to town or something? Rand could drive us in that sled thing he has. He calls it a cuter."

"A cutter," Carly corrected him. Not that it mattered. "And no, not just to town, though we might start out that way. What I mean is we might have to leave here to go live somewhere else. Maybe somewhere far away."

Tommy's face screwed up as if he might burst into tears. "I'm not. I'm staying here."

"I wish we could, sweetie, but—"

"You can go, but I won't. Rand will let me stay here if I ask him."

Tears came to her eyes, but Carly blinked them back. Tommy was too young to realize how his statement hurt her.

"We both have to leave, Tommy." A sob threatened to jump out from behind her words.

"But why?"

How did she explain this? "Remember the lady who was here visiting the last few days?"

"I don't like her."

"That's not nice, Tommy. The Bible tells us to love others." And she was failing miserably when it came to Myra.

"But I don't like her, and what's she got to do with it anyway?" Tommy turned his face away from her. Carly resisted smoothing his hair away from his eyes so he would look at her.

"Miss Cunningham and Rand were engaged to be married once, before we got here. Do you know what that means?" Tommy wiggled his head up and down but didn't answer.

"They couldn't get married then, but now they might want to. Since I'm married to Rand just so I can be here to take care of Mary Jo and Jenna, it might be best if you and I leave so that Rand is free to marry Miss Cunningham." That was oversimplifying it, but Carly didn't care. It was all she could do to get the words out without the dam of tears behind her eyes breaking loose.

"Can Mary Jo and Jenna come with us?"

"No. They need to stay here with their Uncle Rand."

"But they don't like that mean lady either. Mary Jo told me so, and Jenna nodded her head a whole bunch." Tommy looked pleadingly at her, but Carly had to shake her head.

"Can I at least take Mucklededun? Rand said he was my very own dog and I could train him to do good work on the ranch and he would be my best friend, except I think Jenna is still my best friend."

If only Carly could say yes, but how could they take a dog along when Carly didn't even know where they were going? "Mucklededun will be happier if he can stay on the ranch with Vinnie and Bo."

Tommy's tears were falling in earnest. "Can I at least take Polly?"

Carly shook her head, unable to speak. Her tears fell unheeded now, her heart shattered in as many pieces as the picture frame she'd forgotten to clean up in Rand's bedroom earlier. She lay her head beside Tommy's on the pillow and held him as he cried, her own tears mixing with his. How could she do this to her own brother? How could she do this to herself? *How can I do this, God?*

Glad he'd left his boots in front of the fire to dry out, Rand tiptoed back down the stairs. He sank into his chair and let his head fall into his hands. Carly was going to leave. What did he have to do to convince her that he wanted to be married to her, not Myra?

He hadn't meant to eavesdrop, but when he heard Carly speaking to Tommy in his room, he'd been afraid the boy was sick. He'd almost entered the room just when he heard the words "have to leave." He couldn't tear himself away after that.

He couldn't let her leave. He'd have to find a way to make her stay.

The girls would be devastated if she left. That was it. Mary Jo and Jenna. He'd play upon her sympathies with them, tell her how they needed her and had grown to love her.

Tell her you love her.

The voice wasn't audible, but it may as well have been. Rand sat bolt upright. Of course. That's what he would do. He'd even told Myra he loved Carly. Surely, he could tell Carly.

Now, all he had to do was find a way. Would it make a difference? Would she stay if he confessed what was in his heart? Did she have any feelings for him at all? Maybe not, but they would come with time. He'd treat her like a cherished jewel, show her how important she was to him and how much he loved her. He'd make her feel so loved she'd never want to go anywhere else.

The idea was building now. Such a simple solution. Why hadn't he thought of this before? The truth was the only weapon he had. Once Carly knew his feelings, she'd no longer harbor any ridiculous ideas about him wanting Myra. She'd stay, they'd raise Tommy and the girls together, maybe even have children of their own. He'd buy that piece of pasture he'd had his eye on for so long, and that was only the beginning. The Stratford ranch would grow bigger and better, a legacy for the next generation.

Feeling a little less miserable than when he'd crept downstairs, he ascended the stairs once more. Once in his room, the planning continued. Tomorrow, he'd find his mama's wedding ring. It was around here somewhere. It had been Maggie's, and Rand was certain he'd found it among Maggie's possessions and brought it back here thinking one of the girls might want it someday.

It was a beautiful ring, a gold circle set with a single pearl and a deep red garnet on each side. Daddy told him once he'd had the ring special ordered in from the east coast to match one Mama had once admired in a store window when she'd visited New York City as a child.

Where had Rand put that thing? It was around here somewhere. Mary Jo might know. She'd kept Maggie's wedding ring in a trinket box in her room. Maybe the other ring was with it.

He fell asleep planning what he'd say.

Something woke him a few hours later. Rand lay in bed listening. Yes, there it was. Someone was crying. Jenna?

Leaping out of bed, something sharp bit into his bare foot. He ignored it, pulling on pants and a shirt as quickly as he could. By the time he made it to Jenna's room, Carly was already there. Of course she was.

"Is she having another nightmare?" Rand whispered. It had been so long since Jenna experienced a nightmare, he'd almost stopped listening for them.

"No," Carly answered in a low voice. "She feels warm. I think she's fallen victim to whatever we had."

"Oh." Rand breathed a small sigh of relief. He didn't want Jenna to be sick, but at least the nightmares hadn't come back to haunt her. "How can I help?"

"Light the lamp, please. Turn it down low. I'll get her a glass of water from my room and stay with her awhile. She should go back to sleep soon. Hopefully it won't be too long before she's up and about again."

Rand moved into the room lit only by scant moonlight to find the lamp. Why was his foot hurting?

"Are you limping?" Carly's question caught him by surprise.

"I'm fine." He located the lamp, lit it, and placed it back on Jenna's dresser. "Maybe I should go downstairs and get her some fresh water? Or make some weak tea?"

"Good heavens, Rand, you're bleeding!"

He lifted his foot from the floor. Sure enough, a small puddle of blood had formed on the wood floor. Drops of red spotted the room everywhere he'd been, including the braided rag rug by Jenna's bed. Not sure what to do, he hopped to the nearest wall and sank to the floor.

"I'm sorry. I've made a mess."

"Let me look at that." Carly left Jenna, who wasn't crying anymore, and moved to the washbasin on the dresser. She poured a little water from the ewer and grabbed a towel. Sitting on the floor in front of Rand, she picked up his bleeding foot and gently dabbed at it.

"Ouch." He regretted the exclamation as soon as he'd uttered it, not wanting to upset Jenna, but whatever Carly was doing hurt like the dickens.

"I've got to get this cleaned out. It looks like you've got a shard of glass in there."

Right. Thanks, Myra.

A sharp pain that nearly made him cry out ripped through his foot—maybe his whole body. And then Carly was holding the towel against the cut, and the worst was over.

"Got it," she murmured. "But I'd say your foot is going to be mighty sore for a day or two. We'll have to keep the wound clean and bandaged."

How did she get so smart about things like this? Yeah, what she said was common sense, but still, it felt good to have someone else taking care of him for a change. If this had happened before Carly, he'd have been trying to pull something out of the bottom of his foot he couldn't see or reach and bleeding all over the place while he did it. *Thank you, Lord.*

"Here, hold this towel against it with a little pressure so we make sure the bleeding stops. I'm going to go get something we can use for a bandage." Carly waited until his fingers took the place of hers, then left the room.

Jenna whimpered again.

"It's all right, baby." Rand tried to make his voice gentle and comforting, though his foot was still throbbing. "I just got a little piece of glass in my foot, but Carly is taking care of me. You hush now and try to relax. She'll take care of both of us."

Carly returned momentarily with a strip of cloth, which she proceeded to wrap around his foot. "There now. That should do it. You go on back to bed."

He liked it better in here with her, but her tone left no room for argument. He stood, clenching his teeth to keep from crying out in pain, then limped to the door.

"Wait."

He turned to see her. Carly looked thoughtful. "Don't go back into your room. There may be more glass. Why don't you go sleep in my bed for the rest of the night? I'll stay here with Jenna."

Rand wanted to protest. Jenna had a single bed. Carly and Jenna couldn't both sleep in here. No doubt, Carly would spend the night in the hard-backed chair and be achy and sore in the morning. But what was there to protest? It wasn't as if she'd come sleep in her bed with him. Besides, he was feeling a little woozy. Best just do as he was told.

He hopped across the hall to Carly's open bedroom door and fell into the bed, hoping fleetingly that the bandage was tight enough to keep him from bleeding on her sheets. "Nice touch, cowboy," he whispered mockingly to himself. "This stunt will win her heart for sure."

Chapter 21

Of all the stupid things Carly could have done, forgetting to clean up that mess in Rand's room was about the stupidest. When she'd heard him call to Jenna to bring him a broom earlier, she should have come up and taken care of it herself. Wasn't that what a wife was supposed to do? Now Rand was hurt and it was all her fault. Well, maybe some Myra's fault, but it would do her no good to pass any of the blame that direction. Myra was already at fault for most of the things going wrong in Carly's life at the moment.

If it wasn't the middle of the night and she didn't have a sick child to deal with, she'd go after all those offending glass shards Myra left behind and sweep them up but good. Right now though, Jenna needed her.

"Still feeling poorly, sweetie?" Carly laid her hand over Jenna's warm forehead. "Try to go back to sleep. Morning will be here soon, and everything will look a little brighter then."

Jenna's eyes begged her to understand what she wanted to say. She caught hold of Carly's hand and held it tight in her own.

"Don't worry. I'll stay right here." Jenna relaxed, and Carly tucked the quilts in tighter over the little girl, wishing there was something else she could do for her. The illness would just have to run its course. It hadn't taken long with her and Rand, but sometimes children had a harder time getting over a malady like this.

One thing was certain. Carly would not leave this family as long as Jenna needed her.

Morning light found Carly stiff and with a crick in her neck from sleeping in the chair by Jenna's bed, but she was content. There was no better feeling than being needed by a child. Would she ever be a mother to children of her own? That possibility didn't seem very likely in her current situation, but God had surprised her before. If children were in her future, she needed only to wait for His perfect timing.

Carly stretched and rose from the chair. A few dark red spots stained the floor and rug. She'd scrub those out today. She should change clothes, but was Rand still in her room? She tiptoed across the hall, opened the door a crack, and peeked inside. The bed was made neatly, and Rand was nowhere in sight. How did he always manage to wake before she did?

Carly washed and dressed, then checked on Jenna again before heading downstairs. The child still slept.

Rand wasn't in the kitchen, so he must have already been outside or at the bunkhouse. Good. Carly intended to sweep the floor in his bedroom and do it right this time. She grabbed the broom.

Back upstairs, she reached for the doorknob and nearly screamed when the door opened in front of her. Rand stood there in a state of half-dress. His shirt was on, but unbuttoned, his bare chest revealing rippling muscles and black curly hair that made her want to run her fingers through it. Try as she might, she could not draw her eyes away.

"E ... excuse me," she stammered. "I, uh, oh my."

"Not to worry. We do live in the same house, you know." Rand's words further embarrassed her. He quickly buttoned his shirt, and Carly's humiliation increased at his obvious attempts to hide his amusement. At last he grinned at her and Carly let her face relax into a smile.

"I was just going to sweep in here." Yes, and what else would she be doing in his bedroom at the crack of dawn with a broom in her hand?

"I appreciate that."

"Um, how's the foot?"

"Much better this morning. Can hardly feel it anymore."

Rand smoothed his hair with his hands. It didn't do much to tame the tousled reminders of his recent night's sleep. Just the way she liked it. "I ... uh ..." Nothing else came out of her mouth.

"How's Jenna?"

At last, something her tongue could actually form words to answer. "Better, I think. She's still sleeping, but she feels cooler. She coughed some in the night, though. I'm thinking she better stay in bed today."

"Whatever gets her well."

His pointed look made Carly realize she was standing in the doorway, blocking his exit. "Sorry." She moved aside, and Rand brushed past her, touching her hand with his for a brief moment.

"Thanks for taking care of her." He looked as if he wanted to say something else, but then after giving her a quick smile, he was on his way downstairs.

Carly swept the floor thoroughly, finding more than a few stray glass pieces and disposing of them so they couldn't cause further injury. Dried drops of blood still lingered on the floor, marking the path Rand had followed the night before. She'd come up with a bucket of water and scrub the floors later.

If it hadn't been for her carelessness in not cleaning up the mess earlier, she would have spared herself the embarrassing situation of catching Rand half-dressed when she walked into his room. Carly's face turned hot when she realized she didn't actually feel much remorse. She couldn't get that glimpse of his bare chest out of her mind.

As it turned out, Tommy woke not feeling well either, and Carly decided it would be best to keep him in bed today too. It was just her and Mary Jo at the breakfast table, each with a bowl of oatmeal doused liberally with butter and sugar. Mary Jo's even had a dollop of molasses.

"I still can't believe I used to make such terrible oatmeal. That's what we ate every morning. I sure am glad you taught me how to make it right."

"Me too," Carly agreed. "Shall I make some more tea?"

"Save what's left for Jenna and Tommy. I'll just get another glass of milk and start on my lessons." The girl rose from the table and carried her bowl and spoon to the sideboard.

"I was thinking," Carly began, "since Jenna and Tommy won't be joining us today, why don't we make this your free time. We won't worry about lessons, and you can spend the day painting if you'd like."

Mary Jo's grin stretched across her face. "Thanks." She gave Carly a hug that nearly brought tears to her eyes. Had Mary Jo ever hugged her of her own volition before? It would be so hard to leave these precious girls she'd come to love.

Mary Jo started toward the front room, then stopped and pointed at the sideboard where she'd just left her used dishes. "What's that?"

Carly glanced in the direction. The brown paper packages Rand had brought home yesterday caught her off guard.

"Your uncle brought them from town yesterday, and I forgot to open them and put them away. Probably some more sugar and coffee, even though we have plenty." But even as she said the words, Carly's curiosity grew. Those packages didn't look like they held sugar or coffee.

Mary Jo hurried off to begin painting, and Carly, alone in the kitchen, stared at the packages. What caused the odd feeling in the pit of her stomach? She carried the packages to the table and undid the strings.

In a few moments Carly had unwrapped a pair of boots more beautiful than anything she'd thought she would own. As if that weren't enough, she also held the loveliest set of hair combs she'd ever seen. Had Rand meant these gifts for her? Surely he had. That's what he'd said when he brought them in yesterday, and she had sloughed off his thoughtfulness thinking the packages were nothing more than grocery items.

Tears welled in her eyes. She must thank him. She should apologize for not opening them yesterday. She pulled off her shoe and slipped her foot into one of the new boots. It fit her perfectly. How had he known?

Unable to resist, she slid the combs into her hair and stared into the tin cup she'd used at breakfast, hoping to see a reflection of herself.

Overcome with emotion, she sat at the table instead of pouring wash water as she'd intended and cried for a good long while. These beautiful gifts from her husband, what did they mean? Could he care for her? Did he really want her, not Myra?

Maybe she'd been too quick to decide to leave. Maybe she should give Rand a little more time. Maybe … maybe …

A cry from upstairs had her wriggling her foot back into her shoe and yanking the combs from her hair before hurrying to see what Tommy needed.

The snow that had caused so many problems was little more than slush and mud now. Rand kicked at a pile of it before entering the barn, then wished he hadn't. That blamed cut on his foot hadn't healed yet.

Had Carly opened her new boots yet? Rand wished he could have been there to see her expression, but that hadn't worked out like he planned. Very few things did anymore, especially where women were involved. Being a husband was way harder than running a ranch. He'd have to figure it out though, and he was itching to get back inside and find that ring.

Mama would be so proud to know that her wedding ring would be on the hand of Rand's wife. She'd never said so, but Rand wondered if Mama had her doubts that he'd ever get married. She'd tried to teach him the appropriate ways to treat a lady and how to behave in social occasions, but he'd never been interested in anything but the ranch, horses, and cattle.

Rand sighed. He could use some of Mama's advice right now. Best get on inside and look for that ring and muddle through it the best he could.

He rubbed down Dusty and turned him into the freshly bedded stall. It was nigh on dinnertime. Maybe Carly would have something delicious cooking. The smell over to the bunkhouse didn't hold much promise for whatever Tubby was going to dish up for the ranch hands.

When he stepped into the kitchen, he was met with a huge smile from Carly. Then, of all things, she ran to him and circled her arms around his middle. Almost like a hug of sorts. He hugged her back. She felt so good in his arms.

She stepped away from him quickly, cheeks tinged with pink. The new combs were in her hair. They looked as lovely as he'd imagined against her auburn tresses.

"Thank you, Rand. I'm sorry. I had no idea. The boots. Hair combs. It's all so beautiful." Her words tripped over one another.

"I'm glad you like them." He wanted to take her into his arms again but held back. "Soon as the rest of the snow melts off, we'll go for a ride."

Carly nodded. "I'll get to work right away on a riding skirt."

"How's Jenna?"

"She's doing fine. Tommy's ill as well now, so they're keeping each other entertained. Last time I checked, they were both in Tommy's room with their noses in books. I think they'll be well enough to resume their studies by tomorrow."

Rand looked into those green eyes of hers, and as if he had no will of his own, drew his wife into his arms and kissed her. He couldn't have stopped himself if he'd tried. But he didn't want to try. All he wanted to do was kiss Carly.

She kissed him back. Her arms crept around his neck, and he pulled her closer. A slow burn started in his gut and worked its way to the very tips of his toes and fingers. *I love you.* The words almost came out as the kiss ended and she practically melted against him.

No, he'd save them until the moment he could place that wedding ring on her finger and claim her as his wife before anyone who cared to look. His real wife. A tremor went through him. Would tonight ...

"Um, should I come back later?"

Carly jumped away from him at Mary Jo's words.

"No, not at all. We were just ..." Carly flushed a bright red.

"Carly was just thanking me for her new boots." A bit of gray paint smudged Mary Jo's chin. "You painting?"

His niece smiled and nodded. "Carly let me have a painting day. I'm making so much progress on the cattle in a snowstorm picture. Want to see it?"

"You bet I do," he said, although all he really wanted was to kiss Carly some more. "Did you need something?"

"Oh, yes. No. I was just kind of hungry and wondered if Carly needed me to set the table or something." Mary Jo seemed almost as uneasy as Carly, except that she was grinning like crazy. Maybe the idea of seeing her uncle kissing his wife wasn't quite as upsetting as it had been the last time it had happened. Yes, this little family of his was coming together quite nicely.

Carly seemed to recover herself. "Yes, please. For three." She glanced at Rand, and he nodded. Carly continued, "I'll make plates to take up for Tommy and Jenna after a bit." She turned back to Rand. "Now sit down and let me take a look at your foot and make sure we got all the glass out."

He did as she asked, enjoying the caress, however unintentional, of her soft fingers against his foot.

"The wound looks good, already starting to heal over."

"Yeah, I can hardly feel it anymore." Except when he kicked at things that didn't need kicking. Why did it feel so comforting to have his foot sitting in her lap while she inspected it? Maybe because it showed she cared. He could get real used to this.

The three of them dined on leftovers from the night before, of which there was plenty. That fried chicken tasted even better the second time around. Funny how Carly could do that. Anything Tubby tried to warm over tasted like sawdust and felt like rocks in the gut afterward.

After they'd eaten, Rand spent an appropriate amount of time exclaiming over Mary Jo's painting, then lowered his voice to a whisper.

"You remember that ring your mama had that used to be Grandma's? The one with the big pearl and garnets to the side?"

"Mama always kept it in a little porcelain box on her dressing table. We weren't supposed to play with it, but Mama let me and Jenna look at it sometimes. She said it was Grandma's wedding ring."

"Do you remember your Grandma and Grandpa?" Rand asked, suddenly curious. He needed to do a better job of passing down family information. After Maggie died, the last thing he'd wanted to do was talk to the girls about memories that still pained him. But if he didn't talk about them, then the girls would lose their memories. He couldn't let that happen.

"I remember Grandma a little bit," Mary Jo answered. "I don't think Jenna does, though, and neither one of us remembers Grandpa. Mama used to tell us stories about them. She talked about them so much I kind of feel like I know them."

"Do you know where the ring is now?" Might as well get to the point.

Mary Jo shook her head. "I haven't seen it in a long time." Her eyes twinkled. "Are you going to give it to Carly?"

Rand tugged on her braid. "Sure would like to, but I have to find it first. Don't go telling her now."

"I won't."

"Great work on the painting, honey. You go on back to the kitchen now and help Carly get the younger ones fed and wash the dishes. You can get back to your picture this afternoon."

Mary Jo went to do his bidding, still smiling.

Rand didn't know where to start, but he needed to find that ring. A far and distant hope was forming in his mind that told him he needed to find it quick. Before tonight. And if he did, then just maybe …

Chapter 22

Carly watched Jenna and Tommy as they ate. Mostly mashed potatoes that wouldn't hurt their sore throats, but also a few pieces of shredded chicken and some soft bread. The children may not be feeling the best, but there was nothing wrong with their appetites.

Headed downstairs for refills for their water glasses, she nearly ran into Rand when he entered the room. Second time today. The memory of this morning's encounter in Rand's bedroom made heat rush to her face.

"What's this I hear about you two trying to pretend you're sick?" His voice boomed in false gruffness. "Looks to me like you just wanted a day off from all that schoolwork."

Jenna grinned at him, knowing her uncle well enough to realize he was teasing. But Tommy looked up from his plate of potatoes and gravy, his eyes large and round. "That ain't true, Pa." At the last word, his face went beet red.

Carly started to say something to smooth over his slip of the tongue, but Rand continued on as though nothing out of the ordinary had occurred. "Yeah, great idea. You think that'll work on Tubby if I don't want to go range riding someday?"

Both children giggled, and the moment passed. Carly studied Rand as he made a show of feeling their foreheads and having them open wide to peer into their throats. He'd noticed all right. He'd noticed Tommy called him Pa, and he'd liked it. He'd practically melted. And now, Tommy would probably keep calling him that, and Rand would keep letting him.

Carly bit her lip. Tommy didn't remember much about their father, and he needed a pa in his life. She didn't begrudge him that, but just last night she'd explained to him they might have to leave. Was this Tommy's way of fighting the battle? He didn't want to go, and he'd told Carly that in no uncertain terms.

Carly's own mind had undergone a transformation, though. Upon receiving Rand's gifts, and then especially after that breathtaking kiss in the kitchen, she didn't want to go away anymore. Maybe she had it all wrong. Maybe Rand really didn't love Myra. It's what he'd been saying all along. And if there was a chance, even a very small chance, that she and Rand could make this work, she'd stay right here and fight for the right to be his wife—his real wife—despite the obstacles Myra threw in their path.

One major obstacle remained. If she stayed here, she would have to confess her part in Lester's counterfeit operation. She'd come clean, turn the plates over to Rand to do with as he thought best. After all that, and after she'd done her penance, whatever that may be, if Rand wanted her to stay, she'd do it in a heartbeat.

The decision to confess made, a heavy weight lifted from Carly's shoulders. At the same time, a new burden settled upon her. Would she have the courage to do what must be done? How would Rand react? It didn't matter. This was something she had to do, and do it she would.

Tommy wouldn't say anything about their conversation last night. He'd woken up that morning complaining he didn't want to go, and Carly had put him off saying they weren't going anywhere, at least until he and Jenna were well. Now, she'd tell him she was having second thoughts too. Maybe, just maybe, Tommy would get his way after all.

Rand followed her into the hallway and spoke her name. She turned to look at him. "Yes?"

Even though Tommy's bedroom door was still slightly ajar, even though her hands were full of water glasses and an empty pitcher, Rand put his arms around her and gave her the sweetest kiss she'd ever imagined. Was it the sweetness in the kiss or the love in her heart that made her want to collapse into a puddle of tingles and palpitating heartbeats? He kissed her once, then again, and a third time.

With what she perceived to be a great effort on his part, he finally released her and entered his bedroom, gently closing the door behind him. Not a word had passed between them, but his heart had just spoken volumes to hers. Perhaps Rand could find it in his heart to forgive her once she had confessed and her conscience was clear again. She prayed it would be so.

Later, after the chores were done and Carly had helped Mary Jo with some touch-up work on her painting, she wondered if she should make a fresh pot of coffee to enjoy in the afternoon. Where had Rand gotten to anyway? She hadn't seen him in a while. Must have gone back outside, but, oh, the memory of the kisses in the hallway. Her cheeks went hot whenever she thought of it, and that was pretty much constant.

The afternoon passed, and Rand had never come back through. It would be suppertime soon. Would Rand mind chicken leftovers again? Her new boots clicked on the wooden floor as she worked in the kitchen. She hadn't been able to resist putting them on before coming downstairs so that Rand could see her wearing them. Late this afternoon, she'd managed to get a riding skirt cut out of the fabric Rand had brought to her the day Myra showed up.

Think about something else. That day was not a good memory. Think about Rand kissing her this morning standing right in this very spot. Think about him doing the same thing in the upstairs hallway earlier today.

"Mary Jo," she called in an effort to once again turn her thoughts in a different direction. "Time to get your painting things cleaned up and come help me with supper."

"All right," Mary Jo called back. Not even a word of protest. Carly smiled to herself. After days of everything going so wrong, things were finally going right. Now, if only she could cross that last obstacle in her path and make that confession to Rand tonight. *Father in Heaven, help me do what I must.*

The kitchen door opened which such force, a gust of air ruffled her skirts. Carly whirled around to see what had Mary Jo in such a hurry and came face to face with her husband. His eyes blazed with so much fury, Carly backed away until she was crammed against the sideboard.

"I thought you were outside." Her words sounded minuscule and ridiculous as she stared at his red face. "Is something wrong?"

He threw two muslin wrapped objects onto the sideboard. They landed with a deep thud just behind Carly.

"What in thunderation are these?"

Rand stared, shocked at the sound of his own voice, loud as a cattle stampede and echoing off the kitchen walls. Carly looked as if she would faint dead away at any second. At this point Rand was so angry he couldn't even manage to lower his voice, even though the ranch hands could probably hear him all the way from the bunkhouse.

At no answer from his wife, who was staring at the objects as if they might bite her, he continued. "I want to know what those things are and why they're in my house. Speak up."

Mary Jo appeared out of nowhere. "Stop it, Uncle Rand." She looked from him to Carly, then added, "Help me get her to a chair, or she's going to pass out." Mary Jo put an arm around Carly and gently led her toward the kitchen table.

Rand grabbed the chair and pulled it out, making it clatter as much as possible. Carly sat in it, put her hands over her face, and burst into tears. Great. The crying thing. Now he'd never get her to give him a straight answer.

"What's going on?" Tommy, followed closely by Jenna, entered the kitchen, both of them still dressed in their nightwear. They knelt on the floor in front of Carly and tried to console her as best they could while Mary Jo stood behind her, the girl's arms wrapped protectively around Carly's shoulders. Both girls were crying too, and Tommy didn't look too far from it.

Rand stared at the foursome, though not a one of them spared him a glance. How could he feel so outnumbered in his own home with his own family? His anger burned hot, but it was obvious he wasn't going to get anywhere with this until he cooled down.

He sank into a chair across the table and dropped his head into his hands. He was pretty sure he knew what those chunks of metal were and who'd hidden them in the dresser in the attic, but the why of it all eluded him. Still, a few other things were beginning to make sense.

After several minutes of silence but for Carly's sobbing and the disapproving looks the children threw at him occasionally, Rand tried again. To his amazement, his voice came out both quieter and gentler.

"Tommy and Jenna, you two go back to bed. Someone will be up to check on you soon." He couldn't promise it would be Carly based on the way she looked at the moment. Her face had gone white as the snow-covered prairie, and her body shook so hard the teacup on the saucer in front of her was clattering.

Jenna and Tommy looked at Mary Jo, who gave her uncle a withering glance then nodded toward the younger children. "Go on. It'll be all right."

Reluctantly, the pair left the kitchen. Soon, their bare feet padded on the stairway and then overhead. Two doors closed with quiet clicks.

Mary Jo removed the clattering teacup and refilled it from the steaming pot on the stove, then set it back in front of Carly. She fished Carly's handkerchief from the pocket of her apron and pushed it into her hand. After one more warning glance his direction, she hugged Carly again and left the room.

God help him, the girl was only twelve, and already she was handling the situation way better than he knew how. Whatever the case he needed to get to the bottom of this.

Rand took a few more deep breaths. Keeping his voice steady, he asked, "Would you like to go sit in the parlor where our conversation can be a little more private?"

Carly's expression told him she didn't buy the privacy thing, but she nodded and got to her feet.

The back door swung open, and Tubby rushed in, panting hard. "You better come, boss! Fire! Looks like the south pasture."

Rand stared at the remains of the burnt grass and charred fence posts, the wood pieces still glowing. It had been several weeks since he'd lost any steers, and he'd begun to think whoever was thieving from him had given up. Apparently not.

"These rascals ain't just wanting steak to chaw on," Parker drawled. "Appears to me they're trying to put you out of business." That was the same thing Nate had suggested after the last incident. "You reckon we lost any cattle what with the fence being cut again?"

"Hard to say." Rand surveyed the aftermath of a fire that had obviously gone out long before whoever set it intended. The wind had shifted and sent the flames that would have burnt the whole pasture heading to the creek instead. One dead tree still burned along the near side bank. "Looks like someone cut the fence all along that north side intending to run the cattle out of here with the fire. Might have worked too, if the wind hadn't changed."

"You think it was the cattle they wanted then?" Parker asked. "Maybe they didn't know we'd already moved them into winter pasture."

Rand stroked his chin, thick with a day's growth of beard. "Not sure."

He surveyed the grass around him. "Nate, you, Parker, and Clarence take Bo and make sure all the cattle are safe and no more barbed wire has been cut. We can work on fixing that fence later."

After the three men left, Rand stared at the damage. "What was the point of a fire we'd be sure to see and come running? And why all that fence clipping with no cattle to steal?"

Tubby pulled on his beard. "I ain't trying to brew up more trouble than what we already got, but like Parker said, what if it's not the cattle they're after but something else."

"Like what?" Rand wanted to know.

Tubby shrugged. "Anybody you know of that might want revenge for something they think you've done to 'em?"

Myra crossed Rand's mind again, but he didn't dwell on the thought. Myra was a piece of work, all right, but she wouldn't have done this. What would she have to gain by setting a fire?

"No, not that I know of," Rand mused.

"Whatcha want me to do, boss?" Tubby asked.

"Go back and start supper for the boys. They'll be hungry once they get back." Tubby turned his horse toward home, but Rand called after him. "And stop up to the house first. Tell Mrs. Stratford I won't be in for supper. I'm going to stay out here and keep an eye on things for another hour or so." Tubby didn't need to know it, but Rand figured if he took a little more time to cool off before he and Carly had the difficult conversation awaiting them, they'd all be better off.

Rand rode the fence line to determine the damage to the barbed wire and how many new posts he would need. Dark came early these days, but the glow of the still-burning embers of posts and the cottonwood tree by the creek lit his way. Good thing they'd had that wet autumn and all that snow he'd cursed when it fell. Dry pasture grass wouldn't have allowed this fire to stop regardless of any wind shift.

"Hey, boss. You still out here?" It was Tubby's voice coming out of the darkness.

"Yeah, but what are you …"

"Got something you need to see." Tubby emerged from the smoky blackness. He pulled his horse alongside Dusty and handed Rand a folded piece of paper. "Found this in the barn. It was stuck into a pile of hay with the end of a pitchfork." The ragged hole bored through the top of the page attested to Tubby's statement.

Rand squinted as he peered at the paper. Writing was scrawled across the page, but Rand couldn't make it out in the darkness. "What's it say?" he asked, a sense of foreboding enveloping him. "Do you know who put it there?"

"Nope. All of us were out here contemplating this here fire situation. I didn't figger I'd ask Mrs. Stratford about it until I talked to you first. It's addressed to her."

Addressed to Carly? "Tell me what it says."

"Near as I can remember," Tubby drawled, obviously not eager to reveal the note's contents, "it said something about 'give back what is mine or you will pay the price.' It wasn't signed."

Rand's stomach seemed to drop into his boots. "You sure it's meant for my wife?"

"Yep. *Carlotta Blair* was written on the back of it."

Someone had been on his ranch, someone who didn't belong there, someone who didn't want to be seen. Worse, it appeared the reason for the visit was those plates he'd found in the attic. Now his family was being threatened.

Chapter 23

Carly tried to calm the children, but she was far from calm herself. She told them the fire was probably nothing important, but she didn't even try to explain the muslin bundles still on the sideboard or Rand's behavior. She couldn't wait to get those counterfeit plates out of this house. She yearned for Rand to come home and dreaded the moment when he did. Her prayers for help were interrupted when her husband walked in the kitchen door.

"Anything to eat?" He didn't look at her, just rubbed his chin. "I'm starved."

"Tubby said you wouldn't be in, but I can fix a plate for you." Her voice shook as badly as her hands. "He said there was a fire, but it's out now. Do you know what caused it?"

"It didn't burn much. Turned toward the creek and got that old dead cottonwood I had my eye on for winter stove fuel, but other than that, not much damage."

Definitely a strain in his voice. Carly wished she'd moved the plates from the sideboard to get them out of sight, though she had no hope of getting them off Rand's mind. She filled a plate and poured him a cup of coffee. It sloshed onto the table top. He seemed not to notice or care.

"Pour yourself a cup and sit here with me," he suggested. On second thought, it sounded more like a command.

Carly poured another cup of coffee even though she didn't really want one and sat across from him. "Rand, I …"

Tommy ran into the kitchen. "Hey, Rand, where ya been? Tubby said there was a fire."

"You're supposed to be upstairs in bed." Carly's voice carried more of a reprimand than she'd intended.

"I wanna know about the fire. What was burning? Carly said it was probably a line shack. What's a line shack, Rand? Is it bad if it burns?"

"We want to know what happened too." Mary Jo entered the kitchen, Jenna trailing her. "Is everything all right?"

"Everything's fine," Rand snapped. He forked a bite into his mouth, then looked around the room as if surprised everyone was staring at him. He put down the fork. "Just a little fire on the pasture. It's out now, and there's nothing to worry about." His voice was gentler.

"Did it catch the whole pasture on fire?" Tommy asked. "Why did Clarence need his big gun? Ya can't shoot a fire."

"Just a little spot burned. We didn't shoot anything, but all the hands know to be prepared just in case. Now you children hustle back upstairs. I need to talk with Carly." Rand's tone was serious, and the children obeyed without argument.

Carly stared at the dark liquid in her cup, watching it make tiny waves as tremors shook her hands. She swallowed a gulp in a vain attempt to wash away the bitter taste of bile rising in her throat.

Rand pulled a piece of paper from his shirt pocket and handed it to her. "This was left in the barn sometime late this afternoon."

Her name was written on the page. The handwriting alone was enough to make Carly's stomach revolt. It was the same as the writing on the letters from Lester.

"Turn it over."

In big, unmistakable letters were the words, *Give back what is mine or you will pay the price. Deliver to Walnut Point Hotel addressed to LM.*

Even if she could have spoken words around her panic, Carly didn't know what to say. Lester McGraw had found her. He had come all the way to this Kansas ranch to plague her with this threatening note and God knew what else.

The cold hand of fear wrapped around her stomach, gripping it until nausea overcame her. "Excuse me." She raced out the back door and lost her supper over the porch railing.

When she'd finished, she gazed out into the darkness, refusing to meet her husband's eyes, though he stood behind her, his hands on her shoulders. Now was the time to tell him. Rand would keep her and

Tommy safe. Or would he be as disgusted with her as she was with herself that she'd had a part in crafting counterfeit money plates? Maybe she'd go to jail. What would happen to Tommy? Or to Mary Jo and Jenna, for that matter?

"Tell me about the plates, Carly." His tone left no room for argument.

Rand supported Carly as she sank onto the porch steps. He sat beside her and practically had to force himself not to touch her. With what was going to be said between them, she probably didn't want him near her. He stayed close anyway. He had to make her tell him. It was the only way he could help.

Rand's initial anger had faded some, but he was still plenty mad. *God, help me keep the anger under control.* Throwing more anger her way would get him nowhere. *And please help Carly trust me.*

"Can you help me understand what's happened here?"

She didn't look up.

"I'm pretty sure those things I found in the attic are counterfeit money plates. I also know you've got enough art talent you could have drawn the image for them. Is that right?"

Carly nodded, though he was barely able to discern the slight movement of her head.

"You drew the replications, the drawings were transferred onto metal plates, and then you brought them here?"

Another nod. He supposed that was better than no response, but he couldn't have this conversation on his words alone. How could he get her to speak up?

"Why?" he asked at last, the single word filling the night with his wife's palpable fear.

She heaved a sigh. "You knew I worked at a newspaper office. I was engaged to marry my boss. His name is Lester McGraw."

Rand nodded. She'd already told him that much.

"Lester showered me with flattery about my artistic abilities once I had drawn some ads for the paper. I can see through it now, but at the time I ate it up as fast as he could dish it out. My mother had been discouraged from practicing her artwork by my father and felt that my talents would only lead to trouble." Carly dropped her eyes back to the floor.

"Go on." Rand's voice was so harsh it grated against his ears.

Carly squirmed but continued. "After a while he began to present me with things he said were meant to challenge my abilities. He had me copy pictures from other papers, draw landscapes of areas we visited together. I even copied photographs. He would give me lavish praise for everything I was able to reproduce. I guess it went to my head."

Rand wanted to speak, to help her. He didn't know how. The words continued to pour out of her mouth.

"One day, he handed me a five-dollar silver certificate and said he knew I probably couldn't do it very well, but he wanted to see if I could draw a replica. Once the challenge was on the table, I met it head on. I did my absolute best, just like Lester knew I would. I drew the thing, front and back, and Lester asked if he could keep my drawings. It wasn't until later I discovered he'd made it into printing plates. I don't think he'd quite perfected the technique yet, but it was his intention to produce counterfeit bills."

"Then what happened?" Rand managed to soften his voice.

"I found the original drawings, ripped them into pieces, and threw them in the fireplace. I stole the plates so Lester couldn't use them and brought them with me to Kansas. I thought he'd never find me out here."

"Then he's responsible for the note in the barn."

Carly nodded. "And some letters too."

Letters. The man had written his wife letters, and she hadn't said anything? He had to work to keep his voice even. "When were you going to tell me about this?"

A fresh bout of tears kept Carly from answering right away. Rand tried to be patient, but he wasn't very good at it. After a moment she wiped them away and continued.

"I was going to tell you tonight. I know you probably don't believe me, but I was." She turned her face to him, a pleading look in her eyes.

Somehow, he did believe her. It was dark, but he could still see the despair on her face. Saying these words was hurting her too much for them to be dishonest.

Carly dropped her head into her hands and continued, her voice so low Rand had to lean closer to hear her whispers. "I never meant to make counterfeit money." Her voice pleaded with him to believe her. "Lester tricked me. It was my own vanity that caused this predicament. Lester kept going on and on about what a talented artist I was and how he never would have believed I could copy a five-dollar silver certificate with such accuracy. The more he praised me, the harder I tried to get it just right. My own selfish pride put me here." Her head fell into her hands. "God, forgive me."

Every ounce of his anger drained away. All Rand could feel was compassion. Indeed, Carly had made some mistakes along the way, but she hadn't intended to do wrong. It was now up to him to make it right.

He rose from his seat. "I'll take the plates into the sheriff in the morning."

Carly jumped up and grabbed his arm. "You can't." Her voice was little more than a shrill shriek. "I'll go to jail ... or to prison ... or be hanged—"

"That's ridiculous. The only thing you've done wrong is keep those things hidden. Lord knows why you didn't turn them in to the authorities immediately, but it has to be done, and I aim to do it. I won't have them under my roof."

"Boss, you need to get over here," Clarence called from the barn. He sounded upset.

"Be right there." Rand turned to Carly. "I'll take the plates in the morning."

Her only answer was a slight nod.

Carly covered her face with her hands and sank back onto the steps. Rand was right about turning in the plates. If only he were right about her not having done anything wrong. Maybe he didn't know what had happened to Emmanuel Ninger. Even if he did, the plates needed to be turned over. Tomorrow she would face the sheriff. She'd be convicted and sent to prison. Her marriage would be annulled. She couldn't expect Rand to keep up the charade of their marriage. God help her, what would become of Tommy?

She had to protect Tommy. She couldn't count on Rand to take care of him once she was sent away.

She'd just have to put the plan in place that she'd made a few days ago. She would pack their things, leave while Rand was in town tomorrow, and by the time he got back here with the sheriff to arrest her, they'd be where nobody could find them. Maybe she could get one of the hands to drive her into town. It would take nothing less than an outright lie to explain her need to get to town, but next to her part in

Lester's counterfeit scheme, what was a lie at this point? They'd have to take care that Rand didn't see them once they got to town, but he'd be at the sheriff's office, and she'd be on the other side of town at the railroad depot.

What would she do about money? She might be able to return the boots and combs Rand had bought for her at Keller's. She'd worn the boots a little bit, but not enough to be noticeable. Would the store take them back, and would the refund be enough for train tickets for her and Tommy to … to anywhere?

As soon as she found a job and saved some money she could send Rand the price of the boots and combs. Then she could get her and Tommy somewhere far away where the sheriff couldn't find her and no one knew what she had done.

Maybe she could change her name. She might even dye her hair to become a brunette in case her likeness and description appeared on one of those wanted posters. Carly had seen some tacked to the outside of Keller's General Store. She shuddered to think of her image and the word "WANTED" scrolled across her face. Would someone recognize her?

The snow was gone, but the night was cold. She made her way back inside. The plates in their wrappings glared at her as she passed through the kitchen. She left Rand's uneaten supper on the table and said goodnight to Mary Jo, who was painting in the sitting room. Carly didn't give her any time to ask questions before she ran up the stairs. She checked on Tommy and Jenna. Both were asleep, foreheads cool to the touch. They must have been feeling better.

Alone in her bedroom, her thoughts ran through the happenings of the day prior to Rand throwing the counterfeit plates on the sideboard. Holding back the tears as best she could, Carly packed her satchel. She would take nothing but what she had brought with her, which was very little. Most of the worn, threadbare clothing she'd owned before coming to Kansas was now part of her rag bag. So be it. She couldn't take advantage of Rand by taking the things he'd bought for her.

The same with Tommy. She'd have to pack his bags in the morning. This morning, he'd called Rand his pa. Carly hated to take him away now, but what choice did she have?

She dropped her clothes on the floor and slid into her bed without bothering to light the lamp. Tomorrow morning would come too fast. Ignoring her empty stomach and her empty heart, she drew the warm quilts tight around her and closed her eyes. It hurt too much to think, so she tried not to, but the thoughts kept jabbing her awake. Tonight was her last night in this house. She might not ever see the man she loved again. That was enough to keep her awake most of the night.

Rand stared at the man lying on the barn floor in a pile of hay, his hands and feet tied together in Parker's sturdy rope knots. "I thought you were my friend."

Dave Pearlman didn't answer. His eyes were closed tightly against the lantern light.

Rand turned to Parker. "Tell me what happened."

"I was riding the fence line like you told us, and I came upon this old galoot with these here wire cutters in his hand." He held up a metal tool for Rand to see. "I asked what he was doing, even though the clipped fence in front of him made it pretty clear. He tried to run, but he was afoot, so I caught up with him, bulldogged him just like he was one of them steers, and tied him up. I brung him back here." Parker pointed at the man in the hay.

This was not what Rand needed tonight on top of everything else. "You wanna tell me why you're driving off my steers, setting fire to my pasture, and ruining my fences?"

Dave met Rand's glare with a sorrowful expression. "I knew you was a hankering to buy Hawthorne's pasture, and I guess I thought I needed it more than you did. Figured if I kept costing you money by running off cattle and such, you might hold off on buying it until I had a chance to save enough to get it first. Hawthorne said he'd make me a deal if I paid cash money, 'cept I don't have it just yet."

All the trouble, all the cost, because Dave—his friend, his neighbor— wanted more land? "Why didn't you just come to me and tell me you wanted the pasture? We could have worked something out."

"Don't s'pose you'd believe me if I said I was sorry, but I reckon I am." Fear clouded Pearlman's expression. "You gonna turn me in to Sheriff McConnell?"

"Yep." There was no other answer. Dave had thieved cattle and damaged property. Rand couldn't let him walk away. He turned to his hands, who were gathered around him, staring at the man on the hay.

"Untie him enough so he can walk over to the bunkhouse, then tie him again so he doesn't try to run away in the night. Get him a warm supper and a blanket to sleep on. I've got to go to town in the morning anyway, so I'll take him with me. While I'm gone, Parker, Nate, and Clarence are on ranch patrol. Tubby, you stay at the house and keep guard over Mrs. Stratford and the children. I'll be back as soon as I can. Look sharp because this man isn't the only trouble we've got around here."

Rand walked away without another word.

Lying in bed staring at the ceiling that night, Rand wondered how things could have turned out like this. It wasn't exactly how he'd envisioned this night would go when he'd started looking for the wedding ring. Mary Jo had heated up his supper for him when he came in. His belly was full, but eating without Carly made everything taste like sawdust. The chunks of iron wrapped in muslin and lying on the sideboard stared at him all during supper.

He'd taken them upstairs and put them under his bed as soon as he was done eating, but now it felt like they were in his straw tick by the way his back ached. Rand reckoned it wasn't the metal of the plates so much as the pain in his heart that caused him such discomfort. The look of utter fear in Carly's eyes when he'd told her he was taking the plates to the sheriff kept smoldering at him through the darkness of his room.

How in the world had Carly been able to sleep at night knowing those things were in the attic? She seemed to believe she would go to jail or some such thing, but that was silly. The only thing she'd done wrong was take the plates from her boss and run away with them. Wasn't that actually a good thing? McGraw couldn't use the plates to make silver certificates when they were in Carly's possession.

Rand turned over and closed his eyes, but sleep didn't come.

When the first tinge of dawn stole over the horizon, Rand climbed out of bed and into his clothes. Best get Dave and those plates to town and have that errand behind him. Jeb would help him figure out what to do about McGraw. Maybe then Rand could figure out a way to talk some sense into Carly.

Mary Jo was already up and had coffee waiting. Nice change from a few months ago when the girl's coffee rivaled the flavor of spring mud.

"Shall I fry a few eggs, maybe some bacon?" she asked as he picked up the steaming mug.

"Nah, better get going. Maybe you could slice me off a slab of that bread and put a little blackberry jam on it. That'll hold me till I get back."

Mary Jo set about doing as he requested. He took the bread from her, gulped one more swig of the coffee, and headed for the back door, counterfeit plates in hand. Rand didn't want to take a chance on running into Carly before he left. She'd try to talk him out of going. At this point, he was just weak-willed enough she might be able to do it. Whatever it took to get that frightened look out of her eyes and bring her back into his arms. He'd found the blasted ring that started this whole mess, and he meant to put it on her finger.

Just as the door was about to slam behind him, Rand caught a glimpse of Mary Jo sliding into a chair and laying her head on the table. He backed into the kitchen again.

"You feeling all right, honey?" he asked.

Mary Jo made an effort to lift her head and put a smile on her face, but now that she had his attention, Rand could see through the falseness in her actions.

"Just a bit of a headache. I'm sure I'll be fine once I've been up a little longer." Mary Jo ended her sentence with a cough.

Rand laid a hand on her forehead. "You're warm. I'm thinking this sickness that's waylaid the rest of us has finally made it around to you. You get back on upstairs now and get yourself in bed."

"But I need to get something for Jenna and Tommy to eat for breakfast, and I don't know when Carly will be down." Or if she would be down. Rand heard the unspoken words in her voice. Mary Jo understood enough of how this thing was affecting Carly to know she might well spend the morning in her room. "I should make her some tea or something."

Rand sighed. "Nothing doing, girl. You get back to bed. I'll tell Tubby to make something for the children. He'll stay in the house with you while I make a quick trip to town and bring back plenty of tea for you and Carly."

Mary Jo coughed again and headed upstairs without further argument. How could he have been so wrapped up in his own problems that he failed to notice she wasn't feeling well? He should go up and tell Carly.

No, he'd go find Tubby, fill him in and let the old cook tell Carly whenever she decided to come downstairs. Rand needed to go to the bunkhouse anyway to collect Pearlman and give the men orders for the day. Now that he knew McGraw was around, he needed every set of eyes watching the ranch. Rand shoved the bread and jam into his mouth as he stepped out the back door.

A commotion in the farmyard woke Carly. Dogs were barking and men were hollering. She ran to her window and watched as Clarence and Parker helped a man Carly didn't recognize into the back of the wagon. The man's hands were tied together. Myra's trunks had been loaded into the back of the wagon as well. Good. At least they'd be gone from here.

The man who had his wrists tied didn't appear to be struggling with them, just accepting what was happening. As strange a sight as this was, all Carly could focus on was the bundles of muslin Rand was pushing into a leather saddle bag. He jumped into the wagon seat, and off they went toward town. She had no idea who the man was, but it didn't really matter. Rand had the plates, and he was on his way to seal her fate.

She finished packing her satchel as best she could, choosing to leave her trunk and the most threadbare of her clothing behind. Rand could throw it all away if he had a mind to. Packing Tommy's belongings into something they could easily carry would be the hard part. She'd argued with herself over it but had finally decided to allow Tommy to take the things Rand had bought for him since they'd come. He was growing so fast that Carly doubted he'd have anything left he could wear if the new clothing was left behind. It was going to be hard enough on Tommy to leave Muckלededun without having to leave behind his possessions too.

But who was she fooling? Leaving behind clothing or even a dog didn't even come close to the pain involved in leaving behind Mary Jo, Jenna, and Rand. For both of them. Tommy thought of the girls as his sisters and Rand ... well ... she loved Rand in a way that was steadfast and sure. She would love him the rest of her life, even if she never saw him again. She'd love him from a jail cell if it meant she could keep him as her husband. But she couldn't be sure how he would react or if he would care for Tommy. For her brother's sake, she had to run.

Tommy was still asleep when she entered his room. She emptied his dresser, folding the clothes and placing them in a leather bag she'd been using to store her paint supplies. Someday when she could afford it, she'd buy a new one and send it to Rand to replace the one she took with her. When most of the clothes were crammed into the bag, Carly turned to find Tommy watching her. Tears swam in his eyes.

"We're leaving, aren't we?" His voice was barely a whisper.

Carly nodded. "I'm sorry, Tommy. It can't be helped."

"Is it cuz of those things Rand found in the attic?"

Carly nodded again. Someday when he could understand better, she'd explain it to him. Tommy needed to know what his sister had done and make his own decisions about whether or not he could look past her wrongdoing.

"Are you feeling well enough to get up and dressed?" Carly handed him warm clothes to wear.

"Can I eat breakfast before we go?"

"Of course. Mary Jo will probably make some oatmeal or something. Just don't say anything to either her or Jenna about us leaving. Can you remember that?" If Tommy let it slip now, they might not get away with her plan.

"I'll remember." But he didn't sound very happy about it. "What about Rand? Can I tell him?"

"Rand has gone to town. Go on and get ready now. I'll be in my room if you need me."

Carly closed the door to her bedroom just in time to hear footsteps trudge up the stairs. A moment later, a door closed. Sounded like it came from Mary Jo's room. Had she been up and decided to go back to bed?

Concerned, Carly tapped on Mary Jo's door.

"Come in." The girl's voice sounded hoarse.

Carly opened the door and peeked inside the room. Mary Jo had left her clothes on the floor and crawled under her covers.

"Are you all right, sweetheart?"

Mary Jo nodded, but barely. "Uncle Rand sent me back to bed. He thinks I've got what you all had."

Carly laid a hand on Mary Jo's forehead. Yes, she was running a fever.

"Your uncle is right. You stay in bed today. Can I get you anything?"

"I just want to sleep." Mary Jo's eyes were closed.

"You sleep then. I'm right across the hall if you need anything." Carly retreated to her room. Could she leave with Mary Jo sick? She had to leave. Mary Jo would be fine by tomorrow, and by tomorrow, Carly would likely be in jail if she didn't run.

Carly sat on her bed listening as first Tommy, followed shortly thereafter by Jenna, left their rooms and went downstairs. They were probably both hungry after not eating much yesterday. With Mary Jo sick, Carly needed to go down and get them something to eat.

Might as well get that done so she could be ready to leave soon. She couldn't risk Rand getting home before she had left. She tiptoed downstairs expecting to find the two younger children waiting for her in the sitting room. Instead she could hear them laughing and talking in the kitchen, a deeper voice answering them.

Three faces turned to look at her when she entered the kitchen. "Tubby? What are you doing here?"

"Good morning, Miz Stratford. Boss asked me to come on up and make breakfast for the young'uns here. Said Miss Mary Jo was feeling ill and you might be, er, indisposed for a while."

Carly managed a smile. "How kind of you. Anything I can help with?"

"Naw, the children ate some eggs what I fried up and drunk big glasses of milk fresh from the cow this morning. I'm thinking I got 'em filled up pretty good."

Tommy and Jenna nodded, both sporting milky mustaches.

"Thanks, Tubby. I'll clean up in here if you want to get back to your work."

"'Preciate it, ma'am, but Boss wants me to stay in the house with you all until he gets home. He said to tell you we caught the guy who was cutting fence and stealing steers. It were a neighbor man who wanted to buy that pasture Boss has his eye on. He's taking him into the sheriff."

That explained the man who'd been tied up. "Thank you for telling me."

It would be good to have Tubby here. At least Mary Jo and Jenna wouldn't be alone when Carly and Tommy left. It might be harder to get away without him noticing, though.

Tommy looked at her expectantly. She nodded, hoping he would understand she still intended for them to leave soon. Her words belied the gesture. "You two go on in the other room and start your studies. I'll be there shortly. Tubby, would you mind replenishing the wood bins? I think we've got a cold day ahead of us."

"Sure thing, ma'am." Tubby disappeared out the back door, heading for the woodshed.

Tommy and Jenna headed to the sitting room. Carly's stomach was too knotted up with nervousness to face complaints or even to wash the iron skillet Tubby had used to fry the eggs. She filled it with water from the sink hydrant and shaved a curl of soap into it, hoping whoever had to deal with it later would forgive her.

She went upstairs to retrieve the satchel and bag she'd packed. She reread the note she'd written last night.

Dear Rand,

Tommy and I are leaving the ranch for a destination that remains undecided as yet. Please don't look for us. Hug the girls for me and tell them I love them. I am so sorry for all the trouble I have caused you.

Carly

She left the note lying on his pillow where he would be sure to find it. She stowed her bags in the lean-to and made her way to the barn. Tubby had said Rand had the hands busy watching cattle, but surely one of them was around. She was going to have to ask someone to drive her into town.

No luck. The barn was deserted. She tapped on the door of the bunkhouse, but there was no answer.

Carly went back to the barn. She wasn't sure how many horses resided in those stalls lining the sides of the big building, but most of them were gone. If she had to ask Tubby to drive her to town, Mary Jo and Jenna would be left alone at the ranch. She couldn't let that happen. She looked around the barn once more. Old Polly and that odd-looking dappled horse that had brought Myra here were both in the stable.

Carly coaxed the dapple to take the bit and bridled her, then hitched her to the little buggy that Myra had used. It was perfect. Rand had said the horse and the buggy belonged to the livery in Walnut Point. She and Tommy would take the buggy and horse to town, return them to the livery where they belonged, and then head to the depot. No lying about needing to go to town for something, no bothering one of Rand's hands, whom he very much needed just now to ride his ranch.

Carly had a little trouble with the unfamiliar harness, but she figured it out quickly. Back in Baltimore, she'd hitched up Leo's horse and buggy every day to drive to work at the newspaper. She could do this.

Once harnessed, she left the horse and buggy in the barn, hoping Tubby wouldn't see it there. Then she went to get Tommy. She intended to tell Tubby she and Tommy were going to feed the chickens, as they did every morning, and ask him to stay with Mary Jo and Jenna, but he wasn't in the house. He must still be tending to the wood bins. So much the better.

This was it. Good-bye. She would never set foot in this house again. "Tommy, come here please."

When her brother entered the kitchen, she thrust his arms into his coat and herded him out the door, grabbing her bags on the way. Carly made a beeline for the barn, dragging Tommy along with her. She'd started to climb in the buggy when two figures appeared from behind an empty stall.

"Nice of you to hitch it up for us, wouldn't you say, Myra?"

The voice belonged to Lester McGraw.

Chapter 24

"Never seen one of these things before." Jeb McConnell turned the counterfeit plates over and over in his hands as he examined them. "Sure enough looks like it could print a pretty convincing bill if someone knew how to use it."

Rand nodded. "What's the next step?"

Jeb rocked his chair onto its back legs. "Reckon I'll lock them up in the safe for now. I'll send a wire to the federal marshals and tell 'em I got these things here and give 'em the name of this McGraw fellow from Baltimore. Next time they come through, I'll turn them over to them."

Jeb's chair came down with a thud. "Problem is, you know as well as I do they ain't gonna find Lester McGraw in Baltimore. He's out here in Kansas looking for these here plates and threatening your wife."

Rand heaved a sigh. So true. "I'll do everything I can to protect my wife. I doubt McGraw knows I've brought the plates into you, and he may just show up hoping to threaten Carly into turning them over." Rand paused. "She isn't in any trouble, is she?"

"Nah." Jeb turned the plates over one more time before locking them in the safe behind him. "I'll need to question her, and the marshals might want to as well, but I'm thinking they'll be thanking her for taking these plates so they couldn't be used, and for turning in the guy. I'll send a man over to the hotel straightaway to see if he's signed in there."

Rand rose and stuffed his hands in his pockets. "And you can take care of the situation with Pearlman?"

The sheriff nodded. "You sure you want to let him go? You could press charges, and he'd see plenty of jail time if he did all that you say he did."

"Dave made a big mistake, but he realizes it now, and he's made himself plumb sick with how sorry he is. Told me about it all the way into town. I know I've made some mistakes in my life and the Good Lord has forgiven me. Least I can do is forgive Dave."

"Good way to look at it," Jeb said.

"Many thanks." Rand offered a quick nod. "I'd best be getting on home now. Kind of nervous about Carly and the kids being there alone."

"Don't blame you." Jeb stood and extended his hand. Rand gave it a firm shake, eager to get back to Carly. She'd be so relieved to hear what the sheriff said.

Rand left the sheriff's office, then dropped Myra's trunks at the hotel. The desk clerk said she wasn't there but he'd have 'em sent to her room. Next, Rand headed to Keller's. He'd promised to get tea. Sick children at home would be in need of it, though Rand didn't have much use for it himself.

"Mornin', Rand," Matthew Keller greeted him as he walked in the door. "I was hoping you'd be by soon."

"Why's that?" Rand asked as he glanced around the store. Mrs. Keller was busy with a customer in the fabrics area.

"That art stuff you ordered came in. Got a big box with your name on it in the back."

Perfect timing. New art supplies oughta help Carly forget this counterfeiting business and get on with her painting.

"Great. Kind of in a hurry today, though."

Matt Keller's eyes twinkled, and his mustache twitched. "Christmas coming up soon. Reckon it'd make a nice gift."

Rand hadn't even given Christmas a thought, but Matthew was right. "Can I leave it here a few days then? I wouldn't wanna spoil a Christmas surprise."

"Welcome to leave it as long as you need to. Tain't in my way a'tall. What can I get for ya today?"

"Just some tea, I guess."

Matt laughed. "Easy to see you got a house full of females at home. I don't think I've ever sold tea to Rand Stratford afore today."

"That would be true. We got some sort of sickness going through the family, and Carly thinks it's all-fired important to get tea and honey on those sore throats. Better give me a double supply." Rand was tempted to buy even more so he wouldn't have to do this again very soon.

"Sure thing. Better throw in a little peppermint too. I hear tell it flavors that tea pretty nice." Matt's mustache twitched again.

"Sounds good."

While Matthew left to measure the tea, Rand stood at the counter and spun his hat in his hands.

"Hello, Mr. Stratford." Mrs. Keller approached from the back of the store. "Nice to see you this morning. Anything I can help you with, or has Matt got what you needed?"

Suddenly an idea struck him.

"Actually, I think you can. I don't have time to wait for it today, so you can take some time to fix them up, but I was wondering if you might put together something for the girls and Tommy that they'd like for Christmas. I'm thinking maybe material for new dresses and some book for the girls, and how about a small rifle and some bullets for the boy? Time he learned to shoot if he's gonna live out here on the Kansas prairie."

Mrs. Keller gave him a broad smile. "Oh, what fun I shall have putting those together for you. You'll be by to pick it up soon?"

"Probably send one of my ranch hands in for it before too long. Better throw in enough warm socks for four pairs of cold feet and new gloves too. Gotta make sure my men stay warm." Rand grinned along with his next words. "I think they like popcorn and sweets too."

"I'll take care of it," Mrs. Keller, promised. "And it'll be all wrapped up so whoever comes to get it won't know what it is. But haven't you forgotten about your wife?"

"Matt's got a box in the back with them art supplies she's been pining for. If you can think of anything else she might want, throw it in. She sure took a liking to the boots and combs you sent home with me the other day." Rand paused. "Say, you got any women's coats? I know Carly could use a nice warm one."

Mrs. Keller gave him a wink. "To be sure I can find a coat for that sweet wife of yours. I'll have it all ready whenever you send someone into town for it."

"Thank you, ma'am." Rand was starting to get excited for Christmas. He couldn't remember feeling that way since he was a little boy.

"Here's your tea, Rand, and a few peppermint sticks thrown in to give it some flavor." Matt Keller handed him a package wrapped in brown paper. "Put it on account for you."

"Appreciate it." Rand took the package, tipped his hat to Mrs. Keller, and made his way to the door. Good folks, those Kellers.

He untied the team, climbed in, and headed for home. He couldn't get there soon enough to suit him.

Carly's first inclination was to run, but she couldn't leave Tommy alone with Lester and … and... Myra? The two of them were together?

She looked again. Sure enough, Myra Cunningham was standing with Lester McGraw's arm around her shoulders. Not only that, but she held a gun. It was pointed at Carly's little brother.

"What do you want?" Carly could barely get the words out.

"I think you know what I want," Lester drawled.

"I don't have them." Carly drew Tommy close and then shoved him behind her. "I don't have them, and I wouldn't give them to you if I did."

Lester grinned. "Oh, I think you will. All I have to do is say the word, and sweet little Myra here will put a bullet in the head of that little brother you think so much of." Lester dropped his arm from Myra's shoulders, approached Carly, and yanked Tommy away from her. He pulled the boy close to Myra.

Carly tried to appear sure of herself and confident for Tommy's sake.

Tommy's eyes were wide as they bounced from the gun to Myra to Lester to her. His lower lip trembled.

"I told you," Carly said, "I don't have them."

Myra sneered. "Well, *Mrs.* Stratford, I suggest you get them and turn them over to Lester now. It's not only this bothersome kid we can cause trouble for. As I recall, there are two girls you seem to think very highly of, and a husband"—she fairly spit out the word—"who claims to love you. What if we line them all up and see if there are enough bullets in this gun to put them all in early graves?" She waved the gun near Tommy's ear.

Carly would have given them the plates in an instant if she'd had them. But they were in Walnut Point at the sheriff's office. For all she knew, the sheriff would be here soon to arrest her. Maybe she could stall Lester and Myra long enough for Rand to make it back with the law. It might be her only hope.

"I suppose I could see if I can find them," she conceded, trying to sound convincing. "But I don't remember exactly where I buried them."

"You buried them?" Lester nearly shrieked the words. "You put them in the ground, and you don't remember where? You little ... I ought to wring your neck right here and now." He started toward her.

"Lester," Myra hissed. "Watch it."

Lester shot a glance over his shoulder. She couldn't see the look he was giving Myra, but she did see the one the woman returned—a cold, hard stare. With one quick glare at Carly, Lester returned to Myra's side.

They wouldn't hurt her as long as they thought she could tell them where the plates were. But Tommy ... and what about the innocent girls in the house? And if Rand came home? He didn't carry a gun, though his rifle hung on its hooks over the doorway in the lean-to. Maybe she could get to it.

"Put them in." Myra flung the words at Lester as if she were the one in charge. Perhaps she was. "We can't wait around here for Rand or one of his ranch hands to show up. Let's get them over to the old house, and maybe once we get her tied up, her memory will improve."

Lester nodded. "I suppose you're right." He leered at Carly. "Girlie, you're going to be sorry you ever stole those plates from me." He picked up Tommy and dumped him in the back of the buggy. "Don't move or my friend will shoot you." He turned to face Myra. "You sure you know where this place is?"

"It's Rand's sister's old house. I've been there many times. It isn't much to speak of, but it'll suit our purposes as long as we need it to."

Lester nodded and approached Carly, yanking twine out of his back pocket. His sneer was evil, and for a moment, she feared he might strike her. Instead, he grabbed her shoulder and spun her around.

The feel of his hands on her skin caused shudders down her spine.

He tied Carly's hands behind her back. Carly winced when the twine bit into her wrists, but she stayed quiet. No need to anger him further.

"Got the sack of food?" Lester asked.

"Right here." Myra held up a lumpy gunny sack for Lester's approval.

Lester threw Carly in the back of the buggy next to Tommy. It wasn't a space meant for people to ride in, and she struggled to sit in such a way as to not hurt Tommy. They were cramped and uncomfortable. There was nothing she could do about it. Even a protest wasn't possible as Lester stuffed a dirty handkerchief in her mouth and tied it around her head. Carly could barely breathe. She forced herself to calm down, slow her breaths, and resist the temptation to struggle against the gag.

Panicking would only make this worse. At least Lester hadn't gagged Tommy.

God, please let Tubby see us and rescue us. Please keep Mary Jo and Jenna safe. Please keep Tommy safe. Please bring help soon.

Myra threw the gunny sack of food on top of Carly. A metal can inside the sack hit Carly in the head. The world darkened for a moment, and she feared she might pass out. But the feeling was soon replaced by throbbing. Carly continued to pray as Myra and Lester climbed into the buggy seat and slapped the reins on the horse's back.

The dapple started slowly. Lester slapped her again.

Carly tried to think. They were taking them to the house Mary Jo and Jenna had lived in with their parents. It couldn't be very far away, but how would anyone know where to look for them? She couldn't see where they were going. Even if she and Tommy managed to escape, she would have no idea how to get back to the ranch. Where was Tubby? Why didn't he help them?

"Suppose you found my little love note I left for you last night." Was Lester talking to her? Carly couldn't answer even if he was. "I was hiding in the barn loft to make sure it got found, and that man of yours made things real convenient for me. They caught some poor coot cutting his fence and something was said about cattle rustling. Your man stood right there and said he'd be taking that poor sap into the sheriff this morning. He told the men to patrol the ranch. I went back to town, picked up Myra, and we left early this morning so we could be sure and find you alone. It wasn't hard at all to conk that old man in the head with one of his own pieces of firewood. He never knew what hit him. I tied him up and threw him in the woodshed. He'll be there until somebody finds him, and we'll be long gone by then."

They'd hurt Tubby? Oh, heavens, she prayed he was all right.

"Lester, be quiet," Myra warned. "She doesn't need to know any of that."

But Carly knew well enough that Lester McGraw liked bragging. He hadn't changed much since she'd left him in Baltimore.

"It was easy as pie to bribe the little gal at the mail office back home. She gave me the address where Old Anna was sending your letters." Lester laughed. "All it cost me was a little kiss in the back room."

"I said, be quiet!" Myra's voice had a fierceness that sent shivers through Carly.

"Myra said your man kicked her out of his house and made her stay in the hotel. Pretty funny when you think about it. I'm staying in that very same hotel and just happened to meet up with Myra yesterday when we were both eating dinner alone. We got to talking and found out we have a lot in common, including having a bone to pick with a Stratford. Seems we can help each other out here."

"Shut up, McGraw, or I've got ways to make you shut up." Apparently, Myra was fed up with Lester divulging all their secrets. Perhaps they weren't quite as good of friends as Lester would have had Carly believe.

Rand would find them. He would start looking and not quit until he had uncovered this whole devious plan cooked up by Lester and Myra. But what of the note Carly had written to Rand? Her heart sank. Rand wouldn't even know they were in trouble, much less come looking for them, at least not until Tubby was found. She and Tommy were completely at the mercy of these two evil people with no hope of rescue.

Chapter 25

The ranch yard was quiet when Rand rode in. The dogs must have been out with the hands on the ranges. Good. They needed to work for their scraps now and then.

The front door of the house swung open and Jenna ran out, her face streaked with tears.

Rand dismounted and caught the little girl in his arms. "What's wrong, baby? Where's your coat? We can't have you getting sick again."

Where was Carly? Why was she letting Jenna run around without her coat on? If she was still stuck up in her room, even Tubby would know better than to let Jenna run outside in nothing but her cotton dress and stocking feet.

He flipped the reins over the hitching post instead of taking the horses back to the barn as he'd intended and carried Jenna back into the house. He closed the front door that Jenna had left open. Strange, even little Jenna knew better than to leave the door open in winter time.

"Carly?" he called. No answer. "Tubby?"

Jenna was so agitated, she was beating on his shoulder with her fists. "What is it, baby? Where is everyone?"

Of course she didn't answer. He set her down on the sofa.

"Don't worry now. I'm going to go upstairs and find Carly." He headed for the stairway, but Jenna clung to his legs.

"All right, then. You can come with me." Rand picked her up again and took the stairs two at a time. "Carly?"

He swung the door open to her room, but it was empty. Tommy's room was next, but it was empty as well. With Jenna still flailing and crying, he pushed open Mary Jo's door after tapping on it. She rolled over in the bed and looked at them.

"Is everything all right?" Mary Jo's voice was hoarse, and her words were followed by a fit of coughing. She would be no help.

"Everything's fine," he answered softly. "Just checking on you. Go back to sleep now."

He closed the door. What in the world was the matter with Jenna? She kept beating on his shoulder. "Aw, honey, what's wrong?" Rand patted her back. He checked Jenna's room, which was empty, and finally his own. An envelope with his name scrawled across the front lay on his pillow. He tore it open and read the scrawled lines.

No. It couldn't be.

Carly and Tommy were gone.

Rand sank onto the bed, the letter crumpling in his hand. Jenna jumped away from him and ran downstairs. He'd go check on her in a minute, but right now, Rand had to deal with the disappointment seeping through his gut and bleeding into his heart. All he'd had to do was tell Carly how much he loved her. Maybe if he had, she'd still be here. But no, he had to make a big deal about the counterfeit plates and lose his temper with her over it.

Why didn't he just give her the ring last night as he'd intended? Now, she was gone, and he had no idea how to find her.

But how had she gotten to town? Maybe Tubby had taken her. Maybe he'd seen where she went.

He ran downstairs and out the kitchen door. The barn door hung wide open. All his hands knew better than to leave it like that. Where were they? Out riding range of course, just like he'd told them to do.

A quick look in the barn told him the three horses the men usually used were gone. That didn't explain where Tubby was, but his first priority was to look for Carly and Tommy. He slid the barn door closed, then opened it again. Something was wrong, but what? He scanned the barn again.

And then he realized that Myra's horse and buggy were missing. That's why things looked different. He kicked at the floor in disgust. Of course. Carly was smart enough to figure out she could take the horse and buggy, leave them at the livery, and get on a train. He'd made it very convenient for her. Or at least Myra had. Dadgum that woman.

He closed the barn door and started back to the house. He needed to see about Jenna. Something had really upset her. She flew out the back door as he approached, still without a coat or shoes. She held something in her hand. He finally realized it was her slate.

Jenna thrust it into his hand. Written there in scrawling letters was *Bad Man take Calry.*

Bad man.

What bad man?

Heart thumping, Rand picked Jenna up and carried her inside, then set her on the sideboard. He stood in front of her, hands on her shoulders, and looked into her eyes. Even an idiot could see the child was frightened out of her mind.

"A man took Carly?"

Jenna nodded.

"Where did he take her?"

She grabbed the slate again, wiped it clean with her pinafore, and wrote. *Hous.*

"He took her to a house?"

Jenna nodded again. Rand could tell she was getting more frustrated by the minute. Had someone Carly known come to get her and Tommy? If so, why had Carly taken the dapple and the buggy? Jenna seemed to think it was a bad man. Maybe she thought that since the man took Carly away.

He picked her up and hugged the little girl close to him. "It's all right, baby," he crooned. "Carly just needed to get away for a while. Maybe she'll come back soon." Rand didn't really believe that, but he'd say what he had to in order to comfort Jenna. Poor child. It seemed to him Carly could have at least taken a moment to explain to the girls that she had to leave. He'd bet his last nickel that Mary Jo had no idea she was even gone yet.

His heart softened a bit as he held the crying Jenna. How hard would it be to leave these girls? Maybe Carly was so heartbroken over leaving them, she couldn't bear to see their tears when she told them good-bye. Maybe it was just easier to walk out the door and be gone.

Truth was, he wanted to cry along with Jenna. Carly had left him because she thought he didn't love her. That and she didn't want to get arrested. But even if she believed she'd done something bad enough to go to jail, his love might have kept her here. Why, oh why had he been so stubborn? So stupid?

Jenna was making odd sounds along with her sob. He leaned away from her enough to see her face. Her mouth was moving. Her eyes were squeezed shut. Was she sick again? Was she so upset she was having some kind of seizure?

"Hep."

Jenna had spoken! It wasn't a real word, but it was the first time he'd heard something like that from her since the night her parents died.

"Jenna, honey, what it is? Can you tell me?" His own voice came out too loud and shrill. He needed to calm down, or Jenna wouldn't be able to calm down either. Her eyes pleaded with him to understand.

"Hep Cawy."

Rand stared at his niece. She was trying to say something. Could she do it? *Please help her, Lord.*

"Tell me again, baby. I'm listening."

Then it was as if Jenna's tongue loosened and the words she couldn't find before came pouring out of her mouth in torrents.

"Bad man come with Mya and take Carwy and Tommy. He take them away in buwwy."

She was speaking. He wanted to rejoice at the miracle, but her fear had him focusing on the words.

"I seed them in the barn," she said. "He say he was taking her to my old house and keep her there until she tell him where she put somefing he wants. Mya … Mywa had a gun. She pointed it at Tommy. They put rope on Carwy's hands and throw her in the buggy. You have to help her. Please, go help her."

Rand stared, trying to grasp what Jenna was saying, trying to grasp that Jenna was saying anything at all.

"A man and Myra were here?" Had Lester McGraw joined up with Myra?

Jenna nodded. "They take Carwy. They wasn't nice to her. They take Tommy. They say they going to my old house." Jenna beat her fists against his chest. "Go help them."

What should he do? Every instinct in him told him to jump on Dusty and ride over to the old homestead where Dan and Maggie had lived. But if he did that, the girls would be left alone. Jenna seemed to think whoever took Carly was armed. Would he be able to rescue Carly and Tommy by himself without someone getting killed?

What if Jenna had it all wrong? What if Carly had left of her own choosing as her note said and didn't want to be found? As far as he knew, Carly didn't even know where Dan and Maggie's house was. Even if she did, why would she go there? The obvious thing for Carly to do would be to head into town and get on a train. Did she have any money? Could she buy a train ticket?

"Pease, Unca Rand. Go get Carly and Tommy." He wiped her eyes with his handkerchief. How could he not try?

"I will, sweetie. I just need a minute to think."

The buggy stopped after just a few minutes. "You get out and take our wagon. I'll follow you." It was Lester's voice.

"I'll drive the buggy. You get out and take the wagon." Myra was being cantankerous. In less dire circumstances, Carly might have smiled at the argument between the two.

"Don't be ridiculous, Myra. We got these two here in the back. If they tried to escape, what would you do? Now get out and get in the wagon. This old nag of a horse you rented doesn't want to pull all of us so take that bag of food you stole too."

"Lester McGraw, I'm staying right here. And if you don't like it, just remember who's holding this." Carly couldn't see anything but the floor of the buggy and Tommy's shoe, but she was pretty sure Myra was showing Lester the gun she'd held to Tommy's head earlier. Whatever else she was, Myra was no dummy.

"All right, all right. Just you remember who it was made those plates that are going to make us rich. Don't forget who's in charge here." Lester clambered out of the buggy, apparently to get into the wagon he and Myra had arrived in. The bag of food on top of her didn't move.

Myra laughed. "Lester, darling, you need me to pull off this little scheme, and you know it. Better not push me too far."

Either Lester didn't answer or Carly couldn't hear what he said. Soon they were moving again. How far was it to Dan and Maggie's house? How far could she ride with her face in the buggy floor and her legs hanging out the side before she got sick or passed out from her head continually knocking against the front seat?

After what seemed like a long time, the horse slowed. "Whoa," Myra said. "We're here." The rumbling of the other wagon stopped behind them.

"You sure it's empty?" Lester asked.

"Of course it is. Now find some shelter for these horses and get some wood cut for a fire. With those clouds hanging so low, I wouldn't be surprised if we were in for another snowstorm." Myra sounded pretty sure of herself.

"What about them?" Carly could imagine him motioning to her and Tommy piled in a heap in the back of the buggy.

"I'll see to our passengers. Just do as you're told."

"The barn's burnt down," Lester protested. "Nothing but a pile of ashes and black lumber."

"Put the horses in the chicken coop then. We can't just leave them out in the weather. We'll need them to get out of here."

The conversation stopped, so Carly could only presume Lester had strode away to do Myra's bidding. Poor horses. They needed food and water, and Carly was willing to bet there were neither of those in an abandoned chicken coop.

At last, the canvas bag on top of her was removed, though Carly's head still ached from where the can had hit her. The twine tying her hands behind her tightened for a moment then fell away. Myra must have cut her bindings. Next, the handkerchief was yanked over her head, and Carly could spit the gag out of her mouth. Her first inclination was to yell for help, but common sense told her there was no one to hear. Best to save her energy.

"Out of the buggy, Carly," Myra demanded.

Just what Carly wanted to do, but how to accomplish it? With every ounce of effort she could muster, she forced her cramped muscles to pull her upright enough to allow her to drop out of the buggy onto the muddy ground below. Tommy followed, moving closer to her. The first thing she focused on was Myra standing not far away, her gun trained on them.

"Inside," Myra ordered.

Carly and Tommy scrambled to their feet. There was little Carly could do except obey while Myra had her gun pointed at Tommy. She would give her life for her brother, if necessary, but what good would it do if Tommy were left alone to defend himself?

Grabbing her brother's hand, Carly started toward the house. It was a two-story clapboard farmstead not as big as the Stratford house, but at one time, she believed it had been homey and inviting. Now with curtainless windows over empty flower boxes and the porch roof about to fall in for want of repair, Carly was sure Rand's sister would be distraught over the rundown appearance of her home.

She pulled open the front door and cautiously stepped inside. Darkness and dust greeted her. Trying not to think about what creatures skittered in the recesses of the room, Carly made her way to an old sofa covered with a dusty sheet that sat in front of the cold stone fireplace.

She pulled the sheet away, and she and Tommy sat.

Myra stood in the doorway, her gun in her hand. She seemed hesitant to enter.

"Better come inside and close the door," Carly suggested. "It's cold in here and going to get colder with the door open like that."

"Don't tell me what to do," Myra spat, but she came inside and closed the door. "Get up off your pretty little backside and see if you can find a lantern or something. And put this food somewhere." Myra flung the gunny sack in Carly's direction.

"Stay here," she whispered to Tommy. "I'll be right back."

The kitchen was as dark and dirty as the sitting room, but a lantern, still about a third full of oil, sat on the sideboard, a striker nearby. Carly lit the lamp and peered around the room. A broom covered in cobwebs stood in a corner. She took a few swipes at the dirty floor but gave up when so much dust rose, it made her sneeze. She set the canvas bag on the sideboard without looking inside.

Was any of the food intended for her and Tommy? Tommy had eaten a good breakfast, courtesy of Tubby, but she'd had nothing, her stomach too upset at the thought of leaving Rand to eat anything. It growled now, tormenting her. Maybe she could figure out how to get a fire started. From the way the sky had looked, she agreed with Myra's prediction of more snow on the way.

Carly stepped into an empty lean-to and opened the back door a crack. Sure enough, a log pile waited there. It wasn't a lot, but it would start a fire and warm this cold shell of a house up a bit. Carly summoned Tommy, and together they carried in enough wood to fill the fireplace and the kitchen stove, even though Myra stood in the kitchen doorway, her gun turned on them. With smaller sticks and some dry grass, Carly was able to get both fires started without too much trouble. The soft glow was enough to make her feel a little warmer.

The front door opened and closed.

"About time," Myra said. "Your little ex-girlfriend already got the fires going for you." Myra's voice floated into the kitchen where Carly had chosen to sit with Tommy instead of in the sitting room where

Myra was perched on the old sofa.

"And what have you been doing? Supervising?" Lester's voice was sarcastic. "Maybe you could look around this dump for something we can use like cups for coffee or blankets. It's already starting to snow. We might be here awhile."

"We don't have to be here any longer than what it takes for your little artist friend to remember where she put those plates. And I have ways of improving her memory if need be."

This brought no response from Lester. Carly glanced at Tommy. His eyes were filling with tears.

She squeezed his hand. "It'll be all right," she whispered. "Just keep praying."

Tommy nodded but didn't answer.

Lester said, "You going to just let them sit in the other room where we can't see what they're up to?"

Myra laughed. "And just what do you think they're going to do? If they run for it, they won't get anywhere. You said yourself it's starting to snow, and you've got the horses put away. If your little missy wants to run out into a snowstorm in the middle of this godforsaken prairie, I say let her. She'll be back here soon enough once she figures out there's no place to go."

"All I want is for her to tell me where those plates are, and I think it's time we started making her talk." Lester appeared in the kitchen doorway. "You two get in here. Now."

Carly met her brother's eyes and nodded. They rose, and she put his hand in hers as they made their way to the sitting room. They sat on the sofa, still holding hands. Carly looked up to see Lester standing over her.

Funny. She'd once found him attractive. That coal-black hair, those long sideburns, that full mustache. He'd never been big or burly, but she'd been attracted to his intellect. And perhaps the way he'd flattered her so. He'd been a considerate employer and a kind suitor as well. She'd never loved him, but she had cared for him as she would a dear friend.

Now, she couldn't believe she'd ever fallen for his lies. What a fool she'd been.

Her only consolation was that, in this case, it was Lester playing the fool. Unfortunately, she had no idea what he'd do to her when he found out the truth.

"Where're the plates, Carly?" His voice was kind and gentle, so like the way he'd spoken to her back when he'd been courting her.

It didn't fool Carly. Fortunately, she'd been thinking about what she could tell him. If Lester discovered the truth, that the plates were in the sheriff's office in Walnut Point, he would probably leave her here for dead and run. Or kill her himself.

No, she didn't think Lester would be capable of murder. She cast a glance at Myra.

That woman was. She seemed utterly devoid of conscience.

Carly forced herself to smile at him. "I'll show you, but you'll have to take me back to the Stratford ranch. I buried them under a tree in the south pasture. I'm sure you can't find it without me. Just promise me that you won't hurt Tommy."

Lester nodded. "The kid won't get hurt if you do as you're told. I'll take you back tonight." Lester threw a smug look at Myra.

Myra's eyes narrowed. "Just in case you're not telling us the truth, your brother stays here with me while you two go back. If you don't come back with the plates, consider him a goner."

Carly choked back her fear. That wasn't quite the way she'd hoped it would work. "Don't worry. We'll get them." Somehow, she would have to get the attention of someone at the ranch. How, she didn't know yet. *Dear God in heaven, help me.*

Chapter 26

It made no sense to go alone. If Jenna had this thing right and the newspaper fellow had teamed up with Myra, kidnapped Carly and Tommy, and taken them to Dan and Maggie's old house, Rand had to get some help.

Part of him wanted to hug Jenna endlessly and celebrate her finding her voice, but it would have to wait. "Come with me, baby. Let's go back upstairs and check on Mary Jo."

They climbed the stairs and entered her room quietly. "Sorry to wake you again," he said. "We've got a situation here, and I need your help."

"What is it?" Mary Jo sat up in her bed.

"Calwy gone," Jenna spoke up. "And Tommy."

Mary Jo stared at her sister, then at him. "Did she just …"

Rand nodded. "I don't have time to explain now. Carly and Tommy are in danger. I need you to look after Jenna while I go get them and bring them back."

Mary Jo nodded, her eyes large and round.

He turned to Jenna. "Stay here with your sister. I'm going to go find some of the hands to help me, then we'll go get Carly and Tommy. Bring the dogs inside and lock the doors behind me." He focused on Mary Jo. "Stay inside, no matter what. You understand me?"

They both nodded.

Rand left the room. If Jenna was so inclined, she could fill Mary Jo in on what had happened. He still wasn't sure if Jenna's version of the story was correct, but he couldn't take any chances. He had to find some help and get over to the vacant house. He'd been going to dismantle the place and use the lumber but had never quite been able to do it. So many memories there.

Rand grabbed his rifle, made sure it was loaded, and hurried out the front door. The team still stood at the hitching rail. Rand pulled them to the barn then saddled Dusty. He kicked the gelding's sides, trying to think. He'd told Nate and Parker to go west and north. Clarence was to head south. He decided to try the north pastures first. If he could find one of his hands to go with him, it evened things out a little better.

It was an answer to prayer to see Parker riding a fence line not long after he rode into the pasture. Rand waved at him, and Parker rode over. Rand filled him in on what had happened with as little detail as possible. There were just some things his men didn't need to know about this whole business.

"What do you want me to do, boss? Should I ride over there with you, or should I look for Nate? I don't think he could be too far from here."

"I haven't been able to find Tubby, either. Stay with me for now. We need a plan. We can't just go riding in there and demand they let Carly and Tommy go. Someone is liable to get hurt."

Rand thought for a minute, but he didn't want to waste valuable time, and snow had started to fall. "Let's ride over there and stop short of the house in that line of trees on the east side of the place. We'll see if we can see anything from there. You armed?"

Parker patted his scabbard. "I got my hunting rifle and a few bullets. Not a lot of extras, though."

"I'm hoping we won't need any, but we need to be prepared. Let's go."

The snow fell thicker as they rode. When they reached the trees not far from Maggie's old place, Rand pulled on Dusty's reins, and Parker's horse stopped beside them. They were about a hundred yards from the house, where smoke drifted from the chimney. So, Jenna's story had been spot-on. Thank God she'd overheard McGraw and Myra. Thank God she'd gotten her voice back to tell him about it.

He stared at the house. It would be cold, dusty, and dark in there. At least they had a fire going.

He tried to gauge the time. It would have been mid-afternoon by the time he got back from town. Dusk couldn't be that far away, and it would come even earlier in this snow that was growing ever worse. Wind was picking up too.

"You see anything?" Rand kept his voice low.

Parker pointed his forefinger. "Over there behind the burnt-out barn. Looks like a buggy back there. Maybe a wagon too, but I can't really tell."

"Makes sense. The horse and buggy we had in the barn is missing." Parker would have to figure out which horse and buggy he meant because, for some reason, Rand didn't even want to say Myra's name. At this point he wished he'd never met the woman.

"Wonder what they did with the horses?" Parker mused.

Rand shook his head. "Don't know, unless they're behind the house or in the chicken coop? You reckon this McGraw fellow coulda convinced those horses to go in the coop?"

Parker shrugged. "Gentle thing that dapple was, it'd probably go anywhere it was led. The important thing is, the horses aren't harnessed to the buggy or the wagon, so they can't get away except on foot. One, maybe two of 'em could crawl up on a horse's back, but they'd have to leave your missus and the boy behind to do it."

Which would be just fine with him. Rand doffed his hat for a moment and shook off the accumulating snow before jamming it back on his head. "Snow's getting worse." He was beginning to lose sight of the house and barnyard through the storm.

"Starting to blow, too. Wait … what's that?"

Rand and Parker watched as the front door opened and a man stepped outside, pulling Carly behind him. It took all the grit he could muster—and Parker's steadying hand on his arm—to keep him from sprinting across the field to save Carly from whatever wicked deed this man had in mind.

He couldn't though. According to Jenna's story, Myra would still be in the house with the boy, and both she and McGraw were likely armed. Any attempt to save Carly now would end in disaster.

They watched as McGraw stepped into the chicken coop and came out with a large brown horse still wearing a bridle. Rand could hardly believe the man actually put a horse in the chicken coop. McGraw threw Carly over the horse's back and then climbed up behind her. There was no saddle on the horse.

At least she had a coat on. That awful threadbare coat with holes under the arms that was missing most of its buttons.

What did this weasel of a human intend to do with his wife?

"You stay here and keep an eye out for the boy," Rand whispered to Parker. "I'm going to follow them."

Parker looked like he wanted to argue, but Rand didn't care. He couldn't leave Tommy here alone with Myra, and he certainly wasn't going to let this skunk ride off with his wife in a snowstorm.

The horse headed back in the direction of the ranch. Rand waited until they were far enough ahead of him he wouldn't be heard or seen if McGraw glanced behind him, then followed. Somehow, he had to get Carly away from this guy without endangering her. *God, help me save her.*

At least Lester let her sit up on the horse. Carly's skirts were hiked up to her knees as she straddled the animal, and the cold was miserable, but she'd been afraid she would have to ride haphazardly slung over the horse's back all the way to the ranch.

And then what? Lester expected her to take him to a place where she'd buried his plates under a tree in the south pasture. Maybe she could pretend she couldn't find it in the snow. Maybe she could point out a phony place and escape while Lester concentrated on digging. Maybe she could yell loud enough to be heard at the ranch house. Not likely. The wind was blowing fiercer than before.

It was an impossible situation. Carly dared not let Lester return to the house without the plates, for she didn't doubt Myra would make good on her threats against Tommy. And yet, how could she give him plates she didn't have?

Perhaps she could tell Lester the truth. It would be a simple matter of knocking on the front door of the ranch house and having Rand verify her story. No. Lester would never let her do that, even if he believed her about the plates being in Walnut Point. She had no choice but to follow through with letting Lester believe the plates were buried on the ranch and hope against hope God gave her an opportunity to get away and get help before it was too late.

The cold and blowing snow was relentless. Carly shivered and shook until Lester grew irritated. "Stop that infernal shaking, woman," he snapped. "The whole countryside can hear your teeth chattering."

If only. Maybe someone would take pity and come help her.

What if Tommy was even more frightened without her there than he had been before, and what if he annoyed Myra with whining or crying? Would she hurt him? Carly wouldn't put it past her. She breathed prayers with each step of the horse's hooves.

The lights of the ranch house came into view. Or what there was of them. There was a lamp glowing in the kitchen and one in the upstairs room that belonged to Mary Jo. Carly couldn't figure what to make of that. Even the bunkhouse was dark. When she thought about it, it made sense. Rand would have his men bringing the cattle in closer to home because of the snow. She could expect no help from any of the ranch hands.

Carly's spirits crashed about the same time as Lester pulled on the reins and unceremoniously dumped her in the snow at the gate to the south pasture. "You better be telling me the truth, you little snip," he warned. "Because you don't want to see how mad I'd be about being out in this storm for nothing."

His voice was little more than a growl that frightened Carly even more than she already was. How could she not have seen through this man before she discovered the counterfeit plates? She'd never believed herself in love with him, and yet she had agreed to marry him. It had seemed like a way to guarantee she and Tommy would be cared for in the future. She couldn't have been more wrong.

Lester jumped off the horse and wrapped the reins around the pasture fence. "Open that gate and show me where this tree is. Make it quick. You'll have to help me dig because we're not walking up to the house and asking for a shovel."

"With our hands?" Carly was horrified. "The ground is frozen. We'll never get the plates uncovered." With her statement came the slightest bit of hope. Until Lester dashed it to pieces. He reached into the pocket of his greatcoat and pulled out two metal objects.

"Found these in the chicken coop and figured they might come in handy." He handed one of them to Carly. Thick forged hooks of some sort. They'd break up ground easily enough.

"I'd guess those dead people used them to hold the chicken feeders from the ceiling of that coop. One of the nicest places I've ever seen made to just keep chickens in. Too bad they didn't have any left in there. I bet we could have had eggs and fried chicken legs for supper."

Lester laughed at what Carly supposed he thought was a joke.

"Which tree?" The growl was back.

"Over there." Carly pointed through the haze of snow and darkness to the big oak tree at the corner of the pasture.

Lester put his hands on her shoulders, forcing Carly to walk ahead of him and break a path through the snow. Sort of a path anyway. If only she'd worn her new boots. They were still in her satchel where she'd hoped to keep them looking new until she could return them to Keller's store. Was it only this morning she packed them so carefully?

The mammoth oak tree, its branches bare for the winter, towered over them long before Carly wanted it to. She hadn't quit praying since that first moment when Lester had appeared around the back of the buggy this morning. Was God even listening? There was nothing to do but sink onto her knees in the snow and start digging with the iron hook. Digging for something that wasn't even there.

Chapter 27

"Help us." The words were audible, but nobody heard them except Almighty God. At least Rand hoped He heard them. Staying hidden behind the bushes next to the west gate, Rand watched as McGraw pushed Carly into the snow, then followed her to the tree in the south pasture. Here, they both went to their knees. He couldn't quite see what they were doing. The best he could figure was Lester thought the plates were buried somewhere by that tree, and he had Myra holding Tommy hostage while Carly took him to retrieve the plates.

He badly wanted to run into the south pasture, dive tackle the no-good varmint, and beat the tar out of him while Carly watched. Or better yet, while Carly went to the house and got warm. He was miserable out in this storm, and Carly had to be too. But as far as he knew, McGraw had a gun aimed at Carly. The man was at point blank range. Lester could easily take a shot at Carly before Rand ever made it to the tree.

Where was everybody? Vinnie and Mucklededun must be in the house because of Jenna's soft heart for the animals. Just as well. They'd have given him away. Not a soul in the bunkhouse. He'd checked. Probably out rounding up the heifers as he'd had them do in the last snowstorm. They were probably cussing him and Parker for not being there to help. He couldn't just sit here. He had to come up with a plan.

He slipped off Dusty and left him ground tied. The animal was well trained and wouldn't go far. His best hope would be to sneak up behind McGraw and hope he could get close enough to take him down before the scoundrel figured out he was there. Rand supposed the risk was getting gutshot by McGraw, but he wasn't gonna pull his rifle with Carly so near to the man. In this storm and dark, what if he missed? Rand wouldn't let that thought stay in his head another second.

Hisss.

What was that? Probably just Dusty whiffing at the snow. Rand continued to study the two figures in the snow trying to plan the best way to sneak up on McGraw. It would be best if Carly didn't see him either, or she might unintentionally give him away.

Rand headed toward a bush a good ten yards away. It would hide him well enough.

"Boss?" A man whispered out of the darkness.

"Nate? Is that you?" Rand kept his voice to a whisper.

"Whatcha thinking on doing?"

Rand drew a sigh of relief and crouched next to his friend behind the bush. With Nate's help, this might not be so hard. "Where're the others?"

"We found Tubby tied up in the woodshed. He's all right save an aching head where he got walloped. He's in the house with the girls. Clarence rode over to the other house to see if he could help you and Parker. I was supposed to stay here and watch in case this guy came back here. Kinda surprised to see you."

"Yeah, well, we can talk about all that later. The thing is, I think this guy McGraw has a gun. I'm trying to figure out how to get Carly away from him without anyone getting hurt."

Nate's grin was evident, even in the snowy darkness. "I got an idea."

It was a good one, too. Rand let Nate have time to circle around so he could come toward the oak tree from the opposite direction. But not too much time. No telling how long McGraw would dig before Carly broke and told him the truth.

When he thought it was time, Rand crept toward the tree, making sure his footsteps were muffled by the accumulating snow.

A sound cut through the wind, a loud sort of mooing and something that sounded like pawing in the snow. Nate was good.

"Any cattle in this pasture?" McGraw asked, evidently forgetting to keep his voice low.

Good. Now if only Carly wouldn't give them away. Rand was almost close enough. She looked up and seemed to see him lurking in the shadows behind McGraw. *Come on, Carly. You can do it. Catch on to what's happening here.*

"I think so." Carly knew the breeding stock had been moved to the windmill pastures for the winter. The south pasture was empty. She looked away, then at him again. She had to have seen him.

Nate made some more sounds like mooing and pawing. Rand wanted to laugh. Anyone but a city boy would know the sounds were fake, but McGraw was definitely a city boy.

Carly looked back down. "A big mean bull with sharp horns named Cow Boy lives in this pasture. I almost got trampled or gored or something one time, but I don't expect he'd attack at night."

Nate mooed again.

"Didn't you hear that?" McGraw sounded nervous.

"Probably just some of the cows wondering what we're doing in their pasture. They're usually pretty tame ... unless they haven't been fed in a while."

McGraw dropped his digging tool and stood, obviously trying to catch sight of the nonexistent bull. He left Carly and the shelter of the oak tree to peer into the darkness in the direction of the sound. He walked a few steps away from Carly, cocking his head as if listening. Rand held his breath. *Come on, McGraw, a little farther, another step, one more. That's it.* McGraw was almost horizontal to him in his hiding place behind a cedar tree. Now was Rand's chance.

Rand leapt and tackled McGraw, knocking him to the ground before the guy had a chance to react. In another second, Nate was there to help him. Between the two of them, McGraw was hog-tied and face down in the snow before he could even think to yelp.

Rand patted the man's coat pockets until he found a pistol and slipped it into his own pocket. "Teach you to come after my wife."

So much more he wanted to say. So many more places he wanted to lay his fists on the no-good possum-tailed scoundrel. But he didn't. Carly was all that mattered. He reached her in an instant, picking her up from where she'd collapsed in the snow and bundled her close to his chest. "I've got you, honey. You're safe now."

She forced herself to speak. "Tommy. Myra's got Tommy."

"I know, honey. Parker's watching the house. He won't let her hurt him." He jogged toward the house and called back over his shoulder, "Hitch up the wagon, Nate, and throw him in the back."

"Yessir, boss." Nate mooed again.

Rand might have laughed if not for the woman in his arms. "I'll have you inside in just a moment."

"Rand." He had to lean his ear even closer just to hear her. "Thank you."

Sitting in front of the roaring fire and wrapped in plenty of warm quilts, Carly held a cup of hot tea in her hands, and still, she could feel the awful cold penetrating through her very being. But it wasn't from the weather.

Mary Jo sat next to her on the sofa, also wrapped in a blanket and sipping from a cup of tea. Jenna sat at their feet, chattering away as she told and retold the story of finding her voice. Carly allowed herself a half smile at the little girl's excitement. Apparently, she had been so silent so long, now that she could speak, she had a lot to say.

Tubby stoked the fire, his back to them.

"Shouldn't they be back by now?" Carly had asked the same question several times over the last what seemed like hours.

As he had done every time before, Tubby pulled a watch from his pocket, glanced at it, and snapped it closed. "I'd say anytime now, Miz Stratford. Don't you be a worryin' none. Our boys'll take care of that little brother of yours. I'm sure he's just fine."

Lester was no longer a threat. Rand and the other three hands had gone to capture Myra and rescue Tommy. Surely Myra was no match for four grown men, and yet Carly kept remembering the gun she'd brandished about earlier and the threats she'd made. Would Myra follow through with the horrible things she'd promised?

Carly took another sip of her tea and then wished she hadn't. It felt almost traitorous to sit here in the warmth of the fire, her stomach full of Tubby's potato soup, when poor little Tommy was out there somewhere in that storm, maybe fighting for his life.

In the distance a dog barked. Carly listened but didn't hear it again. Could it be Bo? Maybe the men were near. Vinnie, lying with her head in Jenna's lap, suddenly got to her feet and stood alert. In the distance, the dog barked again. It was Bo, Carly was sure of it.

In another minute, Vinnie and Mucklededun were both barking and jumping by the door. Carly threw off her quilts and ran to the back door just as it opened.

Tommy ran inside.

Carly scooped him up in her arms and hugged him tightly.

"Hey, stop, you're hurting me. What's for supper? I'm starving."

"Tommy, darling. You're safe. Are you hurt? Are you cold? Here, come stand in front of the fire and warm up."

"I ain't cold. Clarence wrapped me up in a big blanket and held me real close to him all the way home. He was singing to me, too. A song about Baby Jesus in the manger. Hey, Carly, is it almost time for Christmas?"

Mary Jo and Jenna stood at the door to the kitchen, pushing the dogs aside. When they stepped in, they were followed by Tubby wearing an enormous grin.

"Tommy," Jenna called, "you're home. Guess what? I can talk now, and Tubby says I helped save you and Carly cuz I tried really hard to talk and it worked. It really worked. I told Uncle Rand that bad man and lady came and got you and took you to our old house where me and Mary Jo used to live. Hey, did you see my room? Well, it used to be my room, but now my room is here in Uncle Rand's house. Vinnie and me was just waiting for you to get back so I could surprise you about how good I can talk now. And tomorrow we can ..."

Tubby pretended to clamp a hand over Jenna's mouth.

"Whoa there, little missy. All of us is mighty proud you're talking again, but our Tommy here, I reckon he needs some of that potato soup in him. Now, you go slice him a piece of bread and put some of that apple butter he likes on it. Mary Jo, you get him a glass of milk, and we'll let the lad get his belly full before we start planning tomorrow."

Both girls ran to obey Tubby while Tommy sat at the table. Mucklededun settled at his feet. Carly was so thankful and so relieved he was home, she sank into the chair beside him, silently praising and thanking God for His deliverance. Tommy shoveled in his supper as if he hadn't eaten in a week while Carly watched the back door. Where was Rand? Why hadn't he come inside? She couldn't wait to thank him, to tell him how grateful she was for saving her and Tommy from the evil that had befallen them today. And yet ... with Rand would come the news of her fate. Would Sheriff McConnell be here in the morning to arrest her, or would he wait until the weather had cleared? How much longer did she have? What would she say to Rand about the note she'd left? Surely he'd read it by now.

Tommy's soup was gone, his eyelids drooping.

Rand still hadn't come in.

She patted her brother's head, still damp from the snow. "Didn't

Rand come home with you?"

Her brother rubbed his eyes. "Clarence and Parker brung me home. Pa, I mean, Rand and Nate stayed with that bad man and the Myra lady so as they wouldn't try to escape or nothin' tonight. Rand says he'll haul 'em to the sheriff in the morning. And Nate kept mooing at the man until Pa told him to stop."

Oh. Carly looked around at all the tired eyes. Apparently, she would be the one to make sure they all got to sleep. "All right, then, off to bed with all of you. Mary Jo, you've been ill. Go to bed and make sure you sleep in tomorrow. I'll see to breakfast. Jenna and Tommy, you've had quite a day. Both of you skedaddle. I'll come up and say prayers with you in a few minutes."

The children obeyed, and Carly couldn't resist rubbing her own eyes. She was exhausted beyond anything she could remember.

"Want me to stay in the house with you folks tonight?" Tubby asked. "I'd be glad to lie down on that nice sofa in there and have a look-see at the fires every now and then."

"Thank you, Tubby." Carly was too tired to protest. Anyway, the idea of the old ranch cook keeping watch over things tonight was rather comforting. She stifled a yawn. My, but it would feel good to crawl into her own bed. This morning, she'd thought she would never sleep there again. God had granted her one more night in this place she loved and with the people she cherished.

Rand watched the fire slowly dying in the old homestead where he'd spent so many happy moments with his sister and her family. He really should get up and put another log on the fire. One in the kitchen too. But he was feeling kind of lazy, and perhaps a bit nostalgic. He hated to disturb the moment.

"Want me to get another log on them fires, boss?" Nate asked.

Rand hadn't realized the ranch hand was still awake. "Sure. Thanks." Rand watched as Nate stepped over Myra and McGraw where they slept on the floor in front of the fire, their hands still tied.

"She don't look quite as pretty as usual." Nate's remark after replenishing the fire fuel caught Rand off guard. He stared at Myra's sleeping form. Her dark hair was tangled and in need of washing. Her face was showing signs of aging without her rouge pot to cover up the wrinkles. To think he'd almost married this woman who had lied to him, stolen from him, and betrayed him. *Thank You, God, for Carly.* God had certainly been watching out for him when Rand didn't know enough to watch out for himself.

"Nope, she sure doesn't," Rand answered.

"It's stopped snowing," Nate told him. "Wind's settled down, and the moon's a-shining. Oughta be a simple thing to get to town with the wagon once dawn breaks."

"I'll just throw these two hoodlums in the back end and dump 'em off in Sheriff McConnell's jail cell before I head home."

"Parker was pretty proud of himself, wasn't he?" Nate laughed.

Rand had to chuckle, too, remembering how Parker had puffed out his chest and told the story.

"Yep," Parker had said. "I was watchin' the house from them trees like you told me and all at once the door opens. Miss Cunningham, she hightails it to that outhouse over there. I figured that was my chance, so I was there waiting for her with my rifle pointed at her when she came out."

Rand couldn't stop grinning. "Myra Cunningham defeated by the call of nature."

Nate laughed again. "Yeah, Parker said he took her gun and went to empty out the bullets but found out it wasn't even loaded. Guess she was all show and no blow. All he had to do then was wait until Clarence got here. Hey, you sure ol' Tubby's gonna be all right?"

"He's fine except for a lump on the back of his head and a whole lot of embarrassment for letting himself get caught like that when he was supposed to be taking care of things."

"Wasn't his fault," Nate said. "Coulda happened to any of us."

"I know," Rand assured him. "He wouldn't listen when I told him to sit down and take it easy. He was all about making a big pot of soup for when everybody came back cold and hungry. Say, Nate, I'm much obliged to you for choosing to stay at the ranch and keep watch there instead of riding over here with Clarence. I don't know if I could have got Carly away from McGraw without your help."

Nate guffawed. "Did ya see McGraw's face when he figured out it was just me a mooin' at him? Serves the old coot right."

"Yeah, and that was about the time he and Myra started blaming each other." Rand chuckled at the memory. "I reckon we've got about all the confessions we need to put them both away for a long time."

Nate nodded. "Miss Myra convinced McGraw they should start a lottery business. They would travel from town to town, selling lottery chances, then pay out the lottery winnings in counterfeit dollars. By the time anyone figured it out, they'd be long gone to the next town. Might have worked except they needed those plates."

By daybreak, Rand had the team hitched to the wagon. They were raring to go after spending the night with little shelter except the overhanging trees. Rand hadn't been about to try to get Dusty or Nate's horse in the chicken coop. He couldn't quite figure out how McGraw had done it with the smaller horses. The dapple and the other horse, along with McGraw's wagon and Myra's buggy, would have to wait a day or two to get back to the livery, but the hands would see that the horses got a good bit of grain and a warm stall in his barn for tonight.

"Load up folks," Rand joked as he and Nate shoved Myra and McGraw into the back of the wagon. It'd be a mighty miserable ride to town for them bumping along in the cold wagon, but they'd survive till they made it to the sheriff.

A twinge grabbed his belly at the thought of Myra going to prison, but it didn't stay with him long. She deserved everything she had coming to her. And McGraw, Rand didn't give a squirrel's backside about that scum. Whatever happened to him was well deserved too. He'd have to forgive both McGraw and Myra someday, according to what the Bible told him, but he'd work on that tomorrow. Today was made for celebrating. Just one more thing to do before he set out for town, and it wasn't gonna be easy.

"Um, Nate, you wanna step over here a minute?" He didn't want to be within earshot of their prisoners when he said these words to his ranch hand.

"Sure, boss." He followed Rand to the far side of the wagon. "What's on your mind."

Rand nodded. "First of all, don't be tellin' anybody what I'm about to ask of you. Got it?"

Nate nodded. Rand wanted to wipe the grin off Nate's face, but he could feel his own grin edging out of the solemn expression he'd wanted to show.

"When you get back to the ranch, you march yourself up to the door and knock. If it isn't her who opens the door, you ask for Mrs. Stratford. When you see her, make sure nobody else is within earshot, and here's what I want you to tell her …"

Chapter 28

$\mathscr{T}$he sun broke over the eastern horizon sending millions of glittering specks into the untouched snow cover on the prairie. Carly took it all in from the upstairs window, her feelings a mixture of delight and despair. Oh, what she would give if she could stay here in this place she'd come to think of as home and with the people she loved so dearly.

Sometime between yesterday's horrific events and last night's glorious uninterrupted sleep, Carly had concluded that running away would do her no good. She must accept her punishment and face it with the strength and courage God gave her. It wouldn't be easy, but neither would she be alone. Perhaps if she was taken to prison, Rand would agree to take care of Tommy during her absence. The two of them had grown so close, it almost made her envious.

Carly slipped into one of her newer dresses and went downstairs to make breakfast for the children.

A tap at the back door caught her attention as she was breaking eggs into a bowl. Probably one of the dogs wagging his tail against the door, wanting out. She'd forgotten to let them out this morning. Hurrying to the lean-to, she opened the back door and was surprised to see Nate standing there. Didn't Tommy say he'd stayed at Maggie's house with Rand? Did this mean Rand was back, too?

"Good morning, ma'am." Nate held his hat in his hands despite the cold. He looked quite uncomfortable.

"Good morning, Nate." He made no immediate response, so Carly tried to think of something else to say. "Thank you for your help yesterday with … with everything. I don't know what I'd have done if you men hadn't all come to our rescue."

"Glad to do it, Mrs. Stratford."

Again, the silence stretched to the point of awkwardness.

"Something I can do for you?"

"Uh, no, ma'am. I mean, yes, ma'am." Nate's face flushed to a bright red. "Uh, Boss is on his way to town. He wanted me to give you a message." Nate shuffled his feet.

Apparently, Carly would have to help him. "It's all right. Just tell me what Rand said."

"Well, he said to let you know there aren't likely to be any charges against you, so you're not to worry about that."

Carly's knees turned to jelly from sheer relief, and she nearly fell. No charges? She wanted to run, jump, sing, shout, celebrate, anything but stand here watching Nate have such a difficult time with his words. She clenched the doorframe on either side of her and did her best to keep her countenance staid. Impossible.

"Anything else," she asked, though she felt her grin growing ever broader.

"Well, yes, ma'am, um … fact is, well, I …"

Carly had to lean closer to Nate to hear him.

"Boss said to tell you he loves you." With that Nate turned and hightailed it out of the yard like a coyote tailing a jackrabbit.

Rand had no idea what to expect when he got home. Would Carly speak to him? What would she say? Had she changed her mind about leaving? How could he convince her not to go? The honest truth would be his best option, and the sooner he could look in her eyes and tell her how much he loved her, the better.

He rode into the ranch yard, jumped out of the wagon, and handed the reins to Clarence. Striding toward the back door, he rehearsed the little speech he'd been working on. The first thing he needed to do was make sure she was all right. She'd gotten mighty cold before he and Nate got her rescued. And then … This was where he kept tripping up. And then, what?

Suddenly, the back door opened, and Carly ran out. Without

uttering a word, she flew into his arms and hugged him until he could barely breathe. He hadn't expected that, but he liked it. He hugged her back until the children—even Mary Jo, who looked tired but happy to see him—begged for a turn. Then they hugged him too, sort of like a family hug—if there was such a thing.

At last, Rand shooed them all back inside and out of the cold, keeping an arm around Carly's waist as they went. He had a mind to never let her get too far away from him again.

"Pa, we want a Christmas tree." Tommy was the first to speak.

"Yes," Jenna added, "because tomorrow is Christmas Eve, and we want a really big tree, and we want to make pretty decorations for it, and we want to invite the ranch hands in to see it, and then ..."

"Easy, Jenna. One thing at a time." Rand could hardly keep from laughing, but it was so good to hear her talking again.

"Dinner is ready," Carly announced still standing in the circle of his arm. "You children set the table, and we'll talk about this after we eat." She didn't move. Rand didn't care. There was much to be said between them, but his message by way of Nate must have gotten through. Good old Nate. Now, if the ranch hand could only keep his mouth shut.

Rand was so hungry that the simple dinner of beef stew and fresh bread tasted better than anything he'd eaten in a long while. He was tired enough to go to bed right now and not wake up until morning, but the children were clamoring for a Christmas tree. Anyway, he had plans for tonight, so he'd better get over his fatigue. If Tommy called him Pa one more time, Rand was likely to do anything the little guy wanted.

"Can we go now, Pa?" Tommy asked. "Can we?"

Rand tousled his head. "Tell you what. All you children have been sick, and the prairie's full of snow. How about if I go pick out one of the cedar trees by the gate, and you can watch me out the window, make sure I get the right one. When Carly says it's time, I'll bring it inside, and you all can put those doodads on it." If he remembered right, there was a box of tree decorations up in the attic that had come from Maggie's. Red ribbons, glass balls and the like. He hadn't had a tree in this house since he was a kid, but it sounded like a right fine idea this Christmas.

He still had to talk to Carly about something, and it could be she wasn't going to like it much. Maybe he'd wait to tell her until later this evening. But the children had all disappeared to the attic to search for decorations, and there she stood, the light from the fireplace reflecting in that red hair of hers, and he just couldn't help himself. He drew her into his arms and kissed her. Then he kissed her again.

"You love me," she whispered. It was more like a fact she was trying to believe than a question to be answered, but Rand figured it was time to get this settled once and for all.

"You bet I do," he answered. "I love you, Carly Stratford, and I always will."

He kissed her again just for emphasis.

"I love you, too," she breathed.

Rand couldn't help his sigh of relief. "You'll stay then? You and Tommy? You won't leave?"

"Not as long as you want me here."

Carly's reply made him kiss her again. "You better believe I want you to stay. Stay here for always and be my wife."

Carly nodded, her smile stretching across her lovely features. "Always."

Better get it said. "Sheriff McConnell wants me to bring you into town tomorrow. He needs to question you."

She gasped, and her eyes grew wide. "Nate said you didn't think there would be any charges filed against me."

"That's what the sheriff said. He does need your statement, though, to back up the charges filed against McGraw and Myra."

"Oh. And you'll be with me?"

"Right beside you the whole time," Rand assured her.

She hesitated only a moment. "All right."

Huh. That was easier than he'd figured.

"Will we have time to stop by Keller's for a minute?" she asked. "I might have some Christmas shopping to do."

"Got some things to be picked up myself. Oh, that reminds me. I've still got some tea from Keller's in my saddlebags. Matt said he threw in a few peppermint sticks for flavor. Sounds pretty festive to me."

Carly smiled. "We'll drink it while we decorate the tree. Now you better go out and get it before you have three helpers you probably don't need."

Rand jammed his hat on his head and, after just one more kiss for his wife, stepped outside.

That evening after the children had gone to bed, Rand pulled Carly into his arms. "I have one more thing to ask of you."

"Ask away," Carly teased. "I don't feel much inclined to deny you anything right now."

Rand pulled his mama's wedding ring out of his pocket and placed it on Carly's finger.

She stared down at the pearl and garnets, her mouth forming a little O. "Will you be my wife? Really and truly my wife?"

Carly blushed a beautiful shade of pink, and tears glistened in her eyes. "I would love nothing more. Really and truly."

Rand stood and pulled her to stand beside him. After a long kiss he didn't want to end, he blew out the lamps, and they climbed the stairs, hand in hand.

Christmas Eve found the Stratford family gathered around their beautifully decorated Christmas tree after enjoying a goose dinner courtesy of Parker's hunting skills. Carly's heart was warm as she sat tucked beneath Rand's arm. She couldn't quit staring at her left hand and the ring that sparkled there. He said it was hers now. And he'd proved it to her last night.

As it turned out, the Federal Marshal had authorized Sheriff McConnell to absolve her from all charges. Lester and Myra would both go to prison. Carly asked for leniency for Myra, though her request might not be granted. Somehow, Carly felt sorry for her. "I hope she takes the chance to seek God's forgiveness," she'd told the sheriff. Sheriff McConnell didn't know how it would go, but he promised to pass her request onto the marshals.

God's love and forgiveness felt tangible tonight. He had shown her that she was flawless in His sight, despite her shortcomings. She'd found her refuge in His promises.

Rand leaned over to kiss her, apparently no longer caring that his ranch hands were watching. Her heart was full. She was home, and she was loved.

Author's Note

$\mathcal{D}$espite the frightening implications of such a venture, mail-order brides were a reality in this time period. As men began populating the western part of the country, establishing farms and ranches on the outskirts of eastern civilization, women were scarce. Without cultural activities, dress shops, and an abundance of other women for female companionship, the west was not a popular place for them to venture. Men in need of wives for accomplishing household tasks, helping on the farm, or bearing children would place an ad in newspapers back east in an attempt to find someone to fill the role. Some of the women who answered these ads were, like Carly, desperate to escape from their current situations. Some were widows with children to support. Many were foreigners or divorcees not accepted into the social circles of the east.

Emanuel Ninger, known as Jim the Penman, produced counterfeit bills using his artistic abilities beginning in 1878. He cut bond paper the size of bills, stained it with a diluted coffee solution, then drew the bills, one at a time with ink and a paintbrush. Interestingly, he never included the phrase crediting the Bureau of Engraving and Printing on his counterfeit replicas. It is said he worked weeks at a time on each bill, perfecting it almost to the point of being unrecognizable. He was caught in 1896 when a bill he passed at a bar got wet and the ink began to smudge.

In my attempt to stay true to the time period and locale of this story, I have used terms that may have an unfamiliar context to today's readers. Primarily, lunch was an infrequent word. The term for the noon meal was dinner while the evening meal was known as supper.

Another term not readily used today is cutter. A cutter is what we might call a sleigh. It was a small compartment built with curved runners on the underside so that a horse could easily pull it through snow when buggy or wagon wheels couldn't perform the task.

A sideboard, a flat surface perhaps built under a set of shelves or cupboards, was what we would refer to today as counter space.

A ewer was the pitcher often set in a basin kept in the bedrooms for washing.

With the invention of barbed wire, free range cattle became less popular, but it became necessary to move breeding cattle, like heifers ready to produce their first calf, into safer pastures closer to home come winter.

I hope you have enjoyed the colloquialisms and terminologies from the past, many of which are still used by old-timers of all ages in the Flint Hills area.

I would love to hear from readers. Please contact me at ksucindy@ excite.com and let me know if you enjoyed *Mail-Order Refuge*.

41788697R00143

Made in the USA
Lexington, KY
11 June 2019